THE ABDUCTION

THE SA TSKIR BROTHERS CHRONICLES
BOOK 1

DANIELLE KAHEAKU

PARADOXICAL PRESS

THE ABDUCTION

THE ABDUCTION

THE SA TSKIR BROTHERS CHRONICLES
BOOK 1

DANIELLE KAHEAKU

ONE

"Is the Internet down?"

Samantha did not look up from where she sat on the couch, her eyes focused over the bridge of her straight nose down to her lap. She tapped the screen of her handheld tablet with one thumb to turn the page and wiped at her red nose with a tissue. "I just downloaded a book ten minutes ago. Internet is fine."

"Well, the TV isn't changing channels."

"The batteries in the remote are probably low."

Carly, a petite, curly-haired blonde, pressed the buttons on the remote controller down violently with her thumb, and then smacked the remote against the arm of the coffee table.

"Damn piece...of...shit..."

"Hey!" Samantha set down the tablet and leaned over to snatch the remote from Carly's hand. "Violence and electronics do not mix!" She shook her head and pointed the remote at the small flat screen in the corner of the hotel room, frowning after pressing a few buttons with no response. The newscaster dragged on, spouting something about an alarming number of missing girls from someplace in New York.

"See?" Carly's pink, pouty mouth scrunched into a satisfied smirk as she eyed the slim brunette. Her short gold curls bounced around her heart-shaped face as she flipped her head triumphantly. "I'm not the only one with issues."

Samantha let out a short bark of laughter, her hazel eyes sparkling. "Oh, trust me. My issues are not even in the same ballpark as yours—"

"Well, if we'd just go down to the casino already then we wouldn't have to be worrying about the TV."

Samantha looked up, rolling her eyes. "I just got here after driving seven hours to meet you. I'm tired and need to unwind while the cold meds kick in. Besides," she said, pushing a lock of long brown hair behind one ear, "I still need to go back to the car to get my wallet before I can gamble."

"I can't believe you remembered your stupid eReader but forgot your purse in the car. You know you have horrible priorities?"

The TV shut off. Both girls looked at each other, and then down at the remote.

"Hey," Carly said happily. "You got it to work."

Samantha shook her head. "I didn't do anything."

The overhead lights went out, along with the alarm clock on the nightstand between the two beds and the lamp beside the beds. The hum of the hotel's small refrigerator slowed and then clicked to a stop. Silence hung heavy in the darkened room, illuminated only by the small screen of Samantha's tablet.

"Great." Carly jumped off the bed and hurried over to the window, throwing back the curtain to let in the dying evening light. "The power's out, again. Serves me right for wanting us to stay in one of the new rooms before they finished renovating..."

"Hey, we agreed to save money on the rooms so we can spend it at the casinos," Samantha said, as she settled back with her book.

Carly sighed. "I know. But now I wish we hadn't gotten so cheap and just paid for the Monte Carlo. You know my parents offered to cover the tab. I *really* wanted you to enjoy this trip."

"I don't mind. Besides, they're your parents, not mine. They shouldn't be paying for my vacation."

Carly sat down on the couch next to Samantha, who sighed and set her tablet down and sat up. She reached over and took Samantha's hand and squeezed. "I think meeting some new friends is exactly what you need! I mean, this is the first chance at fun you've had since you dropped out of school after your dad died, and you've been stuck on that farm alone—"

"Well, I wasn't alone for most of it..."

"John's a dick, and I'm glad you guys broke up," Carly cut in, angry. She shook her head sadly. "I worry about you. It's been six months since you left Brown, and this is the first time we've been able to get together —even though I've invited you out multiple times."

"I've been a little busy trying to get settled and fixing things up after the shape my dad left things..." Samantha said, a little defensively.

Carly looked down at her hands. "The house is paid off, Sam, you don't have to worry about too much. I'm just afraid that you're getting so caught up in *his* life, and what he left behind, that you're going to miss yours. I mean, all you dreamed about was becoming a writer."

"Carly—"

"And now that you're not getting married you have so much that you could look forward to."

The couch suddenly bucked and shook, and both women were thrown off balance. They toppled onto the floor together in a twist of arms and legs.

"Oh, my God!" Carly shrieked. "Are we having an earthquake?"

Samantha quickly untangled her legs and forced herself to her feet. She grabbed her tablet and held it out in front of her like a flashlight. She snatched up the foil packaging of her cold medication on the side table and shoved it in one pocket, and then stuck her hand out for Carly. "Come on! We need to get downstairs!"

The shaking stopped, and the girls sat still. After several tense heartbeats, they stood and stepped out into the hall. Doors in the hall opened, and other curious hotel guests popped their heads outside to investigate. Being under renovation, the building was only half occupied, and it made Samantha feel better to see a few other faces in the dark.

"Hello?" Carly called out.

"This way," came a reply from the dim hallway. "You guys OK?"

"Yeah."

Samantha stepped out into the hall and held up her tablet. The light illuminated a small circle around her, revealing the faces of the darkened shapes standing closest. A trio of girls from the room next to them stepped closer.

"Did you feel that?" asked one of the girls, her eyes wide and darting around.

Carly nodded. "That felt like a big one. Do you think we should get downstairs?"

"Not sure," Samantha said. "It doesn't look like there's any damage. If there are no aftershocks we're probably fine—"

A scream from one of the lower floors of the tower stilled everyone into silence. The scream rose in pitch, cutting through the layers of concrete and cheap carpeting that separated the floors to pierce the growing darkness. Another howl followed, and soon several more joined in chorus.

Panic rose in Samantha's throat, quickening her breath and making her heart race as screams—both female and male—suddenly filled the ever-growing darkness of the halls. Several guests dashed through the dark toward the elevators and stairs.

"Don't use the elevators!" someone yelled from the dark.

A race for the stairs left several people nearly trampled, and several screamed as they fought to keep their footing on their way down the steps in the dark.

A hand grabbed Samantha's shoulder, and she turned to see Carly beside her.

"Let's take the stairs at the other end of the hall," Carly whispered in her ear. "So, we can get down in one piece."

Samantha nodded, and they wove their way against the struggle toward the west hall. One of the girls in the trio stood in a frozen panic near the wall, her breathing too quick and eyes too wide. Samantha paused long enough to snatch her wrist and pull her along with them. Soon they broke free and felt their way along the walls until they were around the corner.

They paused for a moment as Samantha tried to calm the raspy hiccups of the panicked girl.

"What's your name?" she asked, pulling out her tablet and holding the light of the screen toward the girl.

The soft circle of illumination seemed to steady the blonde for a moment, giving her something to focus on. "J-Julie."

"Alright, Julie," Samantha said calmly, her training seemingly kicking in. "We're going to get out of here, but I need you to relax and breathe."

"Sam!" Carly hissed. "Let's go, just leave her."

Samantha glared at Carly and held out the lit screen to show their path. "Just breathe, Julie."

Julie nodded, and took hold of Samantha's hand, squeezing her fingers tightly.

They took off running.

Ragged breathing mingled with their footsteps thudding against the uncarpeted halls of the unfinished wing of the new hotel tower. They stopped at the end of the hall, Samantha flicking her screen left, then right, before heading left toward the stairwell. Carly reached the door first and yanked it open.

The sound of feminine screams and shouts from men from the lower floors wafted up to them. Carly started down, but Samantha held her back.

"Something's not right," she whispered.

Carly shook off her hand. "Of course not, you idiot. There's an earthquake and the power's out."

Samantha shook her head. "There was only the one aftershock. And people wouldn't be screaming because it's dark..."

"Maybe someone's hurt," Julie added, starting down the stairs.

Samantha's ears perked forward, and Carly caught the change in her friend's manner.

"Julie's right," Carly said, inching her way forward with a smile meant to be convincing. "Maybe someone needs our help."

Samantha sighed, knowing all too well what Carly was trying to do, but also aware that if someone was in need, she would help if she could.

SAMANTHA LED THE WAY, lighting the path, followed by Carly and a reluctant Julie. Carly pulled out her cell phone and frantically started dialing.

She let out a frustrated growl. "I'm not getting a signal."

Three flights of stairs down, they finally found the door to the main floor. The screams had intensified as they descended, and they paused to listen.

A male voice screamed out, "Don't touch her! Dani—"

A short burst of a single electrical pop rang through the darkness, followed by something heavy falling to the ground.

Carly yipped and covered her mouth with one hand, stifling her cry. Julie shook Samantha's shoulder, pointing to the glowing tablet.

"Turn it off!" she hissed.

Samantha's fingers shook as she fumbled for the off switch, and froze when the screen finally went dark, snuffing out the small, comforting circle of blue light surrounding them. They sat huddled together in the dark, waiting.

The sounds outside the door had stopped, the screams fading down somewhere farther, deeper into the building.

After a few moments, Samantha reached up and felt for the doorknob, grasping the handle.

"What are you doing?" Carly whispered, her voice frantic.

"We can't just sit here," Samantha hissed back. "We need to get the hell out of here."

She took a shaky breath, her heart loud in her ears, and slowly turned the handle. She bit her lip as the latch gave a soft click before releasing, and then opened the door a mere few inches to peer through.

A strange, dim green light bathed the quiet hallway. A quick glance around revealed several flare-like objects tossed about the floor, emanating the eerie glow. A man lay on the ground to their right; arms and legs twitching in small spasms, his half-open eyes reflecting the flickering green flares like angry, trapped fireflies.

Samantha swallowed and pushed the door open farther, squeezing through. She shoved her tablet in the back pocket of her jeans and motioned for the other women to follow.

They made their way slowly through the hall, holding hands, and slowed as they neared the corner that led to the finished end of the hotel. Samantha held her breath and flattened herself against the wall before peering around the corner.

Flares littered across the foyer of the first floor bathed the walls in a radiant deep green. The outlined shapes of men littered the floor of the entry, some still and lying in the awkward positions in which they fell...

Samantha's breath caught in her throat.

Scattered among the fallen bodies of the male patrons, females of all ages and dress rolled around on their backs with their naked legs wrapped around the waists of strangely uniformed men. The girls moaned in ecstasy and begged for more, as if the twitching bodies of the fallen men surrounding them were not even there. The uniformed newcomers obliged them by moving faster, spreading the girls' legs farther apart in order to thrust deeper, harder.

Samantha peered harder at the few uniformed men moving about at the edges of the disgusting orgy. She could not put her finger on it, but there was something about them that was not right. They were all tall and broad shouldered, and they moved fluidly, as if they had joints and muscles where they should not, as they walked about predatorily, staring intently at their comrades pounding away at the women on the ground.

A well-dressed couple appeared at the bottom of the far stairwell, the tears on the woman's terrified face glowing in the light of the flares. They froze at the sight before them, and the man tried to pull the woman back up the stairs. Before they could turn to go, one of the uniformed men to their right moved incredibly fast across the ten feet between then and snatched the woman away, pulling her toward the middle of the room. Her companion yelled and charged at the uniformed man, who nonchalantly lifted one arm and pointed a weapon—a green dot appearing on the man's forehead—and fired. A bright bolt of green energy shot out like a bullet with a *crack*, and the charging man's head jerked backward as an electrical spider web of micro surges enveloped his face and neck before he fell like a sack of rocks to the floor.

The woman screamed, fighting against the restraining grip of her captor. The man jerked her around to face him and grasped her face in both hands. He leaned down, ignoring the flailing arms and scratching nails of the woman as she struggled, and laid a firm kiss against her lips. Almost immediately, she froze, and then melted against his chest, her head tilted upward, and mouth opened to receive the next kiss.

Samantha gasped and covered her mouth.

Two uniformed men standing near the entry doors to the building looked up, their yellow, catlike eyes glinting gold in the darkness, and stared straight at Samantha. Their eyes narrowed, and then they darted forward.

She backpedaled and pushed the two girls behind her, pointing toward the stairs. "Run!"

The flight back up the stairs in the dark was long and terrifying. Samantha felt hot tears slip down her cheeks as she fought to keep her footing on the unfinished stairwell and ignored the pain in her knee as she slammed against the wall, fighting to find the next door.

Julie disappeared to her left in a flash of pale green light as she darted through an open door. Carly clamored past, going farther up the stairs. Samantha hesitated.

"Sam!" Carly called back. "They're already on the second floor!"

Samantha cringed, looking down toward where

Julie had gone, and rushed up the stairs after Carly. "What about Julie?"

Carly panted and faltered, slipping down three steps to nearly crash into Samantha. "You can't help her—"

Heavy footsteps sounded on the stairs below them, and despite the gnawing urge to help the terrified girl, fear gripped Samantha's own chest. She quickened her pace behind Carly before they could see who was behind them.

Once in the hall of the third floor, they paused, panting, looking around in the dark. The floor was silent, save for the random muted screams coming from somewhere below. Samantha jerked her tablet out of her pocket and held it out in front with a shaky hand, and Carly latched herself onto Samantha's back as they quickly but cautiously jogged down the dark hall.

"Can you please tell me what the fuck is going on?" Carly demanded as they rounded the corner toward their rooms. "Did... I mean did you see what those guys..."

Samantha nodded, her throat thick. She had seen.

Samantha nearly tripped on something in the hall, and she shone her light down only to gasp at several pairs of women and uniformed men coupling on the floor of the hall to their rooms.

Women moaned in ecstasy, running their hands up and down the men's backs as they shoved their hips upward in tune to each powerful thrust, as if they could not get enough. The men's bodies jerked unnaturally fast as they roughly ravished the women below them, their pants halfway down their lean and muscular thighs. They did not give the two girls a second glance as they groaned and panted, focused on the females below them.

Carly's fingers squeezing into Samantha's arm snapped her back to reality, and they glanced at each other as Samantha tiptoed forward through the maze of twisting bodies.

"Are you crazy?" Carly whispered.

"They're a little busy at the moment," Samantha reasoned, waving for her to follow. "I'm more worried about the two guys looking for us."

Samantha paused halfway down the hall as they neared a pair lying right beside one of the green flares, studying the man's profile.

He was human in form and basic appearance, but up close she could see the fine differences. Gold, cat-like irises peeked now and then from below heavy lids. What almost looked like stripes ringed his bared thighs, waist, and wrists, fading down fingers ending in thick nails that looked more like short, curved claws. The creature turned his head as they stepped past, and he growled, flashing sharp fangs, as he pumped harder against the short-haired girl below him.

Oh, shit, Samantha's head screamed. *They're not human!*

"Come on!" she hissed and took off running. She barely heard Carly's cry as she maneuvered through the writhing forms on the ground.

"Sam, wait!"

Samantha skidded to a halt in a clearing at the end of the hall, looking back for Carly. She saw the other girl coming, picking her way slowly around the forms with a squeamish look on her face. Tears reflected the emerald glow.

"Samantha." Carly's voice was thick with horror. "Please don't leave me."

Samantha held out a hand. "Come on!"

Carly took another step closer, and then was jerked backward off her feet.

Samantha cried out as an arm wrapped around Carly's shoulders and pushed her up against the wall. Carly screamed as the uniformed man leaned forward, pulling at her pants with his free hand and leaning toward her. He leaned in for a kiss, but Carly turned her head and kicked out, catching him between the legs. The man grunted and staggered, but his hold never wavered. Carly clawed at his hand, and then struck out toward his face. Her nails met skin, raking across his eye, and the man let out a guttural yowl and flinched away, dropping his hand.

Carly spun around, eyes wild, as she sprinted for Samantha.

Samantha turned to go as Carly neared, her hand outstretched to pull her along.

A sharp crack split the air. Hot electricity crackled through the air, tingling Samantha's arm and side as Carly's fingers brushed Samantha's on her way to the ground. Carly jerked twice, her body convulsing as the tiny electrical sparks ran across her face to fade into darkness, and then went still.

Samantha ran. She ran blindly through the dark, her heart pounding wildly in her chest. Her legs burned, and her lungs ached. A scream built in her throat as she heard her pursuer's heavy boots closing in behind her.

Up ahead loomed the door to the stairwell. If only she could make it back to the stairs, then she could at least have a chance of escaping...

A second pair of gold eyes stepped into the hall in front of her, and Samantha's legs gave out as she tried to suddenly slow and turn. Strong arms grabbed the front of her shirt and jerked her to the side of the hall against a warm, solid wall of a body. In the dark, she saw the black shadow of her original pursuer rush past, gold eyes glaring at her as he overshot and skidded across the floor.

The one who had shot Carly spun around and growled at the newcomer, hissing angrily. Samantha cringed against the wall, trying to melt into the drywall. The newcomer shifted his weight, his legs pressing up against Samantha and pushing her behind him. Terrified, she did not argue, and flattened herself between the warm body in front and the cool plaster against her back, spreading her arms out against the wall to be as inconspicuous as possible.

Her fingers felt the edge of a doorframe, and she held her breath as the two creatures growled and hissed at each other. They began to circle, the newcomer turning his back toward her and pushing the other man farther down the hall. The eyes of the first man narrowed and dropped, and then he rushed forward.

Samantha slid across the wall and pushed the door open just as the two creatures collided together into the wall. She rolled onto her side inside the hotel room and twisted to kick the door shut. Something heavy stopped it from closing completely, and she screamed and rammed her shoulder into it, turning the lock to secure it shut.

Gasping, she scrambled back as she listened to the sounds of struggling and guttural roaring on the other side of the door. She felt around in the darkness and managed to make her way to the room's small, single window. She clawed at the blackout drapes, shoving them aside.

Yellow and gold light spilled in from the tall casino next door, and she frantically searched the frame for the latch. She finally found the lock and popped it open, sliding the glass up. She scrambled on top of the shaky dinette table and began pulling herself up and out of the window.

"Help!" she screamed out the open window. "Someone help me!"

The door behind her shuddered under a massive weight. Samantha yipped and nearly lost her grip on the windowpane. The wall shook again, and a hanging picture fell, the glass shattering. Samantha clawed at the window ledge, wiggling through to her waist just as the doorframe burst open.

A wave of relief rushed over her as gravity took hold and she began to fall down out of the window toward the bright city lights below. Damn the fact she was three stories up; she had rather have a few broken ribs or an arm than face whatever demons had taken over their shitty Vegas hotel.

A hand caught her ankle and jerked her upwards, hard. Samantha screamed.

TWO

Warmth, centered on her middle and slowly spreading across her chest, neck and arms slowly brought Samantha closer to the surface of the darkness that held her in a soft, comforting embrace.

She swallowed, eyes closed, not wanting to leave the enveloping sense of peace that swathed every part of her being and seeped into every muscle so that she felt relaxed and at ease in a way she had never experienced before.

Her mind began to stir as the warmth moved across her face and neck, her thoughts rising through the oblivion of contented silence like bubbles in golden honey, struggling to make sense and form reason.

No. This feels too good... too right.

The warmth became wet, swiping across her being and bringing feeling back into her skin so that she was aware of her body once again: the air against her neck and breasts, the soft silver comforter wrapped around her legs and back...

Samantha gasped and shifted, her shoulders pressing into the mattress and grounding her sense of space and reality. She fought against the urge to slip back into the comforting warmth and forced her heavy eyelids to open.

At first, nothing made sense. She lazily glanced around the room, trying to gauge her surroundings. The sparse and modern furnishings were masculine and decorated in monochrome grays, whites, and blacks. The large platform bed on which she laid sat in the middle of the room, bookended by matching side tables. A black armchair sat to the side of a low dresser, just to the right of the single window.

Samantha's eyes widened. Nothing looked familiar. This was not her room.

The wet warmth that had woken her brushed against her cheek, and Samantha gasped and jerked sideways on the bed. She twisted her head around to see a uniformed man sitting on the bed beside her.

No, she reminded herself. *Not a man...*

The creature sat frozen, the washcloth poised in the air above Samantha's head. He gazed down at her with gold eyes, steady and calculating.

When he did not move, Samantha scooted backward and slid off the bed to put the mattress between them. She stood and backed against the wall near the open window, steadying herself against the wall, when her weak legs nearly gave out.

Why do I feel so...

The thoughts froze in Samantha's head and sent chills running down her spine. She looked down, and for the first time realized that she was naked. Her face burned in embarrassment, which quickly grew into horror.

Oh, God... We didn't...

Memories flashed before her eyes: images of people rolling about in the halls on the ground in the throes of passion between fallen bodies, golden eyes appearing out of the darkness to jerk her away...

Her legs collapsed out and she slipped to the cool metal floor tiles. Immediately, the man was in front of her, a clawed hand reaching out. Samantha jerked her arm away, huddling against the wall.

"Get away from me." Samantha's words were weak and dry.

The man hesitated, his eyes quickly roaming over her body as if to assess her condition. Then, to Samantha's relief, he took a step back.

She pulled her legs up to her chest and tried her best to cover her round breasts from view. The cool air wafting in from the window chilled her skin, and she began to shiver.

The golden eyes blinked, and then the man reached behind and pulled the silver coverlet off the bed and held it out. Samantha winced, and when he did not move closer, gingerly snatched the blanket away and wrapped herself from neck to toe. She glared back at him, wary.

"What do you want with me?" she whispered. She waited for an answer but received nothing. Suddenly, the fear from her flight before faded to anger as she remembered Carly falling. "What do you want?"

The cat-eyed stranger—*alien* was the first word that came to mind—just continued to stare, stepping far enough back to sit on the edge of the bed.

With some distance between them, and at a seemingly current moment of peace, Samantha took the time to study her attacker as she struggled to calm her beating heart.

He appeared young, anywhere from late teens to early twenties, and his tan face was angled with a straight jaw and wide, straight nose. Dark brown stripes cut across his cheeks and continued down his neck. Thick lashes and heavy lids outlined gold eyes with cat-like pupils. Short, reddish hair spiked off a deep widow's peak and looked more like fur—*or a mane,* she thought. The black, button-up uniform covered him from the neck down to knee-high black boots.

He's not at all what I expected an alien to look like, she mused, her nerves slowly settling at his silence. *Aside from the cat-like features and strange coloring, he looks incredibly human.*

Sudden image flashes of bare skin and coarse fur made Samantha shake her head to clear away unwanted thoughts. Her throat constricted, and she swallowed as she unconsciously tightened between her legs and warmth built in her stomach, her body responding to a memory her mind was slow to recover.

The man on the bed shifted and leaned forward, nostrils flaring as he sniffed the air. He obviously liked what he smelled, because he slid down onto all fours and crawled toward Samantha like a predatory cat. His muscular shoulders stretched at his uniform, and he moved with a fluid grace that should not have been possible.

Samantha shuddered and shook her head, weakly pulling the blanket tighter around her. "No," she whispered.

She wanted to stand and run. To claw at him and put red slashes across that beautifully sharp and sculpted face. To scream...

Yet her body did not respond, and her heart raced when her hands refused to lift in defense. She could only close her eyes and whimper.

His hands brushed against her jawline. His touch was warm and unexpectedly soft, despite the curved claws. He leaned close until he was only inches from her lips, and his warm, mint-laced breath seemed to fill her head and crack her body's reserves. She felt herself heat up in response, and a thick wetness dripped down her inner thigh.

The man made a deep sound in his throat, something between a moan and a rumble, and pressed his chest against her shoulder, burying his face in her neck. A layer of soft hair covering his cheek tickled her skin, and the smell of kitten fur mingled with overpowering mint. His lips trembled against her neck before his mouth locked onto the suddenly feverish skin of her collarbone, and his rough, hot tongue licked long, wet circles in a slow, unsteady rhythm.

She tried to lift her arms to push him away, but her limbs refused to cooperate. Her breath hitched in her throat as he pulled the blanket away and used one arm hooked behind her lower back to lay her gently on the floor and the other to push her legs apart.

"P-please..." She managed, her voice barely above a whisper.

The man's hands stopped at his waistband and his head jerked up, eyes searching her face. A single tear dripped down Samantha's cheek, and his eyes widened as the first sign of emotion became clear on his face:

Confusion.

Samantha held her breath as she waited on her back. Another tear followed the first as she stared up at him. "Please... don't."

Quicker than she could blink, the man was off of her and standing on the other side of the bed, his eyes narrowed, and brow furrowed. He stared at her a moment, and then began to pace uncomfortably back and forth across the small space of the room.

Control returned to Samantha's hands and feet once he was out of close range, and she scrambled back to her corner of the room and huddled under the blanket. She swallowed and fought against her body's urge to fly across the room and tackle the man to rip his shirt off.

What's wrong with me?

She paused, staring as the very upset alien growled to himself, pacing uneasily around the room.

It seems he's wondering the same thing, she realized after a moment.

She remembered how the girls on the night of the invasion had simply given up—or rather thrown themselves—to the uniformed men at a simple touch and reasoned that the aliens were probably not used to getting turned down.

The panic that had been growing in her stomach settled, enough so that she stopped trembling and could breathe again to observe the pacing alien. Standing, she realized he was smaller than the aliens she had seen the night before—though he stood close to six feet tall and probably weighed just under two hundred pounds. Long legs moved solidly beneath the slim-fitting uniform, and the clasps on the front of his shirt stretched taut across his broad chest. His wide shoulders hunched forward as he moved about like a caged—

"Tiger," she whispered.

The man stopped. Looked over at her with a blank face.

Samantha's heart skipped a beat. She had not realized she had spoken aloud. She sat, frozen, staring back into the golden orbs regarding her. Then her stomach betrayed her and growled, loud and angry. She hunched over, willing it to shut up.

The alien blinked, and then turned on his heel and stepped out of the room, shutting the door behind him.

Samantha blinked, stunned by the sudden silence. Then she shook her head and snapped out of it, standing quickly and glancing around the room. She did not see her clothes, and for all she knew he had torn them to shreds, so she dove into the nearest dresser to see what she could find. One thing was for sure: she was not about to sit around and find out whatever plans he had for her. She was getting the hell out of here. She pulled open the drawers to find underwear, socks, and belts, and thankfully, finally, a silk-like bathrobe.

She yanked out the robe and shucked it on, belted the tie around her waist, and turned toward the window as the door opened suddenly, her captor back with a covered tray in his hands.

He stared at her from the doorway, his eyes radiating disapproval and mouth set in a tight line. A low growl emanated from his chest, growing in crescendo until Samantha stepped back from the window and crouched back into her corner.

Seemingly satisfied with her position, the man kicked the door shut with one foot, not bothering to lock it, and set the tray down on the floor in front of Samantha. He lifted the cover off and stepped back.

Her stomach lurched, screaming as if it had not tasted food in weeks. Her mouth watered, and her hands involuntarily shook in anticipation. She had not realized how hungry she was until the sight of food was set in front of her.

How long have I been out?

Samantha's eyes roamed at the unfamiliar fare,

seeing what looked like a plate of fish and noodles and a bowl of square, purple fruit. Something red and spongy sat on top of a pile of what looked like seaweed, and she decided that she was not *that* hungry, not enough to eat something resembling a giant eyeball. She glanced at the alien, who had taken up a seat on the edge of the bed to watch. She stared at him for a moment, trying to decipher his intentions, and satisfied he was not going to approach, leaned forward and nearly attacked the food.

The food was unexpectedly bland, and Samantha was disappointed in the bowl of seeded fruit that tasted like hard sweet potatoes, though she cleared away half the tray before she slowed.

Samantha glanced back at the man on the bed. He sat, eyes wide and staring, with his mouth turned upwards ever so slightly at the corners. Amused. She snorted at him and snatched up the last square of fruit and a glass bottle of water before settling in the corner against the wall, pulling the robe tight around her legs.

The man had not moved save to turn his head to watch her, and Samantha flicked a flat fruit seed at him, emboldened by her satiated tummy. He brushed at his face in annoyance to rid it of the seed, but he otherwise stayed still.

Samantha glowered at him. *Fine by me.*

They sat for what felt like an hour, both staring, with Samantha's occasional sip of water the only sound to break the silence. Finally, she could not take it anymore.

"What do you want with me?"

No answer.

"Where am I?" She waited, her anger rising once again. "Where is everyone else?"

The cat eyes regarded her coolly.

"Do you even understand what I'm saying?" Samantha said, her voice thick with anger and frustration. She stood, and the bottle fell forgotten from her fingers, the glass clinking against the metal floor panels. She balled her hands into fists by her side. "What do you want?"

Samantha turned her head, willing the tears to not come. She did not want to sit and cry. She had done plenty of crying the past few months, with the passing of her estranged father and the end of a three-year engagement. No—she was done with crying. She had responsibilities, a farm to run... but her body did not seem to give a rat's ass what she thought at the moment, and let the tears roll down her red cheeks.

She glanced toward the shadows of the bed, and from her angle spotted her torn jeans underneath. The top corner of her tablet poked out from the back pocket, and she gasped and lunged for it. She jerked the small tablet out and stepped back, and then her face fell at the cracked screen and frozen pixels showing the lock screen photo of her and her dad on their camping trip to Yellowstone when she was ten.

Samantha fell to her knees, sobbing. She clutched the busted tablet to her chest, as if it were a lifeline holding her to a reality that was no longer hers. She screamed; her entire body racked with sobs as she shook her head, praying that she had wake from this nightmare.

Two hands landed gently on her back, the fingers trembling. Samantha struggled to turn away, but then the arms wrapped around her shoulders strong and firm, and she had no strength to fight against them. The alien pulled her toward him, so that her body rested against the line of his chest. He seemed to hesitate, and then leaned his chin on her shoulder, hugging her closer as if trying to lend comfort.

His attempt to soothe angered her, and slowly pushed away the despair. He was, after all, the one who had caused her this pain in the first place. It was his fault she was here. His fault that Carly was dead. His fault that she was a sniveling mess on the floor of his bedroom in nothing but a thin robe...

Fuck him.

She jerked back, gaining a surprised look from the man kneeling before her, and with both hands quickly swung the tablet up to smack into his right temple. The glass shattered further with an audible crunch, and he fell sideways with a grunt.

Samantha dove over him and sprinted out of the unlocked door.

She burst into the hall and frantically looked both ways, trying to gauge her surroundings, and realized she was in some sort of apartment. The large space looked bare and monochrome, with no signs of person-alization or life. The walls were a contrasting white against the gray, tiled floor. The main room, shaped rectangular and narrow, held a single armchair in one corner by the only window and a low table and long black couch against the nearest wall, opposite of a large, mounted, flat screen monitor. The kitchen had stainless steel countertops and industrial-looking appliances. There stood a closed door on either side of her, which she assumed were for a bathroom and a second bedroom.

Samantha's breath hitched as she spotted what looked like a front door at the opposite end of the apartment, and she darted towards it. Her hand closed on the door handle and turned, and she jerked it open.

A clawed hand slammed it shut before Samantha could exit, and she was spun around and pushed against the metal door.

She blinked, clearing her vision, to face her captor. His gold eyes blazed with fury, and his cheeks burned with an angry blush so deep it was near purple. His hand closed about her throat, and he leaned forward to growl in her face, baring fangs.

"Stirka kit rissat sa," he hissed between clenched teeth.

The man's nostrils flared, and he snorted, then shifted his grip to the back of her neck and proceeded to push her back in the direction of the room she had fled.

Samantha planted her feet and refused to cooperate. The alien hissed at her, pushing harder, but she let her legs go out from under her and dropped to the floor.

"No!" she yelled.

"Tski raka!"

He grabbed her by the waist and threw her over his shoulder, storming down the hall.

Samantha tried to kick and fight against him, slamming her fists against his back and twisting in his grip to get loose. She struggled for a while, until the five claws from one large hand got a good grip on the back of her left thigh. He tightened his hold until she froze, in fear of him breaking skin.

Back in the room, he dumped her unceremoniously on the soft mattress and then turned to slam the door shut. Samantha rolled off the mattress and, as he reached for her, slid under the bed out of reach. He let out a small roar and grabbed the bed frame with one hand, flipping the entire bed over. Samantha let out a cry of surprise and tried to crawl away, but he grabbed her hair and pressed her face down to the floor.

He put one knee in the small of her back to free his hands, and easily ripped off the robe. Then he flipped her onto her back and straddled her waist, holding her arms above her head as easily as if she had been a child. Samantha kicked and tried to lift her hips to buck him off, but his greater weight and strength left her panting. He sat patiently, seemingly bent on waiting her out.

They sat for several moments, Samantha's eyes wide and heart racing, the alien's breathing even and jaw tight. Then he sighed and stepped away from her, straightening his uniform. Samantha scuttled into the corner, dragging the torn robe closer and pulling it up like a shield.

Samantha watched silently as he righted the bed and began fixing the mattress and sheets, her heart slowing to normal and shoulders relaxing.

Why hadn't he continued to...

She shook her head, not wanting to think about that something until he actually tried. Though she knew instinctively that if he had wanted to take her then, he could have—easily. The strength she had felt in those clawed hands left no doubt that she was no match in a struggle, and yet he had made it a point not to strike her. She studied him, noting the tremor in his hands and the slight blush on his cheeks and down the sides of his neck.

"You're not going to hurt me," Samantha said after a moment, "are you?"

The man sat on the edge of the newly made bed, rubbing the back of his neck. His eyes did not quite meet hers, and they held not anger, but disappointment and regret.

Samantha shifted against the floor. "Please, let me go home." Tears welled in her eyes again. "Please. I know you don't want to hurt me."

The gold eyes blinked, an indecisive look crossing the alien features. Then he stood and walked to a small touchpad on the wall near the door. He punched in a code and a panel of the wall to the left of the keypad slid open to reveal a closet. Inside hung several uniforms similar to what he currently wore. He pulled out a silver, metal briefcase from one of the upper shelves and set it on the bed. Another code later and a few clicks of releasing locks, and he opened the lid.

Samantha tensed as he picked up what looked like a small, silver gun with a sharp point at the front, and then looked pointedly at her before quickly approaching. She pressed herself up against the wall as he knelt and grabbed her jaw with one hand and turned her face to the side, pressing the object against her head.

"What..." Samantha struggled. "Don't, please!"

The sharp prick of a needle set off a burning sensation behind her left ear, and for a moment everything became muted and muffled. Her heart beat loud in her ears, the whoosh-whoosh of the blood rushing through her veins drowning out all sound. The man let her go, and she leaned back against the wall. She shakily brought up a hand to feel at her skin, where she felt a nub of cool metal stuck just below her hairline behind her ear.

She curled her fingers to scratch at it, but the man caught her hand and shook his head. His lips moved, but the sound was muted in the whooshing of her blood and pounding of her heart.

Samantha closed her eyes, her head pounding and vision swimming as her heartbeat grew louder and louder, the pressure behind her eyes building as her breathing quickened.

Then suddenly everything went silent, and she opened her eyes.

She looked up at the man before her, so close that she felt his breath against her lips. His eyes studied her intently, before he pulled back to sit on his heels.

Samantha swallowed. "What... what did you do to me?"

Tears welled in her eyes as she thought of the possibilities, conjured up by countless science fiction books read and many nights spent alone watching cheesy horror movies. Mind control. Genetic experimentation. Injected diseases... She reached up again to touch the metal implant behind her ear, but froze at his simple command:

"No."

THREE

Her jaw dropped, and she stared wide-eyed at him. She stared at his lips. "W-what?"

He repeated his command in his sharp alien dialect, and almost at once, his voice came through her left ear, as if his voice were inside her head.

"Do not touch." His lips did not match the voice in her ear, the translation delayed by a fraction of a second.

"How—"

"Translator."

Samantha swallowed, her nerves rattled. Her ear ached, and her head swam again. She felt herself falling and braced for the impact on the cold floor. She sucked in her breath as warm arms caught her and gently lifted her limp form, carrying her to the bed. Her eyes were heavy, and she fought to keep the room from spinning while she looked up at the alien as he laid her on the mattress. She was surprised at the touch of concern in his eyes as he sat on the edge of the bed, watching her.

"It should pass," he said after a moment.

Samantha blinked. "Should?"

He shrugged. "I have never done this before," he said, motioning to her neck. "Most pass quickly."

He turned his head to the side, so that Samantha could get a glimpse of the similar metal nub sticking out of the skin behind his own ear.

The room had mostly settled, and Samantha swallowed and slowly pushed herself to an upright position. She moved to rub at her ear but stopped when the alien lifted a finger in warning, and then twiddled her thumbs in her lap as her focus returned.

"How do you avoid me?" the man asked suddenly.

Samantha looked up. "What?"

"You reject my advances. How?"

She scrunched up her nose. "Arrogant, aren't we?"

"Your species is supposed to react strongly to the..." He trailed off, his calculating stare unnerving. "They said you would not say no."

Samantha peered at him, trying to piece together whatever it was she was supposed to react to, and why, then, she would not be affected. Regardless of the reasons, she was elated by the revelation that she had an ounce of control left in the situation. "Who are *they*?"

The alien looked away, silent, and scooted farther away on the bed. He shifted uneasily.

"What's your name?" she asked. Maybe if she

learned more about him then she could figure out a way to get back home from... wherever she was.

He hesitated, the tips of pointed fangs peeking below his upper lip. After a moment he answered, "Krissik Sa Tskir."

Samantha blinked, not even wanting to try. "Uh... anything else I can call you?"

He tilted his head slightly to one side, as if trying to decide what she meant. "Why do you need to call me? I am right here."

"I didn't mean..." Samantha sighed. "I can't pronounce your name. Is there another name I can use? One that's easier?"

He blinked. "I only have one name."

Samantha fought the urge to scream. *So much for this translation device being a big help...*

"Kreesak Tear—" she began.

"Krissik Sa Tskir."

"Krissik Sa... Can I call you Kris?"

The man stared at her, and then slowly nodded, though he did not seem happy about it.

"Thanks. At least this way I have a name to put to your face instead of Tygra."

Krissik frowned. "What is tee-gra?"

His attempt at pronouncing the name almost brought a smile to Samantha's face. Almost.

"It's a cartoon character from a show..." She trailed off at his confused look. Samantha motioned toward his eyes and cheeks. "Striped cheeks and gold eyes. Actually, the feline characteristics are... pretty amazing."

She looked closer at his face, following the high cheekbones to the straight slope of his jaw line. The stripes that cut diagonally down from his hairline across his cheeks continued down the sides and back of his neck, disappearing into the high, stiff collar of his shirt. His lips were full and tinted a very pale pink, a strong contrast to the angles of his profile. She suddenly had the urge to reach out and stroke the top of his head, wondering if his hair was as soft and fuzzy as it looked.

Krissik just stared at her. Whether he did not agree with the comparison, or he did not understand the compliment, Samantha could not tell. She also really did not care.

"My name is Samantha," she said after a moment.

The golden eyes narrowed. "Ssan-tha."

Samantha perked up. At least he was trying. "Sa-man-tha."

He sat silent.

Well, at least he gave it one shot. "Sam. It's easier."

"I am tired." He looked back at her pointedly. *"You* tire me."

She glared at him, and then her bladder screamed, and she leapt off the bed and headed for the door. "Look, I need to—"

Krissik hissed a warning and slid up beside her. He grabbed her arm and pointed to the bed. Samantha jerked in his grip and pointed between her legs.

"I have to pee!" she said quickly. He did not seem to understand, so she elaborated, "Urinate."

His lip curled upwards, as if disgusted by the idea, and let go of her arm. He opened the door and walked her into the hall, opening the door on their left. Samantha stepped inside, turning in a full circle. In the room stood a tall, glass-enclosed shower, a tall free-standing metal cabinet, and two pedestal vanities with hanging towels.

Where is the toilet? Tell me they don't just pee in the shower...

She spun back to Krissik and was taken aback at the fact he seemed to be grinning at her.

"Where?" she demanded, glaring. Her eyes watered with the strain as she waited. "Where?"

Krissik reached out and brushed the wall on their right with one finger. Another panel opened to a reveal a small separate room, and in the middle sat the most futuristic toilet Samantha had ever seen. There were buttons lining the side, and a small, flat-screen display was mounted on the wall nearby. She shook her head. This was definitely a male's apartment.

I guess it doesn't matter what species guys are...

She shuddered and hurried in, then waved at him to shut the door.

"Privacy, please?"

The alien swiped his hand along the wall and the door between them slid in place.

With the relief of emptying her bladder came the tears. She cried for Carly, who had fallen trying to reach her. Then she cried for herself, unsure what this man meant to do to her, and whether she had ever make it home.

Samantha took several minutes to gain her composure, glad to be away from his peering eyes and the reminder that she was his prisoner. She used half the stack of stiff tissues to wipe at her eyes and blow her nose, and then flushed and made several failed attempts to open the door before finally finding the right spot on the wall to swipe.

Hot steam enveloped her as soon as the door slid open, and she stepped into the main bathroom to the sound of running water. She glanced over in the direction of the shower and her heart skipped a beat.

Krissik stood naked in the glass enclosure with his back to her, hot water pelting him from three showerheads and steam rising off his body. The stripes that decorated his face and neck continued down his wide back, circling around his narrow waist and down the backs of his firm butt and slender thighs, appearing much darker and starker against his tanned skin in the overhead fluorescent light. Soap bubbles slid slowly down his neck and back, following the curve of his hips and down his legs.

Samantha yipped and turned to leave the bathroom. She bumped into the nearest vanity, knocking over a small bottle. The bottle fell to the ground with a clatter and rolled, the clear, mint-smelling liquid spilling out across the metal floor tiles. She flinched and glanced back at the shower, where Krissik had twisted to look at her, his gold eyes piercing and wild.

"Oh, shit," Samantha whispered before bolting.

She made it to the door to the bedroom and reached back to shut the door when his wet body slammed into hers. Soap-covered arms lifted her off her feet and dropped her onto the bed. Samantha squealed and flailed her arms trying to push him away, but her hands slid off his slick chest. He rested his lower half against her legs, his weight holding her down as he pulled at the robe. Samantha gasped as she felt his growing erection, incredibly warm and slick, slide up against her inner thigh.

"No!" Samantha shouted at him. "No!"

"Why not?" he breathed against her neck. His tongue lapped up the water droplets on her neck that dripped from his body. "Why do you say no?" He grabbed her face with one hand and planted a firm, wet kiss across her mouth.

Samantha's vision exploded in a burst of golden stars and honey waves as liquid, minty fire spilled between her lips. Heat rose from her groin, stroking between her legs and radiating up to her stomach and chest. She breathed in deeply to clear her head, but the fragrances of mint, soap and kitten fur barraged her senses, and she felt herself running her fingers through the soft, wet fur behind his ears in an almost frenzied rush.

Soap dripped off Krissik's skin onto Samantha's legs and belly. She felt his slick hips wiggle against her skin, spreading her knees farther apart. The hot, wide tip of his starting erection rubbed up against her inner thigh, and she gasped as he shuddered above her in anticipation.

She turned her head to the side. "Because it doesn't work this way!"

Samantha tried again to push him away, her head struggling to swim out the honey depths. Krissik hesitated, unsure, and then growled and tightened his grip on her chin and leaned forward to kiss her again, his lower half lifting slightly off of her to reach. She managed to get one leg free, and she used all of her strength to ram it hard into his crotch. Her knee hit soft tissue and she felt him buckle over.

Krissik gasped and fell to the side, letting go of Samantha's arms. She used the opportunity to bunch up her legs, place her feet on his chest, and kick. He flew backward and hit the edge of the mattress, rolling off sideways.

Samantha twisted toward the headboard, where the metal briefcase still sat. She grabbed the handle with both hands and spun her entire body as Krissik crawled closer. The case connected with his nose, and Samantha winced at the audible crunch and trail of red sprinkled into the air as the man fell back and disappeared over the side of the bed.

Samantha knelt, gasping, clutching the bloodied briefcase to her chest, her heart pounding. After several moments of silence, she shakily stood to peer down at the floor.

Krissik lay curled on his side, eyes closed, and hands pressed to his nose. Red seeped out from between his fingers, smearing across his face and staining the floor panels. He groaned and rolled to a sitting position, leaning back against the bed. He tilted his head back to rest on the foot of the bed, fingers pinching the bridge of his nose. His breathing sounded labored.

Samantha glared at him. "Don't try it again you son of a bitch! That's twice already—"

"What did I do wrong?" came the voice in her ear.

"You can't just kidnap people and force them to have sex whenever you please!"

"I was not going to force you."

"Really? Because you don't seem to take no for answer."

"I was trying to get you to participate." He glanced up at her, and he did not need to say anything for her to know that he did not comprehend. "They said you would want to..."

"Again with the 'they.' Who are *they*?" The briefcase lowered just an inch. "Look, I don't want to have sex with you."

Krissik sniffed and shifted to sit on one hip, leaning his upper body on the bed so that he faced her. Samantha had done a number on his nose; a large gash cut across his wide bridge and the inner corners of both eyes were bruising to a deep purple. Blood ran down his lips and chin and had dripped onto his chest.

"You do not have a choice."

Samantha's cold began to take the better of her,

and she swooned, lightheaded. She steadied herself against the headboard.

Krissik reached out as if to steady her, concern in his eyes. She pushed his arm away and sat back. Krissik held out his hands, trying to look harmless.

"I will not hurt you."

Samantha snorted, her blood pumping. Though regardless of how or why she was there, she knew that Krissik spoke the truth. Even after she had clocked him twice—drawing blood both times—he had yet to strike at her. And glancing at his claws and the teeth she knew hid behind those full lips. She knew he could cause some major damage if he wanted to.

Now if only he could learn to keep it in his pants...

Her eyes roamed on their own accord from his downcast face down his chest, where a small diamond of white fur trailed in a fine line across a muscled abdomen and dark navel, above where the fur thickened and spread to cover... She averted her eyes, blinking back up towards his torso.

She did a double take as she noticed some deep bruising across his ribs, and a row of fresh, raised slashes across his left upper arm.

"Is that from last night?" she asked.

Krissik twisted his arm to look where she pointed. "You mean when I chose you? Yes. But that was two days ago."

"Two days! I've been out for two days?"

He nodded. "The jump is hard on those not prepared for it. I did my best to keep you comfortable."

Samantha thought back to running through the hotel in the midst of some extraterrestrial orgy, when the gold eyes had stepped out of the dark to take her away from the alien chasing her down the hall—the same man who had shot Carly for rejecting him before setting his sights on Samantha.

Looking down at Krissik's miserable expression, and the state she had left his face in, she was tempted to apologize—and even thank him.

Out of all the aliens who could have abducted me, she thought. *I guess I could have gotten worse than this clumsy sod.*

Samantha stood and swept past Krissik into the bathroom, half expecting him to follow. When he did not, she grabbed two hanging towels and wet one in the sink with warm water before wringing it out. She picked up the small fallen bottle, corked it, and returned to the bed.

She tossed the dry towel to him from three feet away. "Please, could you cover up?"

Krissik obliged her, tucking in the towel around his hips.

Samantha hesitated, and then held out the wet towel. "Here."

Krissik looked up, his eyes lidded and swollen. He reached up and took the towel. He acknowledged her with a nod, and then pressed the towel to his face. He sighed and leaned back against the bed, eyes closed.

"Your arm looks like you should get stitches," she said after a moment.

Krissik shrugged. "It is a battle scar. Probably one of the few I will ever obtain."

Samantha's heart finally began to slow, and she swallowed at the lump in her throat. She played with the little vial in her hands, and then held it out. "Here. I accidently knocked this over."

Krissik glanced at her, and then sat up with wide eyes. His face darkened to red, and then paled as he swallowed and almost started shaking. He held the bottle up to the light and shook it, testing the contents. Less than a third of the bottle remained.

Samantha's eyebrows shot up. "Are you OK?"

Krissik's eyes lowered, and his jaw tightened. He looked extremely unsettled.

Samantha stuck out her jaw. "If we're on talking terms, I'd like to get some answers."

"It is late. You should sleep."

"I'm not tired." Though even as she said it, her eyes suddenly felt heavier and her head ached from the pressure in her sinuses.

He peeked up at her. "Yes, you are." He groaned and pushed himself to his feet, holding the towel around his waist with one hand. "Do not worry. I will not try to touch you tonight."

For some reason beyond her, Samantha immediately believed him. "Where should I sleep?"

"In the bed."

"Where are you sleeping?"

"In the bed."

She bit her lip. "I thought you said—"

"I said I would not try to... what is your word... sex. I am tired."

He walked to the closet by the door, set the small vial down on the highest shelf, and used one hand to push around objects on the lower shelf. He pulled out a bottle of pills and fumbled to remove the lid for a few moments using one hand. Frustrated, he growled and let the towel drop to use both hands.

Samantha averted her eyes from his exposed backside as he shook out two white pills, popped the top back on the bottle, and padded naked into the bathroom.

"How about I sleep on the couch?" she called out.

She heard the sink run as he slurped up several mouthfuls of water before shutting it off. He fumbled around with something against the vanity and cursed something the translator could not relay.

She glanced up as he appeared a few minutes later, dry, and soap-free with a towel tied around his waist. He had bandaged his nose with medical tape, and he glared at her from blackened eyes as he typed in a code on the bedroom door, locking it.

"No."

Samantha sniffed, wiping at her nose with the back of one hand. "You don't have anything for sinus problems, do you?"

"What is wrong with your sinuses?"

"I'm fighting a cold."

There was a pause. "Do you need more blankets?"

"No, I'm not cold. I'm..." Samantha groaned. "Never mind."

She closed her eyes as he clicked the lights off and listened to the rustling sound of cloth sliding against bare skin as he slipped between the sheets.

Krissik gave her one last glance before rolling onto his side, his back toward her. He lay still for several moments, and almost at once his breathing slowed and became even.

Samantha stood, wrapped in the tattered robe, and debated her options. A night lying in the same bed as the naked alien who had tried to bed her twice in one day was not her idea of rest, but hours curled on the cold metal flooring was not exactly inviting either.

I could always try to crack the code on the door panel, she thought, eyeing the little red light glowing in the dark.

And if I got out? Where am I going to go? I doubt I could call a cab to take me home.

She turned to tiptoe to the open window. She looked up at the dark sky to see two moons, one blue and one red, floating above. She stuck her head out into the cold breeze and looked down. The vertical drop was multiple stories down. The blue moonlight reflected off the metal siding of the flat building, showing no grooves or outcrops that she could use to climb down. Below, she could just make out the edges of a street, though she saw no signs of life or movement.

Her eyes burned, and she wiped angrily at her nose and sniffed. Her head ached, her stuffy nose felt raw, and she desperately did not want to be alone, sick, and naked on some alien planet.

She turned to glance at Krissik's form on the bed. She held her breath to listen; his breathing was still slow and steady. He was obviously asleep. The wind picked up outside and swept across the back of her neck, lifting her hair. She shuddered.

Damn.

She hesitated, and then tiptoed over to the bed, slowly lifted the corner of one sheet, and slipped one leg in. She hesitated, and then continued to slip onto the bed. The mattress sunk below her weight, molding around her body to cradle her like a custom fit. Once horizontal, weariness bore down on her chest and shoulders, and she closed her eyes. She lay as close to the edge of the bed as possible, keeping as much distance between them as she could.

I'll just rest for a moment, she thought. *Just enough to keep my strength up so that I can try to figure out how to get home...*

FOUR

Weight pressed down on Samantha's legs, trapping her against the bed and twisting her knees apart. She kicked out, trying to free herself.

No! She screamed. *No, not like this!*

The hold only tightened, and she screamed and lashed out with her hands...

Her eyes snapped open, and she looked around to find herself alone in the bed. Red sunlight poured into the room from the open window, bathing her skin in a warm glow. She looked down. She lay sideways on the bed, her arms out at her sides. The front of her robe lay wide open, her breasts and stomached bared for all to see. The sheets and coverlet twisted tightly around her legs, and she quickly kicked herself free and sat up.

Her eyes roamed the room. Krissik was nowhere to be seen. She slowly stood and padded into the hall but was only greeted with silence.

"Hello?" she whispered. "Kris?"

Glad to be alone for a few moments, she quickly crossed the hall to the bathroom, wanting to take care of personal needs before she was surprised with anything else. She blew her nose several times, her head clogged and sinuses aching. Once finished, she figured out how to turn on the water in the shower and stepped in, grateful that the heat was immediate.

The water felt amazing, and she rolled her shoulders in the heat, closing her eyes. She stood still for several minutes, letting the multiple showerheads beat near-scalding water against her shoulders, back and chest. The thick steam rising off her body helped clear her nose, and she relished being able to breathe deeply. Eventually, her skin screamed for relief from the heat, and she went about scrubbing every inch down with the blue bar of soap sitting on a small ledge. She lathered up her breasts and neck, trying to wash away the lingering scent Krissik had left behind the night before.

She turned the dial to stop the water, and a sudden flow of cold water shocked her and made her cry out. She frantically pressed the controls until the water shut off, and she shivered and stepped out onto the metal flooring. She grabbed the last hanging towel and quickly dried off, wrapping it around her torso as she tiptoed to the doorway and peeked out.

"Kris?"

The silence in the apartment sat heavy like a thick fog. She was surprised he had not returned by now, and her heart began to race. Suddenly, she felt that the presence of her resident alien was not such an annoyance after all. Being on an alien planet with a dysfunctional alien was one thing; being on an alien planet completely alone was something else.

She sniffed and rubbed at her nose, and then froze. She blinked, thinking, and then gasped and rushed over to her torn jeans in the corner. She patted down her pockets and let out a little joyous yip as she pulled out the package of cold medicine.

She closed her eyes and looked skyward, whispering, "Oh, thank you!"

She darted into the bathroom and pushed out two orange, liquid capsules and downed them with handfuls of water from the sink. She wiped her mouth with the edge of the towel, and then walked toward the kitchen as her growling stomach egged her on. She reached up and began poking around in the upper cupboards.

The lock on the front door beeped as someone punched in a code from the other side. Samantha yipped in surprise and stepped back, looking around the room. She snatched up the heavy serving tray on the counter from the day before and held it up like a bat ready to swing. Suddenly, the nonexistence of her captor settled like a cold weight in her stomach. The idea of some new alien stepping through the door in his stead terrified her.

Please be Kris, please be Kris...

The door hissed open and swung inward. A clawed hand grabbed the edge, pushing the door farther open.

Samantha's eyes burned, her throat tight, and she readjusted her grip on the tray.

Krissik looked up and froze, his eyes going wide. The white tape on his nose stood out starkly against the bruising around the corners of his eyes, and several specks of blood had bled through to spot the surface. He stared at Samantha as if she had grown a head in his absence before turning to shut and lock the door behind him.

"What are you doing?" he asked slowly.

Samantha sighed and lowered the tray. She opened her mouth to speak, hesitated, and then shrugged. "I didn't know where you went. You've been gone for a while."

Krissik's face went solemn as he set two bags and a silver paper-wrapped package on the table. "I did not expect you to wake so soon."

"Where have you been?" Samantha set the tray on the counter and crossed her arms.

Krissik stopped on his way to the bathroom. The gold eyes narrowed. "I do not answer to you."

Samantha frowned. "Considering you hold my life in your hands, you owe me some answers."

"Later."

He disappeared into the bathroom and shut the toilet door behind him.

Samantha made a strangled noise as she ground her teeth. She was surprised that she felt comfortable around Krissik enough to feel anything but fear, but not enough so to hold her frustration at bay. Now that the feeling of imminent danger had passed, Samantha's mind was set on only one thing: get home.

She waited until she heard the water flush, and then opened the bathroom door and stepped inside to intersect him on his way to the sink.

"I *need* answers," she nearly shouted. "You assholes kidnapped me from my home, killed my friend, and I have no idea where I am or why I am here!"

"We did not kill. Only stun."

Samantha sucked in a breath, her heart overjoyed. So, Carly was alive!

"You mean... like you tasered them?"

"I do not know that word."

Krissik tried to step around her, but Samantha blocked his path. He frowned down at her.

"Move."

"Not until you give me more answers."

He looked ready to throw her out the window. "Do you think I could not move you?" He lifted one hand, fingers curved to show off his claws.

Samantha jerked back and stepped away. She was fairly certain he would not actually use those claws on her, but the sight of them alone made her body react. Krissik's eyes followed her movements, and Samantha was sure she saw a small smirk at the corner of his mouth.

"Please," she started again, subdued. "I really need you to talk to me."

Krissik finished washing his hands and dried them

on the nearest hand towel before walking back into the living room.

Samantha's cheeks heated, and she balled her hands into fists and followed him. "You abduct me and try to screw me, stick me in the neck with some alien gizmo so I can understand you, and now you don't want to talk?" She sucked in air as she screamed, "You selfish alien bastard!"

Krissik's eyes went wide as he turned from the counter, a package in his hand. His eyebrows knotted together, and his shoulders hunched forward protectively.

Samantha breathed in and out heavily, the blood pounding in her ears. Her eyes dropped from his shocked face down to the package in his hands. She looked back up to meet his eyes—which never left hers as he carefully set the package down on the arm of the couch and stepped back.

"What is this?" Samantha said after a moment, the red in her vision dissipating.

"For you," he said.

Samantha blinked, and curiosity overcame anger. She gave Kris one last glance, and then crossed the living room to the couch and unwrapped the silver packaging. Her fingers met cool cloth, and she lifted up a plain black dress and matching slippers. Relief flooded through her at the sight of something to wear other than the ripped robe, and she clutched it to her chest.

"Thank you," she said after a moment. She looked

up to his expectant stare, and then dismissed herself to the bathroom.

Surprisingly, the dress fit fairly well. Conservative and covering, it was several inches too long, and she suspected that it meant the alien girls—whatever they called themselves—were tall just like the men. There were slits in the sides for small pockets, and she slipped the cold medicine in one and a ball of tissue in the other. She rolled up the ends of the sleeves to fit her shorter arms and ran a finger along the high neckline that reached the bottom of her jaw.

They obviously aren't for showing much skin.

Krissik was sitting on the couch studying his claws when Samantha appeared. He looked up as he heard her near, and he seemed to perk up. He nodded in approval.

"Come," Krissik said, his voice low but stern. "Sit."

Samantha hesitated.

Krissik pressed his lips in a straight line and pointed to the cushion beside him.

Samantha did as she was told, making sure to keep ample space between them. Krissik noticed, and he frowned before looking down at his folded hands.

"My world has suffered a lot since the last war," he began slowly, the translator beeping occasionally at a word that had no English equivalent. He seemed to be carefully choosing his words. "Many men were killed during the invasion, and sickness and famine killed most of the females and children. We have never recovered from the imbalance of genders."

Samantha slowly reclined against the soft cushions, her eyes going wide as she listened.

Krissik sighed. "There are very few females alive of breeding age, and so our race is dying. We have tried to artificially incubate, but the offspring do not... they are not *right*. Mentally. So, in an effort to rebuild our society, our Tsiari has ordered us to bring honor to our families and continue our species..." he spared a sideways glance at Samantha, "take mates of a similar race to continue our blood."

Samantha's breath hitched in her throat, and she wiped at her clogged nose. "And you brought *me* here?"

He nodded.

"Why?"

"Because you are of breeding age." He hesitated, dipping his head to gaze at her face. "And you are beautiful."

Samantha let out a choked sob. She covered her face with her hands. "So, you're just going to lock me in a room and knock me up..."

"You will be free to move around the apartment once we consummate."

Samantha turned and narrowed her eyes as she studied his shameful look. She sat up straight. "Wait..." She hesitated, licking her lips. "You mean we didn't..."

Krissik looked at her, confused, and then blinked and shook his head, a blush deepening on his cheeks and neck. "No. I tried, several times." He let out a half-hearted chuckle. "But you pushed me away every time despite being told you would want to."

"Why didn't you force me?" Samantha stared harder. "All of those women at the hotel..."

"I do not fully approve of such actions. Besides, I think my brother would kill me..." Krissik looked down at his slightly trembling hands, then back at Samantha. "I do not want you to be afraid of me. I will not hurt you, nor force you to do what you do not want to."

Relief flowed over Samantha, and she tilted her head back and let out a long sigh. Even though his stance might not be permanent, knowing he would not force or hurt her gave her hope for escaping this planet. She wiped at her face and nose, her head aching.

"Thank you," she whispered.

Krissik stood and walked into the kitchen, and then pulled out a bottle of pale, yellow liquid from the refrigerator door. He popped the cap off and tossed it onto the countertop, and then took several long, slow gulps. He sighed and rubbed at his eyes before turning back to where Samantha stood.

"Are you hungry?" he asked. "Thirsty?"

Samantha shook her head, even though her stomach betrayed her by choosing that very moment to complain.

Krissik pursed his lips, as if debating calling her on her bluff, yet stayed silent as he walked past her and plopped back down onto the couch, stretching out his legs and clicking on the monitor to what looked like a news channel. He glanced sideways at Samantha, and then settled back to stare at the screen.

SAMANTHA GLANCED OVER AT KRISSIK, who leaned against the other side of the couch with his arms crossed over his open computer and his boots propped up on the low table. His eyes were closed, and she studied his face as she flipped aimlessly through the channels—even though she could not understand a word of what was being said.

They had sat watching the monitor together for two hours, with Krissik unsuccessfully trying to scoot closer and slyly put his arm around her shoulders. She found his bumbled attempts almost endearing, though not wanting the close contact, she repeatedly pushed him away. After a while, he had retreated to the other side of the couch and went to work complaining about being behind on his studies, and they had spent the next several hours in relative silence. Lunch had been a quick and tasteless affair, and Krissik went back to work before falling asleep at his computer.

The gold eyes opened, as if he had sensed her staring. He blinked at her, annoyed, and sat up. "Yes?"

"So, I guess we should get to know each other if we're going to be cohabitating for the foreseeable future." She cleared her throat. "What do you do?"

"What do you mean?"

"For a living. Your job."

"I am an architect," he said proudly, sitting higher up. Then he sighed. "Assistant... architect. I still have one year left in my training."

She eyed him, trying to get a better idea of his age. She was a little surprised to hear the clawed and fanged creature having such a 'normal' career title, and then admonished herself with the idea that every built civilization had architects.

"You said you have a brother?"

"My elder. Rikist Sa Tskir. He is a decorated officer in our military, fighting the resistance on one of the outer islands."

"Resistance?" Samantha's brow shot up.

Krissik nodded and shut his computer. "Since the war, there have been pockets of rebels that have been trying to ignite a civil disruption due to the oppression of cities that did not fight in the name of the Tsiari, among other things..." He shot her a sideways glance. "We have been able to squash them mostly without issue, but lately their numbers have been growing."

Samantha sat back, digesting the news. She wondered what those 'other things' were, and if there were any risk of combat here in the city. Though Krissik did not seem concerned, and she figured that it probably was not as bad as she imagined.

"You said your brother was on an outer island? Are *we* on an island?"

He nodded. "Our planet is mostly water; the land

is divided up in strings of connected islands and small continents. Which has made it easier to quell the resistance because of the distance needed for them to join forces. Hard for them to acquire ships."

Krissik's hand lifted to Samantha's face, and she froze as his claws brushed against the side of her head. The sharp tips ran through her straight hair, gently pushing the hair back behind her ear.

"Do not worry," he said. "I would never let anything happen to you."

He let his fingers linger on her jaw, and then pulled back and reclined on the couch.

Samantha willed her heart to settle. His simple act of touching her hair had made her heart race and palms sweaty, and she pulled out her tissue from her pocket to give her something to keep her hands busy. He had told her he would not hurt her, but the view of his claws and memory of his inhuman strength made his touch feel as if she had been nuzzled by a tiger: he was pretty to look at, but able to lop her head off with one swipe. She stood and walked toward the bathroom, needing some distance. She pulled out the foil package of cold capsules as she pushed the door open, and a hand suddenly caught her wrist. She gasped and looked up to see the wall that was Krissik's chest. She had not even heard him move.

Krissik's gold eyes stared down at the package in her hand. His nostrils flared as he bent down to sniff at the packaging, and then jerked upright.

"What is this?" he demanded. When she did not answer, he gave her wrist a shake. "What is this?"

"You're hurting me." Samantha scowled at him until his grip lessened. "It's just medicine for my cold."

"Your what?"

"My cold. I'm sick."

Krissik let go and stepped back as if she had burned him. A low rumble rolled out between his bared fangs. "You carry sickness?"

"It's not serious." Samantha's eyes widened at his sudden alarm. "My sinuses are just acting up. It is very common at home."

He hesitated, and then held out one hand. "Give it here."

Samantha gripped the package. "No."

He barked out a short string of words that did not translate, his eyes blazing. "That is why it did not work!"

"Why *what* didn't work?" Samantha tilted her head to one side, lost.

"I should have searched you better. There is nothing wrong with me."

Memories of being engulfed in honey waves and near uncontrollable lust boiling in her gut until her lower half felt like it would burst flooded Samantha's mind. She remembered the smell of mint on his breath as he kissed her—the same scent of the bottle she had spilled. Anger rushed under her skin.

Oh, he so didn't...

Her head snapped up. "You tried to drug me!"

Krissik stopped his ranting and glared at her. "No."

"The mint-smelling vial I knocked over. What was in it?"

"I did not drug you."

"God damn it, Kris, quit pussyfooting around and just answer me. What was in the bottle?"

His lips twitched. "Genetically altered human pheromones."

She hesitated. "Come again?"

"Combined with our saliva, it creates pheromones one hundred times more powerful than those naturally produced in the human body."

"You son of a bitch," she breathed. She pushed at his chest. "That's how you nearly pushed me over the edge."

"I was told it was necessary."

"For what? To mate with you? Don't you know you can't just douse yourself in perfume and expect to just start going at it without first..." Her voice trailed off as she stared at him, at the way he hunched his shoulders protectively. His eyes would not meet hers. "You... don't, do you?"

She stared at his sullen face.

"You've never done any of this before, have you?" She paused. "With a woman, or..." She did not have to finish; the deep purple blush that had crept up Krissik's neck and cheeks said everything.

Samantha covered her face with her hands. She let her hands drop with a sigh, and sat down on the armchair by the window, rubbing her temples. Her head absolutely ached, and her nose felt clogged to the point she thought she had need all of the tissue on the damn planet to clear her lungs.

"How old are you?" she asked after a moment. She peered over at him.

Krissik leaned against the kitchen countertop. "Sixty-two seasons." He ignored Samantha's shocked look, and squinted his eyes toward the ceiling, thinking. "In your planet's measure of time... I think it is about a third of that in your years. Our orbital rotations are much faster than the solar—"

"I-I get it. You don't need to explain." She pulled her knees up to her chest, tucking the dress around her ankles. She did the math herself, putting him several years shy of her twenty-six. *He's just a damn kid!* "You've never done any of this before, have you?"

Krissik hesitated, his cheeks coloring deeper, and then shook his head. "This is... the first time I have been eligible for the jump."

"Jump?"

"Going to your planet. There is a specific time frame in which males are eligible to find a mate."

"You mean this whole mate-snatching thing is orga-nized? And the 'they' you keep referring to is your government, isn't it?"

"I... I am not supposed to talk about that..."

"Kris, you at least owe me an explanation."

"I could get into trouble..."

"Please."

The door to the apartment beeped, and they both turned their heads as the front door swung open. A second alien stood in the doorway with a bag in hand, hair billowing out about his head like a fiery halo and eyes blazing.

FIVE

The man stood taller than Krissik by a good several inches and outweighed him by at least fifty pounds of muscle throughout his broad chest, shoulders, and arms, which were accented by the navy blue uniform jacket and sweeping cloak. A gold aiguillette draped across his right shoulder, and a thick, braided cord of gold and silver hung across his chest beneath rows of striped pins. His jaw was square and straight, sliced on the right side by a jagged scar. The faded stripes on his cheeks and neck were barely visible in the tan face framed by wavy, auburn hair that brushed just past his shoulders.

Samantha swallowed as the dark, amber eyes roamed over her in a full once over. She felt as though she had been admiring a massive lion at the zoo, only to realize the glass had disappeared as it licked its chops. She marveled at the strength and feeling of danger radiating off him in waves that made her hair stand on end and her heart pound. She felt terrified at the feral intensity in the feline eyes, yet mystified by the absolute beauty of something so wild and—

Handsome.

She had the sudden urge to pet and run her hands over such an untamed and ferocious thing, to feel the strong muscles and soft fur slide beneath her fingertips...

She jerked her head to shake the thought. *What am I thinking? He's an alien for God's sake. I shouldn't even entertain the thought...*

"Rikist," Krissik cleared his throat and pushed away from the counter to greet the man. "I thought you were on deployment? What are you doing here?"

The dark amber eyes swept between Krissik and Samantha.

"You obviously have not been keeping up on the news." Rikist said, his voice low and smooth. His nostrils flared. "What happened to your face?"

Krissik blanched, his eyes darting for a split second to Samantha, who cowered under Rikist's gaze.

Rikist raised his eyebrows at Samantha, and then sneered at Krissik, showing off long, sharp canines.

"Really?"

Krissik swallowed, his cheeks red, and took the bag from Rikist. "It was an accident."

Rikist let out a deep, rolling chuckle as he stepped into the room and shut the door behind him. Now standing fully in the apartment's light, Samantha noticed the crutch under Rikist's left arm and the thick metal leg brace reaching up to his left thigh.

Krissik stared. "You have been wounded?"

Rikist limped heavily to the small kitchen table and sat into the nearest chair. He grunted and stretched out his leg, the brace creaking.

"A missile took out half of my ship on the east coast of Sitika. I was hit by the shrapnel and tore my anterior cruciate ligament in the fall."

"You did not send word." Krissik looked hurt.

"I figured you were..." Rikist glanced at Samantha and back. "Occupied."

Krissik stepped behind Rikist's chair and helped Rikist unclasp the cloak and shuck out of his jacket. He draped the uniform over the back of another chair and rested his hands on Rikist's shoulders.

"Did you at least win?"

Rikist looked up and grinned smugly. "Of course."

Krissik smiled, flashing fangs. "So how long will you be home this time?"

Rikist frowned and leaned his elbows on the table, rubbing his face. He suddenly looked exhausted. "I have been put on six weeks medical leave."

"Your wounds are extensive enough to warrant a long rest." Krissik frowned. He glanced at his brother's leg. "And why is a break in duty a bad thing?"

"When it means being stuck in an apartment instead of on the water with my ship?" Rikist sighed, and then nodded his head toward Samantha. "Are you going to introduce us?"

Krissik started and stepped closer to Samantha. "Apologies," he said to her when she shied away. He took her hand and turned her toward Rikist. "This is my older brother, Rikist Sa Tskir. Rikist, this is Samtha."

"It's Samantha," she corrected, and then immediately regretted speaking when she felt Rikist's gaze bore into her skull. She forcibly swallowed her heart back into her chest.

Krissik nudged her forward from behind. "He is the house head," he whispered. "You need to greet him."

Rikist tilted his head to look past Samantha at Krissik, annoyance clear on his tired face. Then he sighed and held out his hand to Samantha.

"My brother is into formalities," he explained.

Samantha stepped closer and stared at the small, white crisscrossing of scars that marred the knuckles and wrist of the clawed hand. Her stomach flipped as Rikist growled and reached out to take her right hand hanging by her side and brushed her wrist against the underside of his jaw before laying a gentle kiss on her knuckles.

Samantha pulled her arm back and stuttered, "Ricks..."

"Rikist," he corrected slowly in his resonant voice. He seemed to consider her for a moment, and then gave her a ghost of a smile. "Welcome home, Samantha of House Sa Tskir."

Samantha merely nodded, her head spinning.

Krissik hefted Rikist's bag over his shoulder. "I need to... clear out your room."

The smile left Rikist's face and eyes narrowed.

"It served as an excellent study while you were away," Krissik quickly explained. He shrugged apologetically. "I needed a place to spread out my plans and drawings. I will ready it for you." He turned to Samantha. "Do you need anything?"

She shook her head. "I'm OK."

Krissik nodded, and then carried Rikist's duffle into the bedroom on the left and shut the door. The muffled sound of moving papers and stacking books came through the wall to break the sudden silence.

Samantha fiddled with her hands as Rikist rested his head on his crossed arms against the table. Her sinuses screamed, and she sneezed painfully.

Rikist looked up. "Are you well?"

She hesitated, remembering how Krissik had reacted to her carrying 'sickness.' She shook her head. "I'm... just fighting a cold. My sinuses are clogged." She reached into her pocket to punch out two gel capsules.

Rikist reached out and snatched the foil package from her unresisting fingers and held them up to the overhead light. He frowned and tossed the package onto the counter.

"My brother did not give you *Kisu*?"

Samantha stared blankly at him. *What the hell is kisu?*

Rikist grunted and forced himself to his feet with the help of his crutch, an annoyed set to his jaw, and limped into the kitchen to rummage through the upper cabinets. He pulled out a steel pot and a glass canister of dried herbs and turned on the sink. "Come here."

Samantha pondered the idea of simply curling up on the couch and ignoring him but decided with two aliens in the apartment that it would be in her best interest if she just tried to survive the day with no incidents.

"You really don't have to—"

"I don't believe I asked you."

She frowned and sidled up to him, annoyance burning her ears. "What?"

"Are you going to question everything I say?" he muttered.

Rikist filled the pot half full of water and then crushed a handful of the herbs inside. He set the pot on one burner and turned on the heat. Within seconds the water bubbled and boiled, and heavy steam rose in a thick cloud.

"Breathe in the steam," he said.

Samantha hesitated, wary of the herbs after the revelation of Krissik' use of the pheromones, and then leaned over and breathed in the steam. The smell caused Samantha to sneeze violently. She coughed at the putrid stench but was surprised at the near imme- diate relief. She turned her head to look at Rikist, but his firm yet gentle hand on the back of her neck kept her face down above the pot.

"Stay still," he said, his voice gruff.

"What—" she started, before having to sneeze again. "What is that—"

"Quit squirming."

Several body-wracking sneezes over the steaming pot and Samantha was positively exhausted, though breathing clear and headache-free. She wiped at her face with a clean towel. She watched Rikist lean against the kitchen counter to take the weight off his wounded leg, a pained expression on his face as he breathed through his mouth.

"Are you alright?" she asked.

Rikist straightened and nodded once, then moved to the refrigerator. He opened the left side and pulled out two ice packs and handed them to Samantha.

"Can you carry these to the couch?"

He grabbed three bottles from the door and juggled them with his crutch as he hobbled—slower than before—into the living room. He nearly collapsed into the armchair and propped his wounded leg on the low table.

Samantha followed and handed him the ice packs, and then sat as far away as she could on opposite end of the couch, curling her legs under. She glanced at the closed bedroom door, hoping to catch a glance of Krissik.

As much as she resented Krissik for abducting her, she felt relatively safe when he was nearby. His large and scarred brother, on the other hand, set her fight or flight senses on high alert.

Rikist pressed the ice packs against his knee through the brace. He pulled out a vial of white pills from his pants pocket, shook two pills into his hand, and popped them between his teeth. He twisted the top off the first bottle and downed it and the pills quickly, letting out a satisfied sigh. He caught Samantha staring.

"Feel better?" he asked her.

"Much. Thank you." She frowned, debating whether she should speak. "Should you be drinking while taking pain meds?"

He rolled his eyes at her and twisted off the top of the second bottle.

"I'm just saying—" she began.

"You have a mate you can bitch at." Rikist cut her off. "I'm off limits."

She crossed her arms and focused her attention on the monitor on the wall as he put the bottle to his lips. It was bad enough she had to be here at all; she definitely did not want to spend the next six weeks being roommates with a gorgeous asshole on meds.

The screen showed shaky footage of an aerial camera screening footage of a battle going on between several massive military ships and battlements spread along a rocky coastline. Fiery explosions popped through the low volume of the speakers. A mug shot of Rikist in full battle dress and tilted beret appeared above scrolling alien text. Samantha sat up, trying to listen to the anchor as the shaky image of an exploding ship appeared next to his photo.

The channel suddenly changed as Rikist swiped his hand across the glass remote. He closed his eyes and leaned back in the chair, ignoring Samantha's annoyed look. "Krissik?" he called.

"Almost done," came the muffled reply.

"I was watching that," Samantha said pointedly.

Rikist shrugged. His eyes stayed closed.

She glared at him. "Being wounded doesn't give you the right to be such a dick."

A snort of surprise escaped Rikist's tight lips, and Samantha could see the humor in his eyes when he turned his head to peer at her.

"You're a feisty one, aren't you?"

"I'm not exactly happy about being here." She narrowed her eyes. "So, lay off."

Rikist frowned and looked away without a word.

Samantha curled her hands into claws and looked to the ceiling. The man's mood seemed to flip on a switch, and it irritated the hell out of her.

"Are you going to drink all of those?" she asked suddenly. "The beer. Alcohol... whatever you call them."

Rikist lifted an eyebrow. "Are you wanting one?"

"I could use it."

He seemed to think about it, and then held out the third bottle. Samantha plucked it from his fingers and sat back on the couch. She used the edge of her dress to grip the cap and twist it off before taking several long chugs. The watery brew was very light and barely warmed her throat on the way down to her belly.

This crap makes our light beer taste like shots...

She wiped her lips with the back on her free hand after half the bottle had disappeared. She looked up at Rikist, who stared at her with an openly amused expression.

"Sorry," Samantha said.

He waved her away. "It will help you relax. You seem to need it."

"That obvious, huh?"

Rikist grimaced as he shifted position, one hand moving to press on his wounded leg. He closed his eyes and leaned his head back against the top of the chair. "My brother is a good man. Young. Inexperienced. But he will make you happy if you give him the chance."

Samantha turned away, focusing her attention on the scrolling alien text that looked eerily like her world's stock market channel.

He acts as though I'm his brother's girlfriend brought home for the holidays. Do neither of them realize that I was forced here? Do they care?

"I can't stay here," she said slowly, watching him from the corner of one eye. "I have responsibilities at home. A life."

Rikist sat still, unmoving. If he had heard her, he gave no indication.

Exhaustion from the events of the last two days pressed heavily on Samantha's shoulders, and she leaned back against the couch, letting herself sink into the soft cushions as she finished off the bottle. Her vision wavered. The new anchor's voice sounded hollow and muffled, as if he were speaking underwater, and Samantha closed her eyes to imagine golden-eyed cats swimming about with red and yellow fish in a gray concrete box...

SIX

Samantha's eyes slid slowly open. The monitor was still on, the announcer replaced with a new face and the same scrolling text rolling by tirelessly. Several empty bottles sat stacked on the edge of the coffee table, reflecting the morning light peeking in through the cracks between the closed curtains.

She sighed and shifted against the wall of warmth cradling her side and back, feeling worlds better than she had before Rikist's homeopathic treatment of her cold. In fact, she felt healthy and rested as if she had slept for a week.

The heated bed below her shifted again, and warm breath blew across her brow and hair. Samantha blinked away sleep, lifting her head slightly to look about.

Her heart skipped a beat when she realized she was still on the couch, and not alone. She lay propped up across Krissik's chest as he slept reclined against the armrest, one arm over his head and the other draped around her shoulders, with his legs outstretched along the length of the couch. Samantha's body lay parallel to his; their bodies pressed together in a solid line across the narrow cushions.

Krissik shifted again in his sleep, grimacing as he repositioned his head on his arm before going still. His breathing deepened, and he snored lightly as his hand on her shoulder went limp. His face slackened to peaceful forgetfulness, and Samantha caught herself staring at the strong lines of his jaw and brow.

She twisted her head to look toward the window, where the armchair sat empty, and then to the closed bedroom door where she assumed Rikist had retired. She moved slowly, not wanting to wake Krissik, and began to slide off the couch.

Krissik's arm tightened around her waist and pulled her back down. He shifted onto his side and curled up against her back, rubbing his cheek against her shoulder. He suddenly seemed wide awake.

Samantha cleared her throat. "I didn't mean to wake you."

"I need to wake for work anyway."

"I don't remember falling asleep," she said, trying to wiggle free.

"You were sleeping before I finished clearing out Rikist's room. And you looked... peaceful. So, after I helped him to bed I just crawled up beside you."

In a flash, Krissik leaned over her, his elbows

against the cushions on each side of her head. He lowered his head until their faces were inches apart. He licked his lips.

"K-Kris..." Samantha stammered. She was afraid to move, and her heart pounded. "Kris, I don't—"

Krissik rubbed his cheek against hers, like a cat begging for a rub down. "Do not worry. I said I would not force you." He sniffed at her neck. "I just want to kiss."

She searched his face. She was not sure why, but she just could not bring herself to be annoyed with him. "Just a kiss?"

He nodded.

The request seemed simple enough, and she figured if she humored him enough that he would not persist in pushing further. Samantha pursed her lips, and then lifted her head to quickly peck Krissik on the mouth.

He shook his head. "That was not a kiss."

"What do you mean that wasn't a kiss?" Samantha demanded. "Our lips touched."

He grinned. "I want a *real* kiss."

Samantha hesitated, and then ran her fingers through the top of his fur-like hair before she thought better of it. She smiled; it did feel as soft and fluffy as she thought it would. She rubbed behind his ears, and froze at a sudden, constant rumbling. She looked up at Krissik's closed eyes and crooked smile.

"Are..." she fought to keep from grinning like an idiot. "Are you purring?"

"Hmm?"

Samantha nearly giggled as he rolled onto his side beside her, and she leaned over him and used both hands to scratch behind his ears and the underside of his jaw. Krissik rumbled on contentedly, twisting his head to get her to hit the right spots. Samantha laughed until her eyes watered and bent to kiss him between the eyes.

"Annoying as you are, you can be so damn cute sometimes."

Krissik's eyes opened. "You missed."

"What?"

He smacked his lips together.

Samantha guffawed and shook her head. "You are persistent."

"Is it working?"

Samantha pursed her lips, trying hard not to smile. Krissik caught on, and rolled his head to the side, purring louder than he had before. Samantha laughed.

"Alright, alright, quit it already." She grinned. "I'll give you your well-earned kiss and then you can leave me alone."

Krissik's eyes twinkled, and his lips slightly puckered in anticipation.

Samantha licked her lips and swallowed, and then put her hands on his chest to lean forward. Her hair cascaded down around her face as she leaned into him, and she closed her eyes as she lowered her head. She stopped, their lips just an inch apart. She could feel the warmth radiating off his skin, and she breathed in, testing. There was no smell of mint, just the slight hint of kitten fur above the musk of sleep and man. She smiled, knowing it meant that he had not tried to use the pheromones to seduce her.

Their lips met, and she held the kiss longer than she had planned, enjoying the way he trembled below her in excitement. She smiled against him and began to pull away.

Krissik's hand on the back of her neck pulled her closer, and his tongue slipped between her teeth to run along the ridged roof of her mouth. Samantha gasped as Krissik rolled to pin her down with his upper body. He wriggled lower so that her knees came up on either side of his waist, and he grinned down at her.

Samantha glared at him. "You said just a kiss!"

"No," he said. "I said I want *to* kiss."

"Off." She glared at him. "You're such a child."

"I just—"

"Get off!"

Krissik hesitated, and then nodded and slid off the couch to his feet. He looked down awkwardly. He patted down one edge of the tape on his nose as he padded into the kitchen.

"Are you hungry?" he called from behind the counter.

"No," she said quickly. She sat on the couch and pulled up her knees.

"You have not eaten since yesterday's lunch."

"I said I'm not hungry."

Samantha heard his footsteps approaching, and she

buried her face in her knees. She felt him pause before her, and then his hands touched her neck and back.

"Are you feeling unwell again?"

Samantha shrugged him off. "I'm fine. Now leave me alone."

Krissik stepped back, his face hurt, hands up protectively. His brow scrunched as he stared at her, as if trying to decode her face.

"I am attempting to make you comfortable," he said slowly. "Please, do not—"

"Why?"

He seemed lost, unsure where the questions were taking them. "Because... because I do not like to see you unhappy."

Krissik looked down at her. His face was guarded, but his eyes betrayed his inner turmoil; they danced in his head as he stared at her. His lips twitched as if itching to speak but were unable to form words. He swallowed and looked down at the ground and took a shaky breath.

"I am sorry."

She nearly bounced against the cushion's springs in surprise. That was not what she was expecting, and especially when it sounded so... sincere.

"For what?" she asked hesitantly, her voice no more than the squeak of a mouse.

He sucked in his breath and looked up at the ceiling, as if searching for words. After a moment he sighed and shrugged, his shoulders sagging under some heavy load.

"Everything. For upsetting you. For bringing you here."

Samantha stared at him, watching him struggle for words as he fought to explain past the limitations of the translator. She allowed herself to settle further onto the couch, the tension slowly seeping out of her shoulders and running down into her back to transfer into the cool microfiber of the cushions. The air around them seemed to still as she waited, suddenly patient and no longer angry.

"I know you do not want to be here," he continued. "I do not like to see you unhappy... I just want a chance to..."

Whether it was his being young on a planet lacking in females, a cultural issue or simply the language barrier, Samantha realized he truly lacked the ability to express his apparent care for her. There was no doubt she wanted off that planet, but it was not in her nature to destroy people on the way out. And the kid really did seem genuine.

Letting my anger get the best of me isn't going to get me home. But maybe figuring out what makes him tick will get him to understand why I can't stay.

"I'm sorry for yelling," she said.

Krissik thought for a moment, and then let out a sigh and wrapped his arms around her stiff shoulders, his body molding around hers. He pressed his lips against the top of her head, breathing in her scent.

Samantha felt him smile against her hair, and she closed her eyes and allowed herself to lean into the hug. Regardless of the source, it did feel nice to just be held. She sniffed the air, frowning.

"What's that smell?"

He jerked upright and darted into the kitchen.

Samantha heard the pan sizzle as he flipped the meat and added water. She looked up to see a small plume of smoke billowing around Krissik' head. She laughed and stood to get a better view.

Krissik turned and glared at her. "This is not funny."

"A little." She stifled her chuckle. "I'm sure it's fine."

The smoke subsided, and Krissik picked up the knife to finish chopping the vegetables. "I have to get ready for work. Please go see if Rikist is hungry."

Samantha frowned. She wasn't keen on going into Krissik' brother's room to wake him, especially not knowing what she might run into or what rude greeting she could receive. He could starve for all she cared.

She sighed and walked to the closed door, steeled herself and knocked.

"Rikist?"

No answer. She knocked louder, her other hand reaching for the panel.

"Rikist?"

A grunt and the shuffling of sheets fluttered through the door, followed by a groggy, "Y-yeah?"

"Are you hungry?"

No answer.

Samantha waited, knocked again, and glanced back

toward the kitchen where she could hear Krissik moving about.

"He's not getting up," she called.

The kitchen went silent, and Krissik's head popped around the corner; a look of concern crossed his face, as if sleeping in was a very odd behavior for his brother. He wiped his hands on a towel as he walked briskly past Samantha, and quickly swiped one finger against the panel to open the door, stepping inside without invitation.

"Rikist?"

Samantha held back in the doorway, afraid of what she might see if they had caught Rikist off guard. One naked alien in her mind's eye was enough. She kept her eyes low and slowly roamed about his dark room, looking anywhere but directly to the bed.

The large room's furnishings matched the modern, minimalist theme of the rest of the apartment; a large double platform bed in the center, a nightstand, and a desk and chair to the side of the open closet. Uniforms, both what appeared to be field and military dress, hung in straight lines below shelves that held more military paraphernalia, medals, and a digitally coded safe. Below the single shuttered window on the far left sat a padded, claw-foot armchair littered with clothes and a few shiny medals on ribbons that seemed to have been carelessly tossed from the empty duffle on the floor. Several blankets spilled off the side of the mattress, and a white undershirt lay crumbled by the door by a discarded pair of boots.

The darkness split, and Samantha jerked back as Krissik opened the shades and window before turning back to the bed.

"You need fresh air in here," Krissik said.

Samantha glanced to the bed unconsciously and was glad Rikist was decent. He was shirtless and wore the pants from yesterday under the large brace. His auburn hair was mussed and wet around his hairline, splayed out around his head like a halo. The dark stripes that covered Krissik' body were faded on Rikist's masculine face, neck, and arms so that they were barely visible, but remained a stark brown that crept up his sides and waist. A thin sheen of sweat covered his skin, pooling in the curve of his neck and soaking the thick, wide patch of white fur on his broad chest and the solid line that ran down through his muscled abs and thickened between his curved obliques before disappearing into his waistband.

Samantha's mouth went dry. If she had thought Rikist looked like a wild lion before, then he was an absolute beast lying half naked on his silver sheets. She grabbed onto the edge of the doorframe to keep her shaking hands still against the sudden rush of heat she felt in her core.

Rikist groaned and threw one arm over his eyes. The round muscles in his chest, arms and stomach clenched as he shivered. "Too bright," he rasped.

Images of rolling and twisting lions and tigers snuffed out at the sound of Rikist's strained voice.

Samantha straightened, a sick feeling twisting in her stomach.

Krissik put his hands on Rikist's brow and neck, checking his brother's pulse. He frowned, and then began releasing the clasps on Rikist's leg brace.

Rikist cried out and reached for Krissik as the first support came loose. Krissik pushed Rikist back against the bed and growled when his brother struggled. He leaned his weight to pin Rikist's struggling arms, and the look on his face made it clear he was surprised how easily he was winning.

"You are feverish," Krissik said. "Your leg may be infected."

Samantha took a steadying breath and stepped into the room. Growing up on her father's farm, she was well aware of what infection looked like in wounded animals, and the damage it could cause if left unchecked. Standing closer in the light, she now saw the dark circles below Rikist's eyes and the pallor of his normally tan skin. Several dark patches of bruising were visible on the left side of his ribs and arm, and a four-inch line of stitches cut across his side.

She touched Krissik' shoulder. "Do you need help?"

He turned his head toward her, his eyes distraught. He nodded. "Turn the clasps counter clockwise until pressure releases." He used his chin to point. "Then pull the support loose of the frame."

Samantha's small hands deftly unsecured the brace clasps one by one, then pulled the support straps loose so that the tension eased, and the frames fell away to the bed. By the time she reached Rikist's ankle he was groaning and shaking, his strength spent.

Krissik eased his weight off his exhausted brother, his eyes wary, and then used his claws to easily rip Rikist's pants open over his thigh. He hissed and then tore the entire pant leg off, and both he and Samantha stepped back.

Rikist's leg had been ripped and pummeled so that purple and green bruises mottled his skin, and several lines of rough stitches cut across his calf and shin. His knee swelled severely, pulling at the edges of the two lines of stitches around the kneecap. A large, purple gash slicing nearly the length of his thigh had been stitched and covered with a wide, clear, skin-like bandage. The edges of the wounds on his thigh burned deep burgundy, and crimson lines spiderwebbed outward between the bruising.

"That is definitely infected," Samantha said, eyeing the impressive amount of damage. She looked at Rikist's closed eyes. "Did you have your knee operated on in the field?"

Rikist sniffed and brought up a shaky hand to wipe at the sweat in his eyes. "Y-yes."

"You did not go to the hospital once you landed?" Krissik yelled, his eyes narrowed.

"No."

Krissik let out an angry snarl, his lips curling back to expose his long, sharp canines and his irises narrowing to thin slits. "You idiot. You should have said something. I am going to call a medic." He brushed past Samantha toward the door.

Rikist's arm shot out toward his brother. "No!"

"You need help."

Rikist struggled to sit upright, his face pained. "If they know how bad it is... I cannot afford to be discharged." His eyes rolled, and he swooned, catching himself before toppling off the bed. "Just get me meds, and I will be fine."

"I am not doing this again. You need more than just medication. You need to see a physician."

Something in Rikist's face made Samantha pause. Maybe it was the sheer determination on his face. Or the genuine fear of discharge in his wide eyes. Her heart broke at the sincerity of his plea.

"Kris," she said softly.

Krissik turned to her, his face angry and frustrated. "What?"

"I... If you have antibiotics, I think with medication the infection will be fine. I've seen animals on our farm come back from worse with care." She shrugged. "I can help. At least give him a day or two and see if he improves?"

Krissik let out a snarl, and then turned on his heel and stormed out the door. "I will see what I can find."

Samantha stood silent as Krissik stepped out of sight and began slamming cabinets in the bathroom before making his way to the kitchen. She pressed her lips together and glanced down at Rikist, who had laid back and covered his face with one arm, his chest rising and falling with effort.

"You know antibiotics won't help your torn knee," Samantha said softly. "That probably needs proper surgery and physical therapy."

Rikist ignored her.

"Can I get you anything?" She waited when he did not answer, and then touched his arm. "Rikist?"

He jerked awake, his eyes fluttering open as he sucked in a breath. He blinked, his eyes unfocused, and swallowed. "I'm cold."

Samantha frowned, knowing from the small touch that he was burning up. She nodded and picked up one of the blankets that had fallen from the bed. She tucked it around him, careful not to cover his wounded leg. She hesitated, and then rubbed his shoulder through the blanket.

Rikist shivered and closed his eyes, turning his head away.

Samantha looked up as Krissik entered the doorway with a glass of water and two bottles of pills. She stepped back from the bed.

"You are lucky we still have antibiotics from your last return trip home," Krissik said, his eyes on his brother.

He set the water down on the nightstand, measured out pills from both bottles, and then gave them and the water to his brother. He glanced up at Samantha.

"He is always coming home with new wounds," he

explained. "We keep pain medication in stock. I have considered the fact I should have gone into medicine with all the hands-on training I have completed living with him."

Rikist swallowed half the water and laid back, his breathing heavy. His eyes opened to Samantha, and he forced a smile. "Thank you."

Krissik gently took Samantha's elbow and steered her out of the room. "The medication should work soon. Come, we can eat while he rests."

Samantha nodded and followed him out, though food was the furthest thing from her mind, with the sudden fluttering of butterflies in her stomach as she felt amber eyes on her back.

KRISSIK WENT BACK into Rikist's room after they had finished eating, intent on cleaning and bandaging his brother's wounds. Samantha did her best cleaning up the dishes and figuring out where everything belonged to keep herself busy.

She nearly dropped a glass at a sudden string of screams interlaced with obscenities.

The door to Rikist's room opened, and a very pissed-looking Krissik exited. He slammed the door behind him and hugged his left hand to his chest as blood seeped from between his fingers. He glared over his shoulder and then headed toward the kitchen.

Samantha started. "What happened?"

"He bit me."

"He *bit* you?"

Krissik held up his hand, where a half-circle of indentions and two large fang punctures marred his skin. "See?"

Samantha grabbed a towel hanging near the sink and wet it, and then wrapped it around Krissik' hand, applying pressure. He hissed and tried to pull away, but she twisted and wrapped her arms around his so that the only way he could free himself would be to hurt her.

Krissik sighed and leaned against the counter, letting her work. "It is not severe. We would bite harder as children."

"You guys would bite each other?"

"When we were upset." He looked up, thinking, and then chuckled. "Actually, I did most of the biting. I was a... persistent pest at times."

Samantha grinned. "Oh, now *that* I find hard to believe."

Krissik smiled at her. "Rikist never hurt me, not really."

"He was a good older brother?"

Krissik nodded. "He had just joined his squad when the first attack came and was out on tour at the front lines. He survived, earning his first medal of valor for saving his commanding officer only to come home to a mewling youth that he was then responsible for."

"How old were you?" she asked. "When your parents died?"

"Twenty-seven seas... Nine years."

"And Rikist?"

"Nineteen."

"Where did you guys live?"

He shrugged. "In our parent's home for a season. Rikist had to take leave from his position to make arrangements, and then sold the home to pay for help caring for me so that he could work. And we then moved here."

"Well you came out all right. And Rikist seems to have done well for himself."

Krissik nodded. "He has led his troops into many battles against the resistance and has brought much honor to our house and our parents' names. His work is everything to him."

Samantha pulled the cloth away, checking Krissik's hand. The marks had stopped bleeding. Krissik was right; the blood made the wound look worse than it was.

"Is that why he doesn't have a mate?"

Krissik' hand stiffened in her grip. After a moment of silence, she looked up to see Krissik staring at her.

She frowned. "What?"

Krissik forced a smile, though it was tight-lipped. "Rikist is past the breeding age to make the jump."

Samantha used a clean edge of the towel and wiped away the red stains on Krissik' skin. "I don't understand the age limit part. He looks young enough to pump out a kitten or two. He's got to be what... early thirties?"

Krissik frowned at the mention of kittens, his face confused. "It is not about the breeding ability, it is about surviving the interplanetary jump. After eighty seasons, the rate of survival drops to below twenty percent. Rikist is almost ninety-three seasons."

"Why don't the younger ones bring back the females for everyone?"

He shook his head. "It is not honorable to take a mate from another's efforts."

"Oh," she said softly. "That's... that's sad, actually."

Krissik looked down at his hand in Samantha's and reached out and ran the back of his free hand down Samantha's cheek, a cheerless smile on his lips.

Samantha furrowed her brow. "What?"

"You do not touch me often on your own accord. I wish you were more comfortable around me."

Samantha stared down on the bloodied towel. One of Krissik's clawed fingers under her chin raised her face to his.

"I will do anything to make you happy," he said softly, his eyes sincere.

Samantha tightened her jaw against the sudden sting of tears. "Then send me home."

Krissik' smile faded, and he turned away, eyes closed. "I have to check in at work for a few hours."

He excused himself to his bedroom and slipped on a clean shirt and black coat. He grabbed a glass touch-screen computer and a roll of drawings from the pile in the corner of the living room and hurried to the door.

He braked, turned, and then ran back to the kitchen where Samantha still stood.

"There is a communicator on the dresser for you, and you can call me any time if you need something. Just press and hold the top left button to dial me directly." Krissik smiled and stole a kiss on her lips. "Please see to Rikist while I am gone."

Then he hurried out the front door and locked it.

SEVEN

The morning passed slowly for Samantha. She occupied herself catching up on the news and flipping through Krissik's glass communicator. She was surprised at how similar the interface was to the smart phones at home—enough that she wondered whether either race had stolen the technology from the other—and she was able to navigate to the GPS function to begin studying the maps surrounding their current location, though after two hours her eyes hurt with the endless grid of streets that all looked the same and labeled with names she couldn't read.

A lunch of a single but monster-sized egg and taste-less fruit later, she still had not heard anything resem-bling life from Rikist. She cleaned up and sat on the couch, but a vague sense of worry plagued her, and she found herself standing outside his door.

She knocked before sliding the door open and poking her head in. "Rikist?"

His heavy, even breathing let her know he was still sleeping. She ducked her head to leave, and then her curiosity got the best of her and she stepped farther into the room.

Rikist lay on his back, one arm above his head and the other just in the waistband of his torn pants. He snored lightly through parted lips, his face slack and peaceful despite his strong lines and the jagged scar on his jaw. Krissik had done a decent job bandaging the wounds with a new, transparent, skin-like dressing, and securing the leg brace over padding to support Rikist's leg.

Her eyes watched the steady rise and fall of his bare chest as she approached the bed. She gently laid a hand on Rikist's brow, testing his skin; even without checking his temperature, it was obvious he ran a high fever.

Samantha left and dampened a washcloth in the bathroom with cool water, and then sat on the edge of the bed and patted away the layer of sweat on his brow and neck. Her fingers brushed against his hairline, pushing a stray lock out of his face. She smiled, admiring the masculine set to his wide brow and thick eyebrows. His lower lip pouted naturally and offset the harshness of the slight cleft and scar in his square chin.

Rikist groaned and licked his lips. His bloodshot eyes struggled to open, and he sucked in his breath when he noticed Samantha. His brow knotted.

"W-where's Krissik?" he managed after two attempts to speak.

"Work. He said he would be back in a few hours."

Rikist coughed and grimaced, and looked to the glass of water on the nightstand. He started to sit up, but Samantha's hand on his shoulder stilled him.

"Here." She picked up the glass, and then helped tilt it to his lips. A thin line of water dripped from the glass down his neck, and she used the edge of the washcloth to wipe it up.

Rikist sighed and rested his head back. "Thanks."

"How are you feeling?"

"Like shit."

Samantha lifted one eyebrow and studied him. "How does your translator work so well?"

"What do you mean?"

"Kris's speech is clipped, his words limited by the translator. And he doesn't use contractions or understand my figures of speech... You don't seem to have any problem with them."

Rikist settled further back into the pillows. "It's not my translator."

"Then what?"

"I'm multilingual." He smirked at her shocked expression and closed his eyes. "I travel much—" Rikist said slowly in accented English— "a lot. I have traveled a lot... in the past. For work."

Samantha grinned; happy to see his lips match his words.

Now I don't feel like I'm in some crazy foreign monster flick...

"You've been to Earth?" she asked.

"A long time ago."

"This is amazing. I'm... I just feel so much better knowing there is someone else... Do you think you could speak English when you're around me?"

"I am out of practice, you'll have to correct me," he said, and then slipped back into his native tongue. One eye slid open to peer at her. "Have you eaten?"

"Yes, why?"

"I am starving."

Samantha crooked an eyebrow, fighting a smile. "And are you expecting something?"

"You to start earning your keep."

Her jaw dropped. "What happened to you being off limits from the bitchy mate?"

"I never called you a bitch." His lips quirked, fighting a smirk. "That is you self-assessing."

Samantha fought the sudden urge to sock him square in his wounded thigh. She lifted her chin and smiled and then turned on her heel and left.

Rikist stared after her. "Hey!"

Samantha reappeared and set something large and cold onto Rikist's stomach. He gasped and fumbled to grasp the round weight. He held it up, and then glared at her.

"Why did you give me an uncooked egg?"

"Your breakfast," she chirped in an overly merry tone. "Served like your attitude—raw."

Rikist's eyes narrowed, and the muscles in his jaw bulged as he clenched. Then he smiled, showing a hint at dimples, and used the tip of one claw to tap a hole in the top of the large egg, and then tilted his head back against the pillow and put the hole to his lips. He poked a second hole into the top of the egg and sucked.

Samantha grimaced at the slurping sound of the egg sliding into his mouth but could not drag her eyes away from his Adam's apple. It slowly bounced in his muscular neck as he swallowed. She licked her lips as he sucked the last drops of the egg from the large shell, the tip of his long tongue licking the tiny hole clean.

Rikist eyed her when he was through, and then held out the empty shell with a wide, pleasant smile as if he had not known he was putting on a show. "Now, if you are done pouting, can I get some real food?"

Samantha glowered down at him and snatched up the hollow shell. "Sure. When you get your ass up and make it."

Then she turned on her heel and left, leaving the gaping alien behind. She walked into the kitchen and poured herself a glass of water.

Something fell with a clatter down the hall. Samantha nearly choked. She wiped water from her lips and set the glass down. She strained her ears against the silence.

Rikist cleared his throat. "Samantha?"

"What?" she sighed.

"I..." Rikist paused. "Can you come here?"

"I'm busy."

"Please?"

That made her eyes widen. She tapped her fingers on the counter, considering, and then walked to

Rikist's room. She leaned against the doorframe with her arms crossed.

"Yes?"

Rikist lay sideways on the bed, his upper body propped up on one elbow and his good leg half off the mattress. Samantha's eyes followed the long sweep of his shoulders down to his waist. She swallowed and followed the line of white fur up the center of his abs, between his wide pecs, and up to his waiting face.

He stared at her solemnly. "I need to use the bathroom."

Samantha tensed. "And?"

He opened his mouth to speak, hesitated, and then sighed and closed his eyes. "I... I could use a hand."

"Sorry, what was that?"

He glared at her. "Are you going to make me beg?"

Samantha grinned.

"Fine." He growled. He reached for the empty glass beside the bed with one hand and the band of his pants with the other. "Can you at least bring me a clean glass of water when I'm through then?"

Samantha made a face and stepped back. "That's disgusting."

He growled and slammed the glass down on the nightstand. "Well I am not about to piss my sheets. So, if you are not going to help then I need some other way—"

"Alright, alright," she shouted. "What do you need?"

"I cannot reach my crutch."

Samantha glanced to the side of the bed where the crutch lay fallen on the floor away from the nightstand where it had been propped. She realized he had probably knocked it over trying to stand.

She bent and picked up the crutch and held it out. "Here."

Rikist took it and used it to leverage his upper body into a sitting position. He grunted with effort, and then swung his wounded leg over the edge of the mattress. His eyes rolled, and he swayed, and despite herself Samantha leapt forward and steadied him. She froze with her arms around his broad shoulders as his warm breath rushed against her skin, and she realized their close proximity. She stepped back, holding his arm at length.

"You OK?" she asked.

Rikist blinked and then nodded. His nostrils flared as he took a deep breath and heaved himself to his feet. He stumbled off-balance, and Samantha helped hold him still.

"Put your arm on my shoulder." She sighed. "I'll help you."

He shrugged her off. "I can do it myself."

"I'm just trying to help."

"If I need additional help, I will ask for it."

Samantha seethed. *I should kick that crutch out from under the bastard and toss it across the room.*

"You know you put a whole new meaning to the phrase 'when you marry a guy, you marry his family.'" She stepped back and put her hands on her hips.

Rikist glared at her, and then focused on his feet as he slowly stepped forward. His hand on the crutch began to shake halfway across the room, and he finally slowed to a stop just shy of the door. His breath came out shaky, and he leaned against the wall.

Rikist glanced over his shoulder, a drip of sweat on his temple and eyes pleading.

Samantha did not need prodding, and she quickly stepped up beside him, taking his right arm and resting in on top of her shoulder. Together they hobbled across the short hall to the bathroom, Samantha grunting under his weight, with sweat dripping down her lower back as she led him to the toilet area.

He looked at her expectantly when he stood inside the small room.

Samantha shook her head and slipped out from under his arm. "I am *not* holding you upright while you pee."

He grinned sideways, flashing fang; a welcome sight amidst his pale skin and sunken cheeks. "Don't worry," he said in English. "I don't want you in here."

Samantha helped him lean his shoulder against the wall, and then stepped out and shut the door. "When is the last time you took your pills?" she called through the wall.

"I'm due."

"What are you going to give me in return if I make you lunch?"

The toilet flushed, and the door slid open as Rikist finished buttoning the top of his pants. He shot her a suave, crooked smile that Samantha was sure would have made her swoon if he did not look like he had one foot in the grave. "Pleasure of my company?"

Samantha shook her head but could not resist a smile. "I think I'm getting the short end of the stick on that one."

Rikist's smile stretched to both ears, dimples deep on his cheeks and his sharp fangs glinting in the overhead fluorescent light. "Hardly."

"How so?"

The translator kicked in. "I can give you inside information about our world."

Samantha grinned back. "Now that sounds like a deal."

EIGHT

"So that's why you guys are born with stripes. Now it makes sense." Samantha laughed, leaning her elbows on the table. "And the purring..."

Rikist's fingers stopped on their slow slide across the table toward Samantha's hand. "Krissik purred for you?"

"Yeah... don't you ever—"

"I can't."

Samantha sat up straight. "What... why not?"

He shrugged. "At least not anymore. Like the stripes, it's something we grow out of."

"That's too bad." She smirked. "I have to admit it's absolutely adorable. A sound like that shouldn't be possible coming from a human mouth."

"Not quite human." Rikist smiled, his eyes creasing at their corners. He tilted his head to one side, considering her. "Does knowing more give you a better perspective on our culture?"

"About who you are as a people? Yes."

"Good." He drummed his fingers on the table and then stretched, his legs extending under the table until they brushed against Samantha's. He hesitated in surprise and lowered his arms, but kept his legs extended against hers.

"Are you... feeling more comfortable at all?"

Samantha lowered her eyes. She shifted in her chair, causing her legs to rub against Rikist's. Out of the corner of her eye she noted his stare, and the goose bumps on his skin in response to her touch. She fought to keep her face neutral against the sudden lump in her throat and shrugged.

"Does it matter?"

Rikist sighed, and then shook his head and snatched up her hand. He squeezed gently, his face earnest. "I... my brother wants you to be happy. He *is* trying. He just... needs a little time to adjust as well. This is new for him, too."

Samantha's heart skipped a beat at the warmth in his touch. "The difference is that I didn't have a choice in the matter."

He nodded slowly. "I know being here is hard. And that it's a shock being in such a strange place with—" he twisted their hands so that she could inspect his clawed fingers around hers, "—a different people. But if you give him a chance, you would see we're not really so different."

Samantha guffawed. Unconsciously she moved her fingers against his, until they intertwined. She glanced up into his amber eyes and felt the heat in his gaze. She smirked.

"Thanks, Dr. Phil."

Rikist blinked, confused. "What?"

That made her laugh. "It's a show, back home, about a guy who... never mind. You don't have TV—"

"We have the monitor." He motioned with his free hand toward the living room.

"For news. I can't believe you guys invented planet jumping but haven't realized the meaning of simple entertainment. Like movies or fiction books. I mean you guys don't even have sugar for crying out loud. It's funny how much I've been craving chocolate since it's now out of reach."

Rikist averted his eyes and gently slid his hand free of hers. A wide yawn bared his sharp fangs. He rubbed at his eyes with his knuckles and pulled at the collar of his shirt. His skin held a fine sheen of sweat, and his eyes began to take on a glassy look as they roamed down to stop on her chest. Samantha cleared her throat and stood, crossing her arms over her breasts.

"You look like the pain meds are kicking in." Samantha picked up her plate. "You should probably go back to bed as soon as you finish."

Rikist shook himself as if to clear his head of an image and nodded, a blush creeping up his neck. "I think you're right."

Samantha turned from the table and carried her dishes to the sink. She surprised herself with the sudden feeling of sadness at the idea of his leaving. She realized she truly enjoyed his company, especially after the last few days.

Days? She thought. *Who am I kidding? It's been almost a year since I've been this at ease with a guy...*

"Are you sure you don't want any more?" she asked, almost pleading.

Rikist pushed his half-eaten plate toward the center of the table. He looked guilty about something. "No, I'm not hungry."

"You said you were starving."

He glared at her. "I lost my appetite."

Samantha stared at him, taken aback by his sudden change in temperament. "Why are you being an ass?"

"Thought I was a dick?"

"That too."

"Ass and dick." He forced a smile at her. "I'll be sure to let my brother know your preferences."

"I..." Samantha's mouth opened and closed like a fish out of water. *So much for his pleasurable company.* "Eat shit."

Rikist threw his head back and let out a mirthless laugh. He pointed to his plate. "So that's what this is called."

"You're unbelievable." Samantha shook her head and began filling the sink with water. Her hands shook. "I don't know how your bother puts up with you."

"My little brother could do to learn a few things from me."

"Like what?"

"Like how to pull the stick out of his ass and bed you already."

Samantha whirled around with fire in her eyes, only to see Rikist standing only a few inches away. She bit back a yip of surprise, not wanting to give him the satisfaction. "Screw you."

"No," Rikist said slowly. "That's what you're supposed to be doing to my brother."

"Why are you being such a jerk? I don't understand where any of this is coming from." She squared her shoulders and tried to stand tall, though he towered over her by almost two feet. "One minute we're talking and seemingly connecting... and the next you're in a bad mood like someone spit in your lunch."

He looked down at his hand—the one she had held—and made a fist. "We... Listen, it's not appropriate behavior to—"

"Behavior? You're complaining about my behavior?"

Rikist set his jaw.

Samantha turned back to the sink and ran the hot water, something to keep her from having to look at the beast standing before her.

"I have done nothing but try to keep a straight face and not break down in hysterics after being beamed up to some God-forsaken planet against my will, be told I'm supposed to help populate a feline race..." She slammed a bowl down into the sink, splashing soapy water on the floor.

"That is not what I—"

"And then to be stuck in an apartment with an invalid asshole! So, you could give me a bit of a break about *my behavior!*"

"Look." He held out his free hand as he shifted his weight on the crutch. "I know what you're going through, and I'm..." He forced the next words out in English. "I am sorry I am not being more com... compass—uh... I understand. Sorry, I don't remember some words..."

Samantha wiped at her eyes, her chin trembling. "How could you possibly understand?" She sucked in her breath. "You're this strong, decorated soldier-beast who fights wars, and kills... How could you possibly know what it feels like to be helpless? To feel..."

"Trapped?" Rikist finished, his head down.

Samantha stared up at him through a veil of tears. She nodded slowly.

Rikist lifted his eyes and gazed at her from behind a few locks of hair that had fallen forward, his jaw tight and brow knotted. He stayed silent for a moment, his face torn. He looked about to say something, then clamped his mouth shut and straightened with effort, gripping the crutch. He dipped his head toward her and then turned toward the hall.

"Where are you going?" Samantha asked, wiping her nose.

"Leaving you alone," he said softly.

"Why?"

"Because I've upset you." He let out a frustrated growl. "I have been stuck on a ship full of soldiers for too long and I don't remember how to act civil like a normal person."

"You…" Samantha sighed, watching him struggle to keep his footing. "You don't have to go."

"Actually, I do."

"Really, Rikist. Please stay."

Rikist guffawed. "You are crazy. You can flip on a—"

He turned to look at her, and his crutch slipped on a small puddle of suds. He gasped as he fell forward, reaching out with his free hand to catch his fall. He fell on his wounded side with a thud. The crutch caught against the metal frame of his leg brace, trapping his arm beneath him.

"Ah… fuck."

Samantha stepped forward to help, then covered her mouth with one hand and pressed her lips together.

Rikist growled and struggled to roll over to his back, his face pained and frustrated. "It's not funny."

"I know, I'm sorry." A snort escaped, and Samantha closed her eyes tightly. Her shoulders bounced as she fought to keep silent.

Rikist glared at her. He freed the crutch, shifted his grip on the end and swung it across the floor to hook behind Samantha's heels. Then pulled.

Samantha yipped as she fell back, landing hard on her butt and falling back against his chest. She glared sideways at him, and then elbowed him in the stomach.

"Asshole," she muttered.

Rikist doubled over, chuckling. "Why do you constantly refer to body parts?"

"You stink." She pushed on his shoulder as leverage to get to her knees. "When's the last time you showered?"

"I do, don't I?" Rikist snorted and shook his head, his eyes twinkling with humor. "I could use help with a sponge bath."

Samantha fought back a grin. "I think you'd need a tub of bleach."

Rikist smirked and winked at her. "Feel better?"

She thought about it. "A little."

"Mind helping me up?" Rikist held out one hand.

Samantha glanced between the clawed hand and Rikist's anticipating face, and then used both hands to grab his forearm and heft him to his feet. He swayed and leaned into her, one arm wrapped around her shoulders, and she pressed her body against his to hold him steady. Beneath the scent of sweat and medication rolled an exotic undertone of spices and sandalwood, and she breathed in deeply before tilting her head back.

He smells so good I just want to roll around all over him...

Rikist steadied himself and his hand lowered, resting at the small of her back. He looked down at her and their eyes met. His nostrils flared as he smelled her neck, and a low rumble began deep in his chest.

Samantha swallowed. It was hard to think. "W-what... what were you trying to tell me, before..."

Rikist closed his eyes. "Hmm?"

"About inappropriate behavior?"

Rikist's hand gently pulled her closer, pressing their hips together, as his head dipped lower until their noses brushed, and his loose hair fell against her flushed cheek.

Samantha put a hand on his chest to maintain a few inches of distance. His heart raced under her palm, and it set something off deep in her gut, slowly turning her knees to jelly. She trembled, her own pulse in her throat, as she started to rise on tiptoe.

Wait... what am I doing?

"Rik..." she whispered, barely audible. "Rikist."

Rikist froze, not even daring to breathe, as his eyes snapped open and he stared at Samantha from only an inch away. After a moment he straightened and shook his head, his face a mixture of surprise and regret.

"Samantha..." Rikist swallowed, a deep blush set in his neck and cheeks. "I..."

"Are you OK?" Samantha said, recovering quickly. "Can you stand on your own?"

He hesitated, and then nodded, a little too fast.

Samantha waited, watching him flounder. The look on his face told wonders about how he felt at the moment, so she did not push it.

At least I'm not the only one completely freaked out about what just happened.

"Can... can you help me sit?" Rikist did not look her way. "I'll wait for Krissik before going to bed. I don't trust making it all the way to the room."

Samantha swallowed her heart back down and nodded. Silently, she helped him to the couch and pulled the coffee table closer and helped him prop up his leg.

Rikist closed his eyes, pain etched on his face, and pressed down on his upper thigh though the brace, just above his knee.

Samantha retreated to the kitchen and pulled out the ice bags and a bottle from the refrigerator, popped the top, and sat on the couch beside Rikist. She set the ice packs on his leg, and then handed him the beer.

Rikist peered at her with one eye as his fingers brushed hers around the bottle's neck. "I thought you'd said—"

"You seem to need it."

He smirked. "That obvious, huh?"

Silence stretched between them, and Samantha played with the edge of her dress. She cast sideways glances toward Rikist, dipping her head lower when she caught him doing the same to her. After a few moments, Rikist sighed and leaned back on the couch, head turned toward Samantha.

"I'm sorry."

Samantha started, and she twisted on the couch to fully face him. "You don't have—"

"That... I was inappropriate."

"It's not a big deal."

He shook his head. "I don't want you to feel uncomfortable in your own home."

Samantha stared at Rikist, suddenly calm and at

ease as an idea sprang into her head. She scooted closer on the couch and put her hand on his shoulder. She smiled.

"Funny thing is," she said. "I haven't felt this comfortable since I've been here."

Rikist stared as the red flush began to recede. His left hand slid across the couch, hesitated, and then slid up onto her knee.

The front door panel beeped, and they both looked over as the door opened and Krissik stepped through, his arms loaded with rolled drawings and several packages. Samantha quickly pulled her arm back and stood to help Krissik. She took several of the packages away and set them on the counter as he shut and locked the door.

Krissik emptied his load on the counter and sighed, rolling his neck. He gave Samantha a gentle kiss on the cheek. He hesitated, and then took a deeper sniff toward her skin. He frowned, and his eyes shot toward Rikist.

"Has he been giving you trouble?"

She hesitated. "No. He's been a gentleman. I've been helping him move around the apartment."

Jealousy seeped out of Krissik's pores. "What were..."

"He can barely walk, Krissik," Samantha cut him off. She hesitated, and then brushed his hair back and cradled his cheek with one hand. "I'm just trying to help out."

Krissik stared down at her, surprised, and then

smiled. He sat at the table and began unlacing his boots as Samantha stepped away into the kitchen. He glanced again at Rikist.

"You *are* looking better," he said. "Should you be drinking?"

Rikist took a long pull on the bottle and glared at his brother. "Piss off."

Krissik raised an eyebrow and looked up as Samantha appeared with a plate.

"I am sorry," he said, taking her hand, and kissing her wrist. "I was not expecting to be home so late. You cooked?"

"Yes. Are you hungry?"

Krissik used a fork to spear the sautéed veggies and meat and stuffed it in his mouth. He looked at her sideways. "This is very good. Thank you."

Samantha sat at the table while Krissik ate, mildly fascinated by his fangs as he chewed. Samantha glanced over at Rikist, who sat watching the news on the monitor and flipping through pages on his glass phone. She tapped her fingers on the table, waiting until Krissik had cleared half his plate before speaking.

"Do you think you could take me for a tour of the city?"

Krissik's fork froze midway to his mouth. He sat up and lowered his hand. "Why?"

"Well... I am new here. It would be nice to see what your planet looks like."

"Have you watched the monitors?"

Samantha frowned. "Yes, watching the news is

pretty much all I've been able to do all day. I need to get out and see things for myself."

Krissik hesitated, as if unsure how to answer. He glanced over Samantha's head toward the couch.

Samantha turned to where Rikist sat watching them. She furrowed. "What's the big deal?"

"You can't," Rikist said flatly. "Human females are not allowed on the streets."

It felt like someone had kicked Samantha in the stomach. She swallowed. "Why... you mean not at all?"

"You're not to be seen by other males outside of family." Rikist's gaze did not waver. "Doing so could be grounds for punishment."

Samantha's heart raced. She spoke before she could stop herself, "Like what?"

Something haunting passed over Rikist's features. "You don't want to know."

She swallowed. "So... I'm just supposed to exist in this apartment for the rest of my life?"

"Samantha," Krissik cleared his throat and stood. "I-I have something for you."

He turned and shuffled through the packages he had set on the counter, his hands shaking. He stepped close to Samantha, his hands behind his back, and approached the table.

Samantha stared at Krissik's chest, caught between terror and anger at the new revelation. She counted to ten and forced herself to meet his gaze.

"I... wanted you to have this." Krissik held out a flat, wrapped package. "I know it means a lot to you."

Samantha's hands trembled slightly as she unfolded the silver foil packaging, and gasped. She held up her restored tablet, inspecting it in the light; the glass touch screen had been repaired, and a sleek, brushed steel casing had been attached to the outside, forming a protective ridge around the glass front.

"You fixed it," she said softly, the tension in her shoulders slowly dissipating. "How?"

"At night, when you were sleeping." His dropped to one knee and rested his hand on her thigh. "Anything to make you happy." He leaned forward, hesitated, and then pressed a gentle kiss to her lips.

"Ahem," Rikist coughed, noisily shifting on the couch so the springs groaned.

Krissik broke the kiss and glared at him.

Rikist held out one hand, his face a careful, blank mask. "And where's mine?"

Krissik growled and stood, his hand trailing along Samantha's shoulder as he stepped to grab several packages off the counter. He carried them over to the couch and dropped them on Rikist's lap. Rikist grunted, lifting the items off his propped leg. He hissed and pressed on his thigh, his eyes closed.

"Thanks," he forced out.

"I am going to help Rikist get set up," Krissik said to Samantha. "I brought home more medical supplies, and a wound vac."

"Wound-what?"

"A device to help his wounds heal faster and remove infection and deliver proteins to the muscles..."

Samantha frowned, her eyes glazing over as he went on to explain the medical terminology. "I'm going to read for a while."

Samantha sat at the table with her legs propped on another chair, and grabbed her tablet, leaning it against her knees. She swiped through the menu pages, checking to make sure everything was there, and then settled down with a romance novel.

She glanced up to watch as Krissik helped Rikist remove the dressings on his wounds and pull out a heavy, weighted wrap and a small, portable pump from the silver packaging.

Rikist verbally walked Krissik through the procedure, making it obvious he had used the device before, and Krissik compliantly followed the instructions and placed gauze on the wounds, then covered everything with a transparent film. Rikist shifted his weight so that Krissik could lift his leg off the couch high enough to slide the heavy wrap underneath, and tightly fold the edges around his thigh and knee, securing it with thick straps. Krissik handed Rikist the small, wired pump, and connected a wire from the pump to an input on the wrap. Rikist pressed several buttons, and a small humming sound emanated from the pump as the wrap constricted.

Rikist grimaced and leaned back against the arm of the couch, his face tense. Krissik patted his shoulder and then went ahead to put away the extra supplies.

Samantha watched, a feeling of dread building in her throat, until most of the supplies were packed, and

Krissik bade his brother a good night. She stood suddenly, hitching the tablet under one arm, and headed toward the bedroom.

Krissik looked up. "I'll come to bed soon," he called after her.

Samantha turned, forced a smile, and then veered into the bathroom and locked the door behind her.

She hurried to the shower and turned on the water, letting the hiss of the steam fill the silence of the room. She backed away from the door to the far wall below the thin window slits and sank to her butt, leaning back against the cool tiles. She closed her eyes as hot tears stung her cheeks, and she gripped her knees to keep her hands from shaking.

How am I supposed to escape if I can't even get past these apartment walls?

There was punishment if a strange male saw a female...

After seeing the brutality of the alien males and the mass assault during Samantha's abduction, she could only guess what sort of punishment that could be.

Women were not allowed outside.

Samantha wiped her eyes and took a deep breath.

At least not alone...

NINE

"Damn, asshole shot me!"

Samantha woke with a start in the dim light of dawn, listening to the sounds of gunfire and yelling. She sat up in bed, the sheets pooling around her waist, and she looked around Krissik's empty bedroom, eyes wide.

"Krissik?"

Her breath hitched in her throat when no answer came, and she leapt out of bed and wrapped herself in the sheet on the way to the bedroom door. She slid the door open, and cautiously stepped out.

"Hello?"

"Son of a bitch," Rikist cursed. "Why can't I ever seem to—"

Samantha's eyes widened. "Rikist!"

Rikist looked from where he lounged on the couch with his wrapped-up leg propped on the coffee table, wearing boxer-style underwear and a tank top. He glanced up annoyed in Samantha's direction, and then did a double take at her state of dress and put down the white plastic controller in his hand. He furrowed his brow curiously.

"Did I wake you?" He wiped at his mouth. "Sorry, I didn't realize I was being so loud."

Samantha gaped at him. She looked between the dusting of crumbs on his shirt and the monitor, blinked, and then stepped further into the room to see the screen more clearly. Her jaw dropped, and she followed a blinking adapter box and two wires that hung from the back of the monitor to the floor, where a white box with a glowing green light sat. She turned back to Rikist and pointed to the controller in his hands.

"Is that... is than an Xbox?"

Rikist grimaced. "Don't tell Krissik. He's a bit of snitch."

Samantha tightened her grip on the sheet and hitched it higher around her breasts. "How the hell did you get that here?"

He grinned slyly. "I have my connections."

"And why don't you want Krissik to know?"

"My connections aren't always... becoming of a military man in my position. He would not approve."

"And what do I get out of it?"

"Excuse me?" His face went stoic.

Samantha crossed her arms. "Since you're so afraid of Krissik putting you on time out, what do I get if I keep my mouth shut?"

Rikist glared at her, and then reached behind his back. He tossed something toward Samantha, and she caught it while struggling to hold up the sheet.

She looked down at her hand and then up at Rikist. "Are you kidding me?"

Rikist shrugged and turned his game back on.

Samantha's nostrils flared, and her shoulders bunched. "You mean to tell me," she yelled over the sound of gunfire, "that you've been hiding candy bars in your room this entire time, even after I made you dinner and complained about chocolate—"

"Well if I knew I could use it to bribe you to shut up then I would have pulled them out sooner."

She shook her head. "You are such a—"

"Dick, I know," he said, distracted. His eyes were glued to the screen as he quickly fired with his thumbs. He smirked. "You seemed to have enjoyed some of that last night."

"I don't appreciate all of the innuendos." Samantha stepped in front of the monitor. "And no, for your information we didn't do anything other than sleep. But Krissik hasn't given me any sleepwear—"

"Whatever." Rikist leaned his shoulders to try to see past her. He growled. "Do you mind?"

"I do, actually. I would like some answers—"

A rapid series of fired shots boomed out of the speakers, and Rikist groaned. "Come on, Samantha, move!"

"You're such a child. What else do you have hidden away?"

"Nothing."

"You're lying."

"I..." Rikist paused the game and sat back, frustrated. "I said I would leave you alone. Why are *you* bugging *me* now? I had Krissik fix your tablet for a reason."

Samantha's eyes widened. "*You* had him fix it?"

Rikist hesitated, realizing his slip. "I might have suggested it."

"Why?"

Rikist sighed and tossed the controller to the couch. He brushed off the crumbs on his chest and sighed. "Because as much as my brother seems to love you, he's clueless on how to treat a woman and needs all the help he can get."

"And what would you know about how to treat a woman?"

"I know a thing or two." Rikist gave her his best suave smile and shrugged his eyebrows.

"I doubt that." Samantha turned and started walking back to Krissik's bedroom. "You're just angry all the time because you're stuck in a sausage fest..."

"What did you say?"

Samantha turned. "As a lifetime bachelor you're not in the position to be spewing out marriage advice."

Rikist's face reddened, and his amber eyes nearly glowed with anger. "You have no idea what you're talking about."

"Krissik told me," she continued. "You're so wrapped up in yourself and your work that you never made the jump to find a mate. Now it's too late and—"

"Is that what he told you?"

Samantha froze at the venom dripping in his voice. She held her breath as he glared at her, his breathing heavy. His clawed hands had punctured the couch cushions, and he shifted his weight to sit further upright. A dark, angry blush crept up his neck and over his cheeks and ears.

"Is that what he told you?" he repeated, his voice low.

Samantha nodded, unable to speak. Her heart raced at the sudden flash of rage she had seen in his eyes; an animalistic fury potent enough to burn the paint off the walls.

Rikist growled. "I'm going to kick his fucking ass when he gets home."

"I... What?"

He looked away. "Nothing."

"Like hell it's nothing." She shook herself to loosen the tightness in her shoulders. "Why won't you tell me?"

Samantha crossed her arms when he simply stared at his hands. Rikist sat back on the couch, deflated. Samantha stared at him for a moment, trying to find a hint of reasoning on his face behind his outburst. After a few long moments, she sighed and sat on the couch beside him. She glanced down at the box of cheese crackers by Rikist's side and dug in and grabbed a handful. She popped three into her mouth, savoring the all-too-missed burst of flavor after days of fish and hard roots. She sighed.

"Do you have an extra controller?" she asked.

"Why?" Rikist glanced up at her, an emotion in his eyes Samantha could not place.

Samantha swallowed. "To play with you, stupid. I need something to do."

"Later." He reached forward and unzipped the straps on the leg wrap. "I want to go for a walk."

"You sure that's a good idea?"

Samantha chewed slowly as Rikist ignored her and unwrapped his leg. She was surprised at the state of his wounds; the redness of infection was gone, and the swelling had gone down considerably. She leaned forward to inspect the gash on his thigh, where the transparent bandage had actually started to meld with his skin, as if his body were absorbing it.

"Your leg," she said, astonished. "The cuts look like they've been healing for at least a week or more."

Rikist nodded and tested his leg, flexing his muscles and rolling his ankle. He pointed to the bandage.

"There are proteins in the tape, absorbed through the skin to feed muscle and tissue regeneration. The vacuum pulls out damaged cells and infection, cutting the healing time to a fraction."

"Amazing."

"It's my ACL I'm worried about..." he muttered. He slowly tried to bend his knee and stopped after only a few inches of movement. "Hoping I should be good to go in another week or two with the treatment."

Rikist slipped on a pair of pants lying over the back of the armchair, then stepped into his boots. He grunted and struggled to tie his laces, until Samantha huffed and knelt in front of him to help. He grunted in acknowledgment, and then fit the metal brace on the outside of his leg for support. He scooted to the edge of the couch and hooked the crutch under his arm. He pushed himself to his feet and took a deep breath. He tested his weight on his leg and grimaced but looked pleased that it held. He glanced down at Samantha, his face considering.

"Do you want to go?"

Samantha stood, her ears perked. "I thought you said women aren't allowed?"

He nodded and then shrugged. "It's dawn. There are hardly any residents in the area anyway, and no one will be up this early. It won't be long, probably just around the block. I just want to get the blood flowing."

"Sure. I'd love to."

She stepped toward the door, and the crutch shot out to block her path. She turned to meet the amber eyes.

"You need to stay close," Rikist warned. "For your own safety."

Samantha smiled sweetly, putting her best face forward. "I promise."

SAMANTHA COULD BARELY CONTAIN her excitement as she stepped out of the apartment building and onto the front patio wearing one of the four new dress outfits and sandals Krissik had laid out for her. She closed her eyes and sucked in air, letting the chill of the morning bite her nose and sting her lungs.

She looked around and realized that Krissik had not been exaggerating about how hard their world had been hit; the tall, metal buildings stood in long city blocks devoid of color or character. Blackened smears of what could have been from explosions or enemy fire broke the dull uniformity of the gray landscape. Almost no foliage or greenery could be seen anywhere, save for a few dying potted plants on the deserted balconies of the apartments across the street.

She frowned, and then held out her elbow for Rikist, helping him down the trio of steps to the sidewalk. He grunted as his feet hit the sidewalk, and she looked up at him.

"Are you alright?" she asked.

Rikist nodded. "Yeah. Come on."

He took them to the right, and she kept her pace slow to stay by his side as she gazed up at the metal buildings illuminated by the red glow of the rising sun, for a moment bringing color to a world drowned in shades of gray.

Samantha was happy to see Rikist moving around much better; he still needed the crutch with his heavy limp, but he seemed much more energetic, and color had begun to return to his face. She caught him looking at her from the corner of his eye.

"What?" she said.

He shook his head. "Nothing."

She poked him in the arm. "You were staring."

"I wasn't." He smiled. "That dress looks good on you."

Samantha smiled back, and then frowned when she felt a slight blush heat her cheeks. "Thanks." She stared at the quiet streets, void of life. "Is it always this quiet around here?"

"It's still early." Rikist shrugged as they rounded the second corner of the block. "But yes, for the most part this is a quiet sector. Many of the apartments are vacant."

"Why?"

"Many moved to the main cities after the resistance started." He snorted. "They seemed to think being in a higher populated area meant more safety."

"And you don't believe that?"

He hesitated. "What I personally believe doesn't matter."

"Why not?"

"Because our leaders decide what we should believe, how we should act, and who we should fight." His grip tightened on the crutch. "Their will is law."

Samantha eyed him curiously. She was very surprised this was coming from a decorated officer in their government's military, a man who fought against those rising against those in power and strove to squash the rebels from starting a civil war. The medals and ribbons strung across his bedroom walls declared his loyalty to his leaders and willingness to risk his life for his duties... but his current actions said otherwise, and Samantha was not sure which to believe.

"You don't sound like you care for that law."

Rikist glanced at her, and then went back to focusing on his feet. "A soldier is not supposed to act on what he agrees, but what he is told."

"That's not answering my question."

Rikist chuckled. "No, I guess not," he sighed, and his pace slowed. "Though I will say I'm glad this is the last corner before we make it back."

"Is your leg hurting?"

He nodded. "I'm going to need some meds when I get home."

She patted his back and slowed to keep pace. She continued their conversation with general small talk, asking questions about the neighborhood, locations of ports, and transportation.

If I can get him to open up, then maybe I can figure out how to get out of here.

Her ears perked when he mentioned the foreign embassies visiting at the convention center a few miles from the apartment and tried to explain some of their ongoing policy discussions. Apparently, Earth was one of the few planets out of the intergalactic loop, and there were multiple alien races throughout the galaxy who traded, interacted, and fought together—or against each other, depending on the current state of rule.

She blocked his monologue out as her mind whirled with possibilities.

Even though I'm pretty positive none of the ambassadors are human, I'm sure I could find one who would be sympathetic to my escape. At least I have to try!

"Sorry," Rikist's words broke through her thoughts. "I know you wanted to see more on your first outing."

Samantha moved to his left side and smiled sweetly at him, gently squeezing his arm. "Thanks for letting me come. It's been a wonderful opportunity."

Rikist's brow furrowed, his eyes growing wary. "Sam—"

Samantha jerked down on his arm and kicked at the crutch simultaneously as she spun on her heel and sprinted off. She heard Rikist's startled cry as he stumbled behind her but did not dare look back.

Rikist's roar pushed her legs faster. "Samantha!"

Samantha ran. She skidded to a stop at a crossroads, trying to remember the vague maps she had studied on Krissik's phone. She hesitated, and then turned left. Half a block down she came up short against a fenced-off area and had to retrace her steps to the right. Several times she turned, trying to orient herself.

Her breathing quickly became labored as she entered an even more dilapidated street filled with rusty dumpsters full of debris and rolls of wire and metal fencing. Never one for running, her lungs ached with the unfamiliar thin atmosphere, and she gasped desperately for air. She hesitated at the dumpster nearest her, which was marked with white slashes of graffiti.

I swear I've seen that before...

She slowed and pressed her back against the cool side of a crumbling building and closed her eyes to catch her breath.

A rock bounced along the ground to her right, and she gasped and turned left, only to have strong arms wrap around her and shove her against the metal wall.

Rikist's sweating face glared down at her, and he bared his fangs and growled. His nostrils flared as he struggled to breathe evenly.

"What..." he swallowed air. "The fuck?"

Samantha closed her eyes, blinking away angry tears. "How did you—"

"You ran in circles."

Samantha tightened her jaw and tried to jerk free. Rikist's right hand shot up from her arm to wrap in her hair, and he pulled her head back just far enough that he did not hurt her but forced her to freeze.

He grimaced. "Don't. I'm about three seconds away from throwing you off the nearest roof, but my brother would be devastated." He took a deep breath. "So, you are going to behave and come home without any trouble, because I'm not in a position to deal with your shit right now."

Samantha dropped her gaze and noticed the way he leaned heavily on his good leg. His left hand shook on the grip on the crutch; his knuckles white with strain. She frowned and glanced up at his face.

Rikist closed his eyes and breathed hard. Two lines of sweat dripped down his temples, and a speckled 'V' stained the front of this shirt. He swallowed and glanced over at her, his eyes mirrors of the agony he must have been feeling.

"You're a bitch."

She looked away from him, her eyes burning. Yeah, she deserved that. She felt horrible for the pain she had put him through, but hell if she had not tried escaping this nightmare. She had been so close!

She mentally shook her head. *Close to what, escaping? What if the embassy had just sent me back? Or... what if they* didn't? *What sort of trouble would I be?*

"I'm sorry," she whispered.

Rikist's eyes wavered, and he loosened his grip on her hair and settled on trapping her upper arm in a vice grip. He limped back a step, turning her as he moved.

"Let's go."

He started walking them back to the apartment. Halfway down the block, his grip transformed from pulling her along, to having to use her for intermediate support between steps with the crutch.

Samantha inwardly kicked herself. Rikist's sweaty hand on her arms shook, and his face had paled around his dry lips. She had not expected him to follow her—first, she had expected that he would not want to, and second, that he would not be able to. She sighed and shook her head.

Guess he proved me wrong. He is the most stubborn ass I've ever met in my life. She fought a smile. *Even excruciating pain won't keep him from getting what he wants.*

She pursed her lips. "How far did I make it?"

Rikist looked down in surprise, and then gave her a wry grin. "Two blocks."

Her eyes widened. "I ran forever!"

"Like I said, in circles." He motioned with his chin ahead of them. "The apartment is down this block and to our right." He gave her an almost appraising look and opened his mouth to speak, then shook his head and looked away.

Samantha glanced away to glimpse a figure duck behind the side of a building across the street. Fear nipped at the back of her skull, and her senses went on high alert. Goose bumps spread across her skin, and she scanned their surroundings as she pulled Rikist to a stop.

"Rikist?"

An alien in a black uniform—much like the ones the men had worn on the night of Samantha's abduction—stepped out from the building in front of them, a length of steel tubing in one hand. His gold eyes flashed, and fangs bared beneath tight lips.

"A long way from your ship," he growled out. "Are you not, *Captain?*"

Rikist roughly pushed Samantha behind him and pressed her up against his back. Tension rolled off him in waves, and he shifted his weight to both legs and hefted his crutch like a club.

"Sirtis," Rikist said, almost as a curse.

Sirtis's eyes narrowed, and two more men joined him from the shadows of nearby buildings, the long metal pipes in their hands glinting in the red light.

"I... did not expect to see you here," Rikist said slowly.

Sirtis bared his fangs. "You mean you never expected to see us *alive*." He motioned to the other two, and the three aliens spread out in a half circle as they crossed the street.

"Where are you going with this one?" the second man said, his voice deep and gravelly, as he used his pipe to point at Samantha. "Are you so arrogant you think you can just walk out here with a female?"

"You won't get away with this," Rikist hissed.

"Oh, yes we will." Sirtis wagged his pipe in the air. "Because the police will think that the well-paid captain was mugged by a few hungry beggars. And once the truth comes out, they'll be scouring the planet for the heroes that took you down."

Rikist pulled out a key card from his pocket and pressed it into Samantha's hand. "Samantha," he said slowly. "When I say so, run to the apartment."

"Why are—"

"Shut up." His breathing quickened. "Do as I say, do you understand? Lock the door behind you, and call Krissik."

"Rikist, I—"

Sirtis growled as he and the men neared. "Those were your men, you bastard!"

Rikist widened his stance, trying to place most of the weight on his good leg. "They died honorably—"

"It is not an honor to die at the hands of a traitor!"

Rikist roared, his lips pulling back to reveal rows of sharp teeth and long fangs. The other men roared in response and charged forward. Rikist swung his crutch upward, catching the nearest man in the jaw and sending him flying back against the building with a sickening crunch. Rikist spun around, his eyes wild.

"Samantha, run!"

Her legs moved on their own accord, and Samantha found herself running toward the apartment, even though she hated the idea of leaving Rikist behind. She glanced over her shoulder as she rounded the corner, long enough to see him block two swinging pipes aimed at his head, only to take a hit across his back from another. Rikist swung at the nearest man, and Sirtis kicked the brace on Rikist's thigh.

Rikist's wounded leg gave out, and he fell to his knees.

Samantha skidded to a halt and turned, her heart pounding. Frightened tears streaked her face as she glanced between the gate to the apartment building and the fight.

Three against one that's already wounded is not a fight.

It's murder.

She clenched her hands into fists and looked around. Nothing she saw resembled a weapon, but there were bits of debris on the ground below a charred building across the street, and she quickly darted across the pavement and snatched up a long, bent piece of rebar and sprinted back toward the men.

Rikist snarled and lunged at Sirtis, his claws swiping air as the man rolled to the side and kicked out, catching Rikist in the shoulder. The second man snuck behind Rikist, lifted his pipe, and swung.

Even from a distance Samantha heard the pipe connect against Rikist's skull, and saw his body stiffen as he fell forward.

"Rikist!" she screamed.

The men looked up, surprise on their faces. Sirtis pointed one clawed finger.

"Get her."

The third man with dark hair hung past his shoulders in thick waves stepped toward her as Rikist twisted around to look.

Samantha gasped. Rikist's face was red, his left cheek busted open and lower lip split, and blood dripped from between his teeth. Red filled the white of his right eye, and his right temple was caked with blood. His eyes widened as he saw her, and his lips pulled back into a snarl.

Rikist reached out as the long-haired man stepped past, his claws digging into the man's thigh and side. The man screamed as Rikist swiped upward, tearing open flesh, and ripping a hole in his stomach large enough for intestines and other organs to slip out and splatter to the concrete. The man screamed and crumbled to the ground, hands scrambling to push his insides back where they belonged. Sirtis dove at Rikist, and they collided and rolled across the pavement, snarling, and snapping their fangs.

Samantha screamed and hefted the rebar as the second man stalked toward her. She swung when he reached for her, but he moved fast and easily ducked and caught her wrist. He growled and squeezed until she cried out and let go, and the bar clattered to the ground. His other hand came up to grab her neck, and he turned to the side to press her against the side of the building.

She fought against him, clawing at his fingers, and trying to kick, but his greater arm length kept him safe from her swinging feet, and he ignored her useless nails. Samantha twisted in his grip, fighting to breathe. His fingers tightened around her neck, and his fanged sneer leaned in to her ear.

"Once he's dead, and we've had our fun, you're going to the pits with the rest of the human bitches."

He shifted his grip and grabbed both of Samantha's wrists with one hand, holding her arms above her head. His heavy hips ground against her own, and he began lifting her dress as he leaned forward to lick a thick, wet line across her neck.

Samantha tried to cry out, but a clawed hand covered her mouth, muffling her screams. She squeezed her eyes shut and writhed against the strength in his grip, desperately trying to break free. A finger found its way between her lips, and she bit down with everything she had. The alien screamed and slapped her across the face. The blow rocked her head back against the wall with a sharp crack, hard enough to blur her vision and make her head spin.

Rikist and Sirtis rolled around on the ground, their claws slashing and jaws snapping just inches from each other's necks. Sirtis twisted enough to reach Rikist's leg and dug his claws into skin. Rikist howled and loosened his grip, long enough for Sirtis to shift position and shoot his hands toward Rikist's throat.

Samantha struggled. "R-Rik... Rikist!"

Rikist jerked back at the last moment and rolled, twisting Sirtis's arm and flipping the man onto his stomach, pinning his arm backwards. He twisted Sirtis's arm violently until there was a sharp crack, and then grabbed the length of dark hair in one hand and used it to slam Sirtis's face into the pavement again and again until the alien's face turned to pulpy meat and his movements ceased. Rikist's amber eyes spun around, and he roared and leapt toward the man that held Samantha.

The man let go of Samantha to bring up his pipe, but Rikist was on him before he could fully turn. Rikist's mouth opened, his jaw spreading and extending to give him another two inches of opening and clamped down on the man's screaming throat. Blood squirted from between Rikist's lips as he bit down, and the man's scream garbled before going silent. Rikist let go and stepped back, and then grabbed the man's hair and twisted, snapping his head around completely.

Samantha slid down the building to sit on the concrete, covering her eyes with shaking hands. Her breath hitched in her throat, and tears dripped onto the sidewalk from her hanging head.

Rikist spit out blood and gasped for air, barely managing to slow his descent as he sank down beside her. He groaned and stretched out his legs, leaning his head back against the metal building. He swallowed and fought to control his breathing.

"Are you alright?" he gasped.

Samantha shook her head and let out a sob.

Rikist wiped his bloody mouth on his shoulder and grabbed Samantha around the waist, hefting her onto his lap. He wrapped his arms around her and hugged her to his chest, resting his cheek against her hair.

"I'm sorry," he whispered. "I'm so sorry."

Samantha stiffened at his touch, and then grabbed fistfuls of his shirt and buried her face in his neck. Her body shook as she sobbed, and she pulled up her knees and tried to melt into the warmth radiating through his red-stained shirt.

"I thought they were going to kill you," she breathed. She rubbed her cheek against his shoulder. "And then he grabbed me..."

Rikist cradled her against his chest, and he wiped his eyes against her hair. He kissed her temple and then tilted her face up to meet his, pressing their foreheads together.

"I will never let anything happen to you," he said, his lips trembling. "Do you understand? I promise."

Samantha nodded, closing her eyes to let two fresh tears drip hotly down her cheeks. Rikist used his thumbs to wipe them away. He brushed the hair back from her face and turned to glance at the still bodies on the pavement.

"We need to leave," he said, panic at the edge of his voice.

Samantha wiped at her nose and nodded. She crawled off his lap and stepped away to fetch his crutch near the body of one of the men. She brought it back to Rikist and helped him stand. He cried out when his leg gave out, and he caught himself against the building. Samantha shoved the crutch in his armpit and wrapped her arms around his waist and helped him slowly down the street.

They walked in silence down the silent block and up the steps to the apartment.

"HOW MANY PILLS DID YOU TAKE?"

Rikist's eyes slid open lazily, his movements sluggish and delayed. He swallowed and shifted on the mattress, turning his head toward where Samantha knelt beside him.

"Um... I think four?"

"You were only supposed to take two!"

"Three?"

"Rikist!"

"My leg hurts." He closed his eyes. "Whole body hurts..."

"Maybe you should throw them up—"

"I'm fine. I just want to sleep."

Samantha's hand held the washcloth, poised over Rikist's bruised ribs, where she had just finished washing away the last of the drying blood. She had already helped him bandage his leg with the healing wound-vac and iced his knee and the cuts on his face.

Neither had called Krissik.

"Why did they call you a traitor?" She scooted higher up on the bed so that she could look down into his sweating face. "Rikist?"

"Not right now."

"No, you're going to talk right now. You just got your ass kicked by three guys jumping you outside your apartment, and I almost got my throat torn out. I deserve some answers."

"You don't understand—"

"Of course, I don't," she cut in. "That's why you need to explain to me what the hell happened. Why did they want to hurt you? What are the pits?"

His eyes snapped open. "What about the pits?"

"The man that had me said that... when you were gone they were going to send me to the pits. What is that?"

Rikist sighed and shook his head. "My head hurts. Not now, please."

"Now! Or I'm going to tell Krissik everything." Samantha leaned onto his chest. "Please, Krissik!"

He looked to the ceiling, and then leaned back and closed his glassy eyes. "Top drawer," he whispered.

"What?"

"In my nightstand. There's something you need to see."

Samantha slipped off the bed and circled around to the nightstand on the other side of the bed, wondering at the possibilities of what could be inside the drawer. She tapped her fingers on the handle, and then jerked the drawer open. She froze at the sight of a picture frame, face down, and picked it up. The cool, silver edging of the frame felt smooth and crisp in her hands as she turned it over.

Her eyes widened as she took in the smiling face of a younger, striped-cheeked, and short-haired Rikist, his amber eyes shining as his arms held a woman about Samantha's age with blue eyes and long, blonde hair. The woman's face turned to gaze up at Rikist; her bright smile wide and genuine. Samantha was not sure which she was more surprised at: that the couple looked incredibly close and in love, or that the girl was—

"Human," she whispered.

She clutched the frame to her chest, and then stared down at Rikist. "Who is she?"

Rikist turned his head toward Samantha, his eyes red and weary. "Her name was Lindsey."

"Your mate?" Samantha's heart flipped in her chest. "Wait, you said *was*... what happened?"

His jaw tightened. "She's dead."

"I'm sorry." Samantha pressed her lips together. "How long were you together?"

"Five years. I was on the first jump to your planet."

Samantha sat on the edge of the bed, her eyes never leaving Rikist's. "I... When did she die?"

Rikist swallowed. "Two years ago."

Tears sprang to Samantha's eyes, and she looked to the ceiling to blink them away. "Oh, Rikist. I'm so sorry. Why didn't Krissik tell me?"

Rikist shook his head and wiped at his eyes. He could not answer, so he shrugged.

"And you never made the jump again before it was too late?" she asked slowly, watching his profile.

"I never wanted to."

"I'm sorry." Samantha wrung her hands. "But what does this have to do with the pits?"

Rikist's face darkened. "Two years ago, our leaders enacted new policies..."

Samantha's hands shook against the picture frame. "What sort of policies?"

"Imported mates are not meant to be companions, but breeders to extend the bloodline."

Samantha's skin turned to ice. Her stomach dropped to her feet and her throat constricted. She tightened her grip on the picture frame to hide her shaking hands. She glanced down at Lindsey's smiling face.

"And... and what if the mate could not bear children?"

He took a shaky breath. "She is taken to the pits or sold as a slave."

Samantha's heart nearly stopped.

Rikist closed his eyes and breathed. "The pits are where those over breeding age or found unable to make the jump can... enjoy the company of the sterile females for a modest amount of credits. This frees up the jump-eligible males to find new mates."

Samantha paled, and she sat back on the bed. She closed her eyes to block out the spinning room. "Is... is that what happened to Lindsey?"

"We knew she couldn't get pregnant early on, and it didn't matter to me." A single, fat tear trailed slowly down Rikist's temple. "When the new law went into place, the leaders conducted a planet-wide audit..."

"And she was taken," Samantha finished, looking at him.

"She fought back when they came for her. And they shot her." Rikist's face crumbled, and he covered his eyes with one arm. "I was deployed on my ship and I didn't even find out until three weeks later that she was gone..."

Samantha scooted closer on the bed. She lay down beside him and wrapped her arms around his shoulders, leaning her forehead against his neck. Her eyes widened in surprise when his hands came up to pull her closer. She held him tighter as he buried his face in her hair.

"I couldn't help her..."

"It's OK, Rikist," she cooed. "It's OK."

Rikist held Samantha for a moment longer, and then kissed the top of her head, gently pushing her away. He used the back of his hands to angrily wipe at his eyes. "And here I almost got you hurt too—"

"Don't." Samantha sat up and grabbed his face in both hands, forcing him to look at her. "That was not your fault. I took you down the alley. They came at you—"

He shook his head and relaxed against the mattress. He let out a disheartened sigh. "Because I *am* a traitor."

Samantha's eyes snapped to his face. "What?"

Rikist's eyes became unfocused, and his breathing deepened. Samantha leaned over him and tapped his cheeks.

"Rikist. Damn those pills... Rikist!"

His lids fluttered open and gazed at her bleary-eyed.

Samantha shook his shoulder. "What do you mean, Rikist?"

His eyes slid shut as he shifted position. "I'm a soldier. I fight..." he whispered. His breathing deepened and became even.

Samantha closed her eyes and hung her head. She leaned down and kissed his brow.

He twitched at her touch.

"...For the resistance."

TEN

"Sam-tha?"

Samantha sat at the table nursing her third beer when Krissik came home after noon with lunch and a physician. She had finished off one bottle, quickly reaffirming the fact their alcohol was not much stronger than iced tea, but kept at it, hoping to take the edge off.

So far, it had not worked.

Samantha had spent the morning cleaning up the living room: brushing up the cracker crumbs, throwing away chocolate wrappers, and unhooking and hiding Rikist's Xbox under his bed. Then she had taken a shower, changed into a new dress, and brushed her hair down around her neck to hide the slight bruising from her attacker's fingers before calling Krissik. She had not wanted to, but the sudden return of Rikist's fever worried her, and his leg had swelled again, the knee bruising to a deep purple and nearly bursting at his stitches.

She hoped he would not be too angry...

Krissik's face brightened when he saw her, and he smiled and greeted her with an eager kiss. Samantha feigned a smile and kissed him back.

"Thanks for getting here so soon," she said.

Krissik set the foil tray of food on the counter and nodded to the physician as she helped carry his equipment and led the gangly man into Rikist's room.

Samantha waited at the table until Krissik returned, grim-faced, and retrieved plates from the cupboard. He began dishing out portions of fish and transparent noodles for the two of them as he grumbled to himself.

"I do not know what he was thinking trying to exercise so soon." Krissik growled as he brought the plates to the table. "How was it you found him?"

Samantha had run the story through her head a thousand times. "He'd asked me to sit at the top landing to watch in case he fell, and I'd agreed." She poked at the food on her plate. "I didn't expect him to try sprints up and down the stairwell..."

Krissik sat across from her and shook his head. "And the idiot fell and probably permanently damaged his leg."

"It was an accident."

"He should know better. If he gets discharged he deserves it."

Samantha's hand shook, and she forced herself to take a bite of the tasteless noodles. She swallowed. "So how has work been?"

"Tiring. It is hard getting back into the routine after being off for nearly two weeks."

Samantha frowned. "I've only been here for a few days—"

"It takes time to prepare for the jump: medical tests, fasting, physical training, and immunizations. This way, we do not pass out upon arrival in a new environment."

"Like I did?"

"Yes—because this is not your planet and you are not used to our atmosphere. It would be the same for me on your planet if not prepared."

The door to Rikist's room hissed open, and the physician stepped out. He shut the door behind him and stepped up to the table as Krissik stood.

Krissik wiped his mouth on a napkin. "How is he?"

"He did not wake during my examination," the man said. His frown relayed his concern. His eyes flicked to Samantha. "How many *Singrah* did you say he took?"

Samantha swallowed. "Three... maybe four."

Krissik growled. The thin man sighed, rubbing his long neck. "I performed a limited magnetic imaging and x-ray to the leg and found that his anterior cruciate ligament has nearly completely torn through. In light of his refusal to refrain from exercise, he has also caused severe damage to his medial collateral and ripped the circumference of his medial meniscus."

Krissik's face darkened with each of the physician's

words. He cursed under his breath and crossed his arms. "What are you recommending?"

"Surgery, for one, and physical therapy will most likely take several months." The physician's frowned deepened further. "You are aware that I have to report this to his master chief."

Krissik's face twitched, pain and regret reflecting in his gold eyes. "What if... Are you able to postpone your report to see if he can recover on his own? This... could be devastating to his career."

The physician narrowed his eyes. "You realize the longer he postpones treatment the greater chance of developing osteoarthritis and deteriorating the full use of his leg?"

Samantha's heart stopped, and she fought back tears as she took in the doctor's words.

He might have permanently crippled himself protecting me. And what does he have to show for it?

"I need to go clean up," she said suddenly. She looked away from the inquiring stares of the two males. "Your brother bled on me."

Krissik nodded, and turned back to the physician, dismissing her. Samantha took her cue and slipped away into the bathroom.

THE SHOWER FELT WONDERFUL. Samantha breathed in, letting the heat fill her lungs and mist collect on her eyelashes. She fought to think of something—anything, besides her recent escape efforts and the fact that she probably ruined Rikist's career. She smiled at the sudden memory of Rikist's warm breath against her skin as he held her in the street, the strength of his arms as he pulled her close...

Her hands slowed as she soaped up her front, her hands caressing her neck and cupping her small, round breasts. Her nipples tightened as she rubbed her palms back and forth over the small nubs, and her breath quickened as her body heated in response. She closed her eyes and let her hand drift down across her flat and slicked-up stomach to the triangle patch of curls. She swallowed against the lump building in her throat as her fingers played with the shaved edges of her bikini line.

It's been so long since I've even thought about a man besides John...

Her body ached to be in the arms of a man again, one that actually tried to please and serve her because he *wanted* to. With the burden of the newly inherited farm, dropping out of school, ending her engagement, and being kidnapped, she wanted to be able to let go and just...

But that's not going to happen with Rikist, she knew. *He would never do that to his brother.*

She thought of amber cat-like eyes staring down from above her as warm hands caressed her breasts and arms. She closed her eyes as she imagined the press of pink, kissable lips against her neck, then moving lower...

A cool breeze met her back, and she gasped as hot lips found the side of her neck. She brought her arms up instinctively to cover her breasts. Two clawed hands rested on her shoulders.

"Don't stop," Krissik said, his voice low.

"Kris..." Samantha twisted to look sideways at him. Heat rushed to her cheeks as her eyes met his bare chest, and gold eyes bent down to enter her line of vision.

"Please," he whispered, his breath smelling strongly of mint. "I just want to watch."

Samantha raised one eyebrow, knowing full well where that hint of minty freshness came from. "Really?"

At least Krissik had the decency to blush as he smiled sheepishly. He dropped to his knees, his bandaged face nearly level with the bottom of her breasts. Spray from the showerhead pelted his hair and chest, and water rolled down his skin.

"Please," he said. "I could have taken you at any time, but I did not. I..." His eyes locked onto her triangle of curls and his nostrils flared. "I need you."

Krissik leaned forward an inch, and then hesitated, rolling his eyes upward as if for approval.

Samantha swallowed. "Kris, I..."

The scent of wet fur and mint rose within the billowing steam, and a gold halo surrounded Samantha's vision. Her mouth went dry and her vision swam against the sudden ache in her core, her body seeking a need that she had left unfulfilled for too long. She knew that it was the pheromones pushing her reserve to the edge, and yet... Tears sprang to her eyes as she fought against swirling emotions of fear, need, and desire, for a moment unsure to which she should succumb.

Krissik's hot lips kissed away the first tear that dripped down her cheek, and his hands turned her face toward him.

"Do not cry," he said, his voice guttural and forced as he stood, as if it pained him even to speak. He kissed her gently on the cheek. "We can stop."

For a brief moment, her heart surged toward Krissik's kindness, and she wrapped her arms around him and leaned against his chest, ignoring the fact that they both stood naked.

"I'm sorry," she whispered. "I can't."

His arms tightened around her, and he rested his chin on her head. "Do not be. It has been a rough day with Rikist, and I have been neglecting you."

He reached behind them and turned off the water. He stepped out and fetched two towels and wrapped one around Samantha's shoulders before tying the second around his waist.

"I need to get back to work." He smiled apologetically. "But I will be home for dinner. Will you eat with me?"

Samantha nodded.

He smiled and gave her a slow, gentle kiss on the cheek. "I just want to see you happy, Samn-tha."

Samantha forced a smile, knowing his heart was genuine. "I know."

He sent her one last look before excusing himself to get dressed. Samantha stood dripping in the bathroom, listening to him move about in the apartment before hearing the front door close and lock behind him.

RIKIST WOKE with a start when a glass of cold water splashed his face. He gasped and sputtered, struggling to sit up. He coughed and wiped at his face and dripping hair, searching the room until his eyes fell on Samantha beside him.

"Sam... What the hell?"

She threw the cup at him, and it bounced off his chest. "What the hell is right! Do you mind elaborating on what you told me before you passed out?"

Rikist looked at her blankly. He shrugged, lost. "I don't... I don't know what you're talking about."

"We were attacked by three men outside your apartment building, and they said it was because you were a traitor." Samantha crawled onto the bed and kneeled beside him. "After we got back, and I cleaned you up, you said you *were* a traitor, and—"

Rikist's face went stoic. "I am a captain fighting directly against—"

"Oh, cut the crap," she snapped. "I know what you said this morning. I've also been watching the news for the past two hours, and it seems they're investigating the cause of the explosion on your ship. They don't think the amount of damage could have been accomplished from one missile."

He pointed to his leg. "I was there, I should know what kind of damage a missile can do."

"There are the rumors that it was an inside job, to kill off those that were the biggest threats to the uprising in one sweep." She leaned closer. "What did you do, Rikist?"

Rikist stared at her, and his nostrils flared. His cheeks reddened, and he narrowed his eyes. He pushed her back, and not gently. He grunted and pushed himself to a sitting position.

"I can't speak to you when I can smell my brother all over you." His jaw clenched. "Go clean up."

Samantha balked at him. "Isn't this what you wanted? For me to screw your precious little brother?" she shouted and punched the mattress. "I don't give a damn if you're uncomfortable right now. I am uncomfortable every freaking minute of the day spent here, and I just want to go home!"

Rikist frowned, and then reached out to touch her arm. Samantha slapped his hand away and pressed the heels of her hands against her eyes. She sucked in a ragged breath, and then looked to the ceiling.

"A physician came by today to see you," she said softly. She closed her eyes when his face paled. "I called him."

"Why would you do that?" Anger flooded his face. "Samantha, why would you do that to me?"

"Because you're sick!"

"You had no right—"

"You took too many pills, and you started breathing funny and your temperature shot up, and your leg... God, your leg looks horrible..."

"This wouldn't have happened if you hadn't tried to run away!"

"I wouldn't have had to run away if your brother hadn't kidnapped me!"

"You probably ruined my career."

"Well, screw you and your brother and your career." She fought the urge to grab his leg brace and just shake the hell out of it. "You've both managed to ruin my life."

Samantha could not remember when she had started crying, only that she had to wipe away the wetness on her cheeks. She sniffed and shook her head. She met Rikist's eyes, and nearly lost her composure at the hint of pity amidst the smoldering anger. She searched his face, remembering Lindsey's smiling blue eyes, and the rabid lust in her attacker's eyes back at the hotel and in the alley. Her heart ached with fear and uncertainty, and her hands shook as she edged further away on the bed.

"Please," she whispered, "tell me you didn't..."

"Did not what?"

She forced herself to meet his eyes, wanting to gauge the truth to his words. "Tell me you aren't like the others... When you took Lindsey." Her lips quivered. "When you look at me. Tell me you wouldn't..."

Recognition flickered in his eyes and he reached out to take her wrist. He let her pull away and kept his hand out, palm up. "I have never forced a woman, if that's what you are asking. That's not in me."

"All of the other soldiers—"

"Are not *me*. And I made it a point to teach my brother the same morals."

A knot loosened inside of Samantha's stomach. "Do those morals include always telling the truth?"

Rikist sighed. He rolled his tongue around in his mouth and let his hands fall helplessly into his lap. He looked up, defeated. "I did it."

"Did what?"

"I blew up my ship."

Samantha gaped. "Wha...Why?"

"Because it was my job to get rid of the three high-ranking dignitaries who wanted a front-row seat to view the slaughter."

"I don't understand."

He frowned. "How do you think I got the chocolate, and the crackers, and the games onto my planet?"

Samantha shook her head. "Your connections?"

"Yes."

"Yes, what? What does that mean?"

"I'm a smuggler, Samantha. I use my position in the military to gain access to information and weapons and turn those over to the rebel forces."

"Why?"

He guffawed. "Because I like being able to pre-order the next Call of Duty—"

"I'm serious, Rikist!" She slapped his arm. "Why are you so—"

"Because they took away the only thing that I cared about!" he shouted. His nostrils flared, and his chest heaved. "Because everyone else on this fucking island blindly listens to whatever the leaders say and takes it up the ass without a thought."

Samantha sat still, her eyes wide. Rikist glared over at her, his wounded eye tearing in the swollen corner. He wiped it dry and punched the pillow.

"I am tired of being told what to do. Who to fight. What to feel. After Lindsey..." He clenched his jaw. "I couldn't just sit back and watch lives be destroyed by those currently in power. So, I switched sides."

"And Krissik doesn't know."

He snorted. "Of course not. My brother is so loyal to our leaders that he would never go against a direct rule."

"Krissik wouldn't turn you in, would he?"

"If he knew about my after-hours hobby..." He shrugged. "Let's just say I like my head between my shoulders and would rather not risk it."

Samantha took his hands in hers and squeezed, her eyes pleading.

"Help me," she begged. "You know what it feels like to feel trapped. To care about someone so much that you're willing to do anything for them. And you are the only one I feel that I can trust because as much as you try to blow it off, I know that you understand me." She took a shaky breath and wiped at her eyes. "I am scared, Rikist. I am scared of your world, of your rules, and I just want to go home to my boring life on my father's boring farm. To see my sister. I want to feel safe and be free again."

She gazed at his amber eyes and the hard set of his jaw and leaned forward to press her lips against his. When he did not resist, she moved her mouth to part his lips and slid her tongue across his. Rikist lifted a hand to the side of her face, and his lips parted against hers in the beginnings of a return kiss. He made a small sound deep in his throat as he angled his jaw for a better fit against her lips, and then he suddenly dropped his hand and turned his head.

"You are my brother's mate." Rikist finally met her gaze, his face torn and eyes red. "And you are off-limits."

Samantha's heart dropped. She pressed her lips together and nodded, and then slid off the bed. She hugged her arms around herself, and then hurried out of the room and into the bathroom, shutting the door behind her.

ELEVEN

Samantha woke to breakfast in bed. Krissik watched her eat as if mesmerized by her every movement and purred contentedly as she gave him a chaste kiss and an ear rub afterward. His eyes closed as he laid his head in her lap. He ran the back of his hand down her side fondly through the nightshirt he had gifted to her, his claws tracing the curve of her hip.

Samantha forced a smile down at him. The effort he put into trying to make her feel comfortable and needed was more than she had ever gotten from all the men she had ever dated combined, and despite her own feelings, she had no doubt that he really did love her. It made her heart ache as she remembered Rikist's soft touch on her cheek, and the need she had felt against her lips before he had pushed her away.

If only the older brother had swept me away instead...

Yet Rikist had made himself scarce the past week,

keeping mostly to himself in his room, spending his time on his phone and—when Krissik was not around—his games in the living room. When Samantha came near, he usually came up with an excuse about needing to sleep or use the bathroom.

His avoidance hurt, but she could understand his anger; a man in uniform had appeared at their door the day after the physician's visit, letting Rikist know that his medical file was under review and he would be having an evaluation with his master chief in three weeks. Physically, Rikist seemed to be healing, though his mood had grown increasingly sour toward her, and downright hostile toward his brother. Krissik, as positive as ever, blew it off by blaming it on the additional medication Rikist had been prescribed, but Samantha knew something more ate at the man.

She leaned back on the pillows, idly rubbing Krissik's head and neck, wondering if she could get used to the idea of affections from the young man in her lap since she was apparently stuck on this planet. She had been there going on two weeks now, and as much as she did not like the idea of staying, she had reserved herself to the fact that this was most likely her new life. Krissik had kept true to his word and had not forced himself upon her while she 'adjusted', but she could tell that his patience was wearing thin.

I should at least make the best of it.

"A physician is coming by this evening for you," Krissik said suddenly. He twisted his neck to look up at her. "To perform a physical."

Samantha froze, and her hands twitched against his skin.

Krissik sat up. "Do not worry. It is very minor and will not hurt." He touched her face. "I will get off work early so that I can be here for you."

"I... do I have to?"

"Yes," he said. "It is a required procedure for all new mates."

"For what?"

"To check your health."

Samantha looked him square in the eye. "And what if they found something to be wrong?"

Krissik hesitated; uncertainty flashed in his eyes. He smiled at her. "I am sure nothing is wrong. Do not worry."

He kissed her cheek, and then stepped off the bed. "I must get ready for work. I will need to study through lunch so that I can return home before he arrives."

"Guess I'll see you later then."

Krissik dressed and tied on his boots. He kissed her once more before opening the door. "I care deeply for you, Samantha. I hope you know that."

Samantha nodded. "I know you do."

Krissik smiled and left, the sound of the front door locking strangely loud amidst the morning peace.

Samantha smashed her face into a pillow and let out a frustrated scream, and then wrapped the sheet around her and opened the door to the bathroom. She dropped the sheet to the floor and stripped off her nightshirt as she shut the door behind her and walked to the shower to turn on the water. She shivered in the cool air, hugging her arms around her bare breasts.

The door to the toilet slid open, and Rikist limped out in a rumpled shirt and sweats, the brace around his leg stretching against the cotton material. He looked up at the sound of Samantha's gasp, and his jaw dropped. He stood unblinking, unable to move or look away.

"Rikist!" Samantha turned sideways and covered herself with her arms. "Well don't just stand there!"

"I-I'm sorry, I-I didn't know you—"

"Turn around!"

Rikist ducked his head and covered his eyes with one hand. "I shut the door. Don't you knock on your planet?"

"I didn't know you were up!" She stepped sideways and reached for a towel. She let out a frustrated groan when she realized none hung on the pegs. She glanced at the sheet and nightshirt on the other side of Rikist. "Hand me that sheet behind you."

Rikist turned his head to look back. He hesitated, and then reached down. His left leg wobbled with his fingers inches away, and he straightened to catch his balance. He grimaced and shifted his stance to bend at the waist.

"Rikist, don't," Samantha said, realizing he did not have his crutch. She leaned sideways to make sure he was not looking, and then walked closer. "I'll get it."

"I can get it."

"I don't want you to fall."

"Leave it, I'm fine—"

Rikist bent and grabbed the sheet just as Samantha pulled on the other end. The movement jerked him off balance to pitch forward against her legs. Samantha yipped as she fell backwards, with Rikist riding her down. She landed hard on her back and grunted as his weight fell across her stomach and legs. They lay still for a moment; Samantha wide-eyed on her back and Rikist's face pressed against her belly just below her breasts, his eyes closed, and hands held harmlessly out at his sides.

"Samantha..." he began.

Samantha blinked and pushed on his shoulders. "Get-off-get-off-get-off!"

Rikist put his hands on the floor and lifted his upper body so that he balanced on his good leg in a push-up position above her. "Samantha, I'm not a cripple. You don't need to act like I can't—"

He opened his eyes as he moved to twist away and froze. He swallowed with effort and lifted his eyes to meet Samantha's.

Samantha's breath stilled under the heavy weight of his amber stare. Desire and guilt swirled within the predatory eyes, his cat-like pupils dilating and shrinking as he focused. His breathing quickened, and the muscles bounced in his tight jaw. Samantha lifted a hand to rest against his shoulder, her heart leaping at the feel of his firm, heated skin through the thin material of his shirt.

"Rikist," she whispered shakily.

Their sudden closeness after a week of avoidance

hit her in a rush, and her skin tingled with excitement at every point of contact with his. His scent of musky sandalwood and rich spices of cinnamon, cardamom, and cloves spilled around her like a warm fur blanket, and she leaned closer to brush her nose against his neck and breathe in. She swallowed down the multitude of terrified butterflies clawing their way through her insides and pulled up her knees to scoot away from him, and her thighs brushed against his sides.

The sudden touch seemed to wake something within him. Rikist walked his hands further up on the floor in a fluid motion, so that the length of his body covered hers, and then kissed her. His lips were dry, and Samantha ran her tongue over his lips until they were moist and supple. The next kiss was harder, and Rikist bit lightly along her lower lip, bringing a small sound from deep within Samantha's throat. She kissed him back, sliding her hands to either side of his face and gripping the hair behind his ears, pulling him closer.

Rikist kissed her as if he were drinking her down, eager and hungry from years of pent-up sexual frustration. His hands shook as he slid them down her slim sides, cupping her ass and lifting her hips to press against the taut front of his pants. He moaned as Samantha broke the kiss and jerked his hair to tilt his head back, sucking at the edge of the jagged scar on his jaw.

Rikist shook his hair free from her grip and rubbed his cheek against Samantha's like a feline scent-marking his property. He licked a slow circle around the outside ridge of her ear and then down her neck. He suddenly rolled to his back, rotating Samantha on top of him so that she straddled his hips.

Samantha's mouth went dry as she sat over him, looking down at his heavy-lidded eyes and feeling his hard erection pressed against his pants between her legs. She leaned forward, running her hands up his hard stomach and firm chest through his shirt, letting her breasts hang temptingly close to his face.

Rikist hooked one arm around her shoulders and pulled her lower. He lifted his head, and his lips slid over her right breast, carefully taking most of the small firm mound in his mouth. He moaned against her skin as he circled his tongue around her raised nipple, and pulled his head back, letting her breast slide out from between his lips until he held her tip within his teeth and let it stretch until she cried out.

Samantha lifted Rikist's shirt to bare his muscled abs. She scratched her nails down his skin and through the white line of soft fur, watching him writhe and hiss. She scooted higher on his torso, so that she straddled his bare waist. She felt her own desire dripping from her center, and she rotated her hips in a slow figure eight, letting him feel that she was already hot and slick.

Rikist let out strangled groan as Samantha rotated around, giving him a clear view of her backside as her fingers slid inside the elastic waistband of his sweats.

"S-Sam... Samantha, stop."

Samantha froze, her skin on fire and heart pounding. She twisted to look at him, confused. "What?"

Rikist pressed the heels of his palms against his eyes, his mouth in a stretched grimace. His chest rose and fell unevenly, and his wounded leg twitched.

"I want nothing more than to bed you right now," he said slowly, forcing the words out. "But I can't. As much as I want to, I can't."

Samantha slid off of him and sat on her heels. She lifted one arm to cover her breasts. "But I thought..."

Rikist swallowed and did a sit-up, then used his arms to scoot back toward the wall, sitting out of reach. His cheeks and neck burned crimson.

"I'm sorry." He hung his head. "I have been trying so hard not to look at you like this, to stay away, but—"

"Rikist..."

"—It's just been so long since... and now I finally have the chance..." He closed his eyes and let out a short, defeated laugh. "And you're screwing my little brother."

Samantha set her jaw and stared at him through a watery haze. "That's not fair. That's not fair at all."

"Fair or not, it's true."

"And we haven't."

Rikist's eyes shot open. "What?" He stared at her incredulously. "Are you serious?"

She nodded. "He's... still giving me time."

He hesitated, as if considering his options, and then shook his head. "It still doesn't matter." Rikist closed his eyes, and let his head lean back against the wall. "You're *his*."

"I am not personal property!" Samantha's voice rose, cracking with emotion.

"On this planet you are." He paused at her shocked look. "You *are* his. If it weren't for us being brothers and you unmated, I shouldn't even be able to see you. To do so is banishment for me, and... slavery for you."

"I'm already a slave," she spat. "Unable to leave the apartment, only meant to breed. Right?"

"I'm trying to keep you alive."

"Sometimes just being alive isn't enough. Isn't freedom what you're fighting for? To be able to feel or love whoever you want without being told what to do?"

"In a few weeks, I will either be sent back to duty on a ship across the ocean or sent off to some recovery hospital after discharge—"

"And what about me?"

"And you will be here, becoming heavy with child and in the arms of my brother."

Rikist sniffed and looked over at Samantha, his eyes letting her see his regret and disappointment. He frowned, and then used the wall to push himself to his feet. He stared down at her, his jaw tight and shoulders set in a straight line, looking very much the stoic military man that had walked into the apartment almost two weeks ago.

"There's nothing I can do. And no matter how much I try, I can't avoid you while living so close. I think it's best that I move back to the barracks so that you can focus on Krissik," he said softly. "I'll leave in the morning."

He nodded at her, eyes filled to the brim, and then left.

Samantha sat in the middle of the cold bathroom, letting the escaping steam from the shower rise and plume around the ceiling to mist down on her cooling skin as she pulled up her knees and cried.

A KNOCK on the door startled Samantha from her book. She looked up from where she sat on the couch, freshly showered, and dressed. She listened and jumped when the knock came again. She stood and walked toward the hall.

"Rikist?" she called. "Rikist?"

The door to the bedroom opened, and Rikist stood in the doorway in clean shirt and trousers, the metal brace stark against the khaki material. He glared at her. "What?

She licked her lips, taken aback by his rough delivery. She glanced past him to his bed, where his bags and folded clothes laid spread out as he packed his things. "There's someone at the door."

Rikist's face blanched, and he ducked back into his room before limping to the front door with the crutch, one hand behind his back. He pressed several buttons and then looked out of a slit that appeared in the center of the door. His shoulders stiffened, and then he stepped back and opened the door.

"Yes?" he asked, wary.

"Krissik Sa Tskir?"

Rikist shook his head. "What business do you have with my brother?"

"He requested a preliminary health check on his new mate. I am the physician for the area."

Rikist glanced over his shoulder at Samantha, his brow furrowed, and then nodded and stepped to the side. The man stepped inside carrying a silver case, and Rikist shut the door behind him before slipping into the kitchen.

Samantha stood still as she assessed the newcomer. Tall and thin, the hunched alien appeared old; his skin wrinkled around his eyes and his gray and white streaked mane reached the middle of his back.

Rikist limped from behind the kitchen counter; whatever he had been holding in his free hand left behind. His eyes were wide, and pupils narrowed to slits, and his claws clicked against the crutch nervously in a startling resemblance to his younger brother.

"Captain Sa Tskir," the man held out his hand and rubbed his age-spotted wrist under Rikist's jaw in greeting. "I was not aware you were living here as well during your recovery. It is an honor to meet such a brave and devoted soldier to our people."

"Temporarily." Rikist nodded. "I was injured during my last deployment and required assistance."

"So, I heard." The physician bent stiffly to peer

closer at Rikist's leg. "I could inspect your wounds if you should need it."

"No," Rikist dipped his head in respect. "It is nearly healed. Thank you."

"As you wish." He looked at Samantha. "Is this the female?"

Samantha paled.

"Yes," Rikist answered after a moment. His tongue rolled along the inside of his cheek. "You had an appointment?"

The physician nodded. "Yes, but not until later. I had an earlier stop cancelled, and so I wanted to push this one up so that my old bones can return home earlier this evening."

Samantha's pulse pounded in her ears, and her palms grew sweaty as she watched Rikist considering, and the room spun dangerously when he nodded.

"I'll show you to their bedroom," he said, his voice low. He held out a hand toward Samantha, though he would not look her way. "Samantha?"

Samantha froze, her feet rooted to the floor. She stared at the silver case in the physician's hand and her breathing quickened.

She jumped when she felt hands on her arms and looked up to see Rikist staring down at her. His face was an unreadable mask, and his eyes did not quite meet hers as he gently pushed her forward.

"Please don't make this harder than it needs to be," he whispered. His grip on her arms tightened as he gently squeezed. "It will only take a few minutes. Then he will leave."

Samantha looked around Rikist. The physician was shuffling toward the hall, his attention focused on his feet. Her eyes pleaded upward.

"Can... can you stay?" she whispered.

Rikist's eyes darted to the unsuspecting physician, a trace of fear flitting across his face. Then the emotion quickly disappeared as he brought the walls back up. "That is a highly inappropriate thing to ask of me." He whispered. He pushed her forward, faster, and pointed to Krissik's door. "In there."

He reached around the physician to the keypad and opened the door, pulling Samantha inside. He forced her to sit on the bed and then stepped back, barring the door with crossed arms.

The physician set his case on the bed beside Samantha and flipped it open to reveal a small metal box, test strips, several empty vials, long swabs, and a metal speculum.

Samantha squeezed her eyes shut and forced herself to breathe, knowing exactly what type of exam this was going to be.

The physician noted her discomfort and patted her arm with a kind hand. "Do not worry, I have been performing this procedure for nearly two hundred seasons, and I have a gentle touch. You will not feel a thing."

He finished prepping his equipment, and then had

Samantha lie back on the bed. He glanced over his shoulder at Rikist and nodded.

Samantha tilted her head to look at Rikist as he stepped back with a frown and then closed the door.

SAMANTHA SMOOTHED out the front of her dress as she sat on the edge of the bed while the physician typed in his notes on his tablet. He muttered to himself as he pressed the tips of the swabs to the test strips and dropped blood from the vials onto small glass discs that he pressed into the top of the small metal box. He swiped a command onto his tablet, and the small box hummed to life and began spinning rapidly as it hovered above the case.

She looked toward the door, where she could hear Rikist's muffled voice through the door as he spoke on the phone; his words were a quiet rumble below the whir of the box and the clicking of the physician's claws on the tablet.

The box slowed to a stop, and a reading appeared on the screen of the tablet. Samantha's heart leapt into her throat as the man paused to read, his eyes widening. He flipped through the notes again, and then moved to the row of three test strips. He inspected each one, focusing more attention on the last as he compared it to his notes.

After a moment the physician straightened and

replaced all of his items in his case, stepping back. "It has been a pleasure."

He turned to leave, and Samantha stood as he reached for the door.

"What..." she started. She took a shaky breath. "Is everything alright?"

The old man glanced at her over his shoulder, then opened the door and stepped out.

Samantha stared after him as the man walked down the short hall toward the front door. Rikist came into view, lowering his phone to his side. He looked toward Samantha, and then addressed the physician.

"Well?"

The old man frowned at him. "It is not my place to discuss these matters except with her mate."

Rikist's eyes narrowed. "This is my house, and what goes on inside these walls is my business."

"Captain, with all due respect, this is not the first female I have inspected and know well the rules in place."

The physician moved toward the door, and Rikist stepped in his way. The man frowned.

"I also know that men in your position," he continued, "while you tend to believe so, are not above the law. Bar my way again, young soldier, and you shall receive a rude awakening on how little sway your title brings in the upper rings of court."

Rikist hesitated, and then stepped back with lowered eyes.

The physician opened the door and patted Rikist's shoulder. "I know you are concerned for your brother. Speak with him on the matter after I send him my report."

Rikist shut and locked the door after the man left and stood looking down at his feet.

Samantha stepped out of the bedroom, wringing her hands. "Rikist?"

He raised his head, his eyes vacant. "Hmm?"

"What—"

"I'm sure it's nothing," he said quickly, snapping out of his thoughts. "I called Krissik while you were in the room. He's on his way."

"When will we know?"

"Krissik will most likely have read the report before he gets here."

Samantha shuddered, and her shoulders sagged as she leaned against the wall and slid down to sit on the floor. Her hands shook as she hugged her legs to her chest. She squeezed her eyes shut and pressed her forehead to her knees.

"He didn't look happy," she whispered.

Rikist stood still, his amber eyes staring down at her. He tapped his fingers against his legs, a nervous twitch in his right cheek. He swallowed and took a step toward Samantha, decided against it, and walked into the kitchen.

Samantha heard him open the refrigerator, open a beer, and gulp it down. The bottle settled on the counter, and a second cap hissed loose and clattered across the floor as he grabbed the gun he had left on the counter and limped past Samantha, slamming his door shut.

KRISSIK ARRIVED at the apartment an hour later, his face flushed and eyes wide. He dropped his tablet and drawings on the counter and shucked off his jacket, tossing it onto the table. His eyes darted around the apartment and stilled when he found Samantha seated nervously on the couch with her hands in her lap.

Krissik quickly crossed the space between them and knelt before Samantha. He took her hands in his and kissed her knuckles.

"I am so sorry that I was not able to be here while the physician inspected you," he said. "He came much earlier than I had expected—"

They looked up as Rikist appeared from the hall and took a seat at the table.

"It's fine, Kris," Samantha put a hand on Krissik's arm. "What... what did he say?"

"Not much." Krissik swallowed, his eyes haunted. He leaned forward and kissed Samantha on the cheek, his hand brushing against the metal tip of the translator behind her ear, and then stood and motioned for Rikist to follow him.

"Tsik ark satiks?"

Samantha's blood ran cold and she touched the translator stuck in her skin, realizing Krissik had somehow disabled it. Tears sprang to her eyes as the reality of the potential trouble she was in dropped on her shoulders like a ton of bricks.

Rikist glowered at Krissik, a frown etched deep on his features. He grunted and pushed himself out of the chair, and then passed Krissik on his way toward the bedrooms. Krissik turned and gave Samantha a forced smile.

Samantha's blood ran cold as Krissik disappeared behind Rikist into his bedroom and strained to hear their conversation through the closed door.

She did not have to wait long before the yelling started. She could not understand their words, but even in their harsh tongue, the anguish in Krissik's voice was unmistakable—as was the anger in Rikist's.

The door to the bedroom suddenly opened, and Krissik stumbled backwards into the living room, followed by a red-faced Rikist. Krissik stepped to stand in front of Samantha and raised his clawed hands.

Rikist stalked forward—his limp ignored—as he rounded his shoulders and bared his fangs. He growled something in their alien tongue, and Krissik hissed back, his lips pulling back to reveal his own fangs. Krissik took a protective position in front of Samantha and let out a tiger-like roar.

Rikist gnashed his teeth roared back. His deep and resonant voice vibrated off the walls and sent chills down Samantha's spine, drowning out Krissik's higher-pitched cry.

Krissik lunged forward and Rikist dove to the side, barely dodging the blow as Krissik swiped his hands out. Claws caught Rikist in the shoulder as Krissik spun around, splattering blood against the wall. Rikist dropped to all fours and sprung, his fist rocketing out to slam into Krissik's stomach.

Krissik crumbled over his brother's arm, and he let out a gasp as his knees gave out and he slipped to the ground. He sucked in air, his face pained. Then he spun and swung his leg out to kick, connecting with Rikist's side.

Rikist snarled, seemingly more pissed than hurt. He blocked Krissik's next kick with one arm, trapped it against his side, and slammed his free elbow into Krissik's thigh. Then he used his leverage to flip Krissik onto his stomach and pin Krissik's arm far behind his back.

Krissik groaned and thrashed as he tried to free himself. He screamed at Rikist, trying to claw his brother's eyes out with his free hand.

Rikist kept his upper body hidden and head down behind Krissik's twisted shoulder in a practiced manner, staying free of the raking claws. He barked a series of commands, hesitated when Krissik did not answer, and then repeated himself.

"Rak tsi kist tra!" Krissik shouted, his face red.

Samantha cowered behind the arm of the couch, her eyes wide. Her heart raced, watching the two brothers tear at each other. Even wounded, Rikist was by far the better fighter, and watching from the sidelines, Samantha could see that Rikist was doing his best to tire the untrained Krissik without quickly ending the fight with violence like he obviously could.

"Stop!" Samantha screamed. "Both of you stop it!"

Rikist shifted his hands, and Krissik twisted away and struck. His claws dug deep into Rikist's wounded thigh. Rikist howled, releasing his grip, and fell back holding his leg as he let out a guttural yowl that was a mix between a cat's scream and baritone yelp. His amber eyes flashed in fury and he toppled into Krissik, and together they rolled across the living room floor, biting, and clawing.

"Rikist, please! You'll kill him!"

The brothers separated, and Rikist stepped to the side as Krissik lunged. He reached out and pulled Krissik's shoulder to redirect his momentum, twisting Krissik sideways and down to smack his head hard against the stainless-steel counter top.

Krissik's head hit with an audible crack, and he crumpled backward to the floor unmoving. Rikist stood over him, breathing heavy, and then stepped back and sunk onto the couch. He leaned back and pressed on his thigh, blood seeping between his fingers.

"Raki sutari..." he breathed, his face taut.

Samantha's hands shook as she stood and crossed the room to Krissik. She knelt down and felt for a pulse in his neck. It was there, strong and steady. She rolled him over on to his back, gasped at the puddle of blood beneath his head, and then spun on Rikist.

"Why did you do that?" she screamed. She clenched her fists and stormed up to him. "You could have killed him!"

Rikist glared at her. "I saved you," he said in English. "And you defend him?"

"Saved me? I..." Samantha stopped, and her eyes widened. She put her hands to her mouth. "What are you..."

"You are stir... sturl... um..." He seemed to search for the right word. "Cannot carry—"

"You mean sterile?"

He nodded.

The bile came up without warning, and Samantha doubled over and threw up on the floor. She shook and leaned against the counter as she stumbled to the sink to rinse out her mouth. She closed her eyes and took a shaky breath.

"Oh, my God... Is he going to send me away?"

Rikist grunted as he forced himself to his feet. He staggered against the wall, and then limped toward his bedroom, his brace creaking.

"He does not want to, but he is stupid. He plans to plead to our Tsiari to keep you."

"What will that do?"

Rikist shook his head grimly and disappeared into his room.

Samantha stood, torn between helping Krissik and following Rikist. Tears slipped down her cheeks as she stood trembling with fear of the possibility of being taken away to a place as gruesome as the pits, or being sold...

Samantha darted down the hall and into the bathroom. She grabbed a hanging towel and wet it in the sink, then hurried to Rikist's bedroom.

"Rikist?" She poked her head in.

Rikist had taken his brace and shirt off, revealing the bloody scratches that adorned his right shoulder. He struggled to step out of his trousers. He groaned through clenched teeth as the pants stuck around the boot of his wounded leg, and he could not bend to pull it off. Blood seeped out of the puncture wounds from Krissik's claws through the gauze bandages on his knee and trailed down his thigh and calf. He glanced up as Samantha entered, his eyes red. His hands shook as he sat on the edge of the mattress.

"I..." He closed his eyes. "I did not want to fight. I have never struck him before."

Samantha knelt in front of Rikist and undid his laces, gently pulling off his boots and then pants. She pressed the wet towel to his thigh and applied pressure with one hand. Rikist hissed, and his claws dug into the mattress.

"Did I kill him?"

Samantha looked up at his question. She saw the dread in his eyes. "No. He'll wake up eventually." She used her other hand and the edge of the towel to wipe at the blood dripping down his leg. "What am I going to do?" She looked up at him, pleading. "Rikist."

He shook his head and reached behind him to grab a folded pair of uniform pants and bandages from his half-packed bags. He pushed Samantha's hand away and unwrapped the torn bandage on his leg before applying the new dressing. He shook out the new pants and handed them to her.

"Help me. We need to leave."

Samantha helped him step into the pants and pulled them up around his waist as he stood. Rikist's hands shook as he fumbled with the button fly, and after several attempts, Samantha shoved his fingers aside and deftly buttoned him up. He grunted in acknowledgement and slipped on a new shirt, then sat again to put on his boots with her help before attaching the brace to his leg.

"Go see to Krissik," he ordered. He hesitated, his face clouded. "He loves you."

"I know."

Samantha went back into the living room. Her heart fluttered when she saw that Krissik had not moved, and she felt his chest and pulse again to be sure he was still breathing. She snatched a towel from the kitchen and pressed it to the gash on his head, wiping the drying blood off his cheek and away from his closed eyes.

Rikist's uneven, heavy footsteps made her look up. He had a rifle-like weapon in hand, a laser gun strapped to his waist, and his military cloak thrown over one shoulder. He stared down regretfully at Krissik, and then motioned for Samantha to move.

"Come," he said, walking toward the door. "Before he wakes."

Samantha stood, holding the bloody towel in her hands. She wrung it between her hands. "Where are we going?"

Rikist opened the door and turned. "You are going home."

TWELVE

Samantha sobbed against the window of the transport vehicle as it slid silently across the barren landscape outside of the suburban sector of the island. Once they had gotten past the edge of the brother's neighborhood, the dilapidated buildings had seemed to sink into the broken ground around them, testimonies to the ongoing war and lack of community support from their leaders.

Samantha sniffed, wiping at her eyes, and looked over her shoulder at Rikist. He stared out the window in silence, his face dark and expression bleak. He had just gotten off the phone after spending half the ride in a heated conversation she could not understand and propped his wounded leg up against the front dash, absently rubbing at his upper thigh.

"Why?" Samantha asked after a moment, straightening in her chair. "Why are you risking everything to help me?"

Rikist almost jumped, startled from his thoughts. He swallowed, his eyes swimming with conflicting emotions, and then looked down at his hands.

"I cannot have a repeat of Lindsey," he said. "I could not live with the guilt."

Samantha nodded, and reached out a hand to rub his arm. She smiled and fought back another round of tears. "Thank you."

Rikist nodded, tight-lipped, and looked back out the window. His throat bounced, and he clenched his teeth, the muscles in his neck and jaw bulging. He took a deep breath and turned in his seat to face her squarely. He held out his hands toward her face.

"Come."

Samantha leaned forward, and Rikist gently turned her head to the side so he could inspect her translator. She winced as his fingers prodded the metal nub and tensed when she felt his hand on her jaw tighten so that she could not move. A sharp stab of pain laced down her neck, and she cried out.

"Ouch! What was that?"

She looked down to see the thin translation device between Rikist's fingers, the smooth metal of the needle end tinged pink with blood. He snapped it in half and lowered his window, then tossed it out.

Samantha gaped. "Why did you do that?"

"It is linked to Krissik's," he said. "He can... what is the word... locate you."

"Even on Earth?"

Rikist nodded. "When we arrive at the jump point,

you need to be fast." He pulled the gun from his belt and handed it to her. "There is a man on the other side. You need to kill him."

Samantha's eyes bugged. "What?"

Rikist pressed the gun in her hands. "Like this." He moved her fingers into the correct positions on the silver weapon, pointing out the obvious trigger and flipping the safety on and off.

"I can't kill anyone, Rikist!"

He eyed her, annoyed. "Do you want to go home?"

Samantha nodded.

"Then you do not have a choice. The jump needs two ends to work." He paused at her confused look, and sighed, frustrated. He held up one finger on each hand. "We are here. Jump point is here. Both need to activate at the same time to make the jump. If one is missing—"

"Then the jump point won't work, and no one can follow," Samantha finished, her eyes going wide.

Rikist nodded. "Yes."

Samantha hefted the gun in her hands, turning the shiny contraption over in the light from the window. "I... I don't know if I can do that."

Rikist put a knuckle under her chin and tilted her head back to look him in the eyes. "You have to. Or he can follow."

Samantha closed her eyes and nodded, hugging the gun to her chest.

THE CAR SLOWED to a stop near the end of the line of buildings. Samantha sat up, peering out the window at the darkened sky and shadowed ruins. Rikist leaned forward and held a hand out to silence her.

"Stay close," he said.

He hefted his rifle and pressed the panel near his head to open the door. He stepped out carefully, and then limped away from the door and held out his hand. Samantha gripped the handle of her gun and took his hand and stepped out of the car. Rikist limped toward the building quickly, pulling her behind.

They circled away from the street to the back of the building, and Rikist led her up a short flight of stairs to a reinforced metal door. He knocked twice, paused, and then knocked again. He stepped back, shielding Samantha, as the sound of footsteps and clicking panel buttons drifted from the other side of the door.

"Si ta, Rikist?" came the muffled voice through the intercom.

"Tsir," Rikist answered, his hand tightening around Samantha's. "Rik stra irk tsi?"

The lock turned, and the door swung open. A short-statured man with gold eyes and long hair peeked around, his eyes widening at the sight of Samantha, and then stepped back so they could enter.

Samantha pressed up against Rikist as they entered the building, the darkness closing in around them as the short alien closed and locked the door behind them.

Rikist led her down the narrow hallway and turned down a hall to their left. The walk opened up to a large warehouse-style room, filled with electronic equipment and military weaponry.

Rikist paused, leaning against what looked like a tank, and glanced at Samantha. "Are you well?" he asked.

"I should be asking you that," she said. She reached up and felt his sweating brow. "You're hot again."

"I am fine." He leaned away from her hand.

A trio of aliens in green and gray uniforms approached them, and Samantha huddled behind Rikist, who stood tall and set his shoulders back to stand evenly on both legs. Samantha closed her eyes and focused on settling her heart as the four men spoke, knowing she could not follow anyways, and tried to breathe. Her eyes jerked open when Rikist pulled on her wrist.

"They will charge the portal," he said. He grimaced and shifted his weight. "We... borrow our Tsiari's jump site."

"You hacked into your government's portal?"

He frowned. "I do not know that word."

"Hacked—tap into." She shrugged. "Borrow."

"It will only take a few moments. It should be ready when we get there."

Samantha nodded and looked around at the men milling about the large space. She saw that most of them looked worn and thin, a stark contrast to Rikist's strong and solid stature and confidence. She looked at his profile and the etched grimace on his face as he fumbled to pull one of the small containers from his pocket. She moved his hand aside and fetched the bottle, opened it, and handed him two pills. He nodded and swallowed them before shoving the container back into his pants.

"What are you going to do now?" Samantha asked. She waited until he had turned to look at her. "Once I'm gone, what's going to happen to you?"

Rikist hesitated, and then shrugged and looked away. "I am marked now. I will probably have to... converge—uh, convert—fully to..." he used his hand to motion toward the room. "I will not join my ship again."

"I'm sorry."

He stared sadly at her, and then shrugged as he pointed to his leg. "I will not pass the medical interview any way. Even after all I have done, they will discharge me."

A sudden explosion rocked the building, and frantic yelling and gunfire outside shocked them to silence. Samantha clung to Rikist's arm, and he pulled her further into the room. Samantha screamed as the front door exploded, sending smoke and debris in all directions.

"We were followed." Rikist roughly shoved her forward. "We need to go!"

They ran as fast as Rikist could go toward the east corner. Rikist stumbled as they rounded the bend, and Samantha steadied him as they made it down the short hall to another room that held a control panel next to a recessed, hexagon-shaped space with curved metal rods mounted at each point.

Rikist pushed Samantha toward the green-lit center of the shape as he stepped behind the control panel and began typing in codes. "Go!"

Samantha walked to the edge of the ledge, and then spun around and nearly dove at Rikist. She wrapped her arms around him, ignoring his grunt of pain as she buried her face in his shirt.

"Thank you so much," she whispered. "I'll never forget this."

Rikist hesitated, and then his arms wrapped around her shoulders and back, and he breathed against her hair. His hug tightened, and then he pushed her back long enough to press his lips against hers.

"And I will not forget you," he said, his amber eyes glinting wetly. He forced a smile and pushed her back. "Go."

Samantha nodded, and jumped down onto the lowered platform. She wiped at her eyes as the metal rods surrounding her began to glow, and a high-pitched whine filled the room. The glowing floor beneath her feet brightened, the green intensifying. She swallowed and lifted a hand to wave goodbye.

Sharp cracks of gunfire erupted behind Rikist; electric bursts of green currents shot out amongst bullets ricocheting off the walls. Rikist ducked and turned, lifting his rifle as men in black uniforms rounded the corner, and he mowed them down as they entered the room.

"Samantha," Rikist yelled over his shoulder. "Stay there! Only a few more seconds!"

Samantha crouched down in the center of the platform, the green glow casting her shadow on the ceiling above. The humming grew and drowned out the men's yelling.

She screamed as the bullets hit the metal rods and pinged off in all directions and reached out to Rikist.

"Rikist!"

"Sam-an-tha!"

Samantha's head jerked up at the sound of her name, and she gasped to see Krissik entering behind a trio of heavily armed soldiers with shields. Blood covered his temple and stuck in his hair, and his eyes were wide and horrified in his anguished face.

Krissik held out a hand, his expression hurt. "Samantha!"

Rikist roared in frustration and lowered his rifle from Krissik, unwilling to shoot his brother. Krissik shrieked and the man beside him lifted a weapon toward Rikist and pulled the trigger. A bolt of green, electrical energy shot out from the barrel and hit Rikist in the chest.

Rikist jerked and fell onto his back at the edge of the platform. His body convulsed in a seizure, first doubling over and then jerking backward to arch his spine. His hands clenched into contorted shapes and his legs shook, his boots squeaking against the concrete floor. He twitched as two soldiers approached with their guns held at the ready.

Samantha screamed, "Rikist!" The green light suddenly brightened to white in a sudden flash, and without thinking Samantha threw herself at the edge of the platform and grabbed Rikist's nearest arm. She put her feet against the wall and kicked with all of her might, pulling Rikist off the edge and down onto the platform with her, just as the light winked out.

THIRTEEN

Samantha opened her eyes to a quiet room, void of gunfire and soldiers. Rikist lay on his side beside her, his body still and eyes closed. She twisted on her knees at the sharp intake of breath behind her and gasped at the sight of the surprised alien in a black uniform sitting at a computer-laden desk in the corner of the room.

The man stood and reached for the weapon on his belt. Samantha yipped and lifted the gun Rikist had given her and pulled the trigger.

The gun kicked in her hand, and the bullet went wild and buried into the nearest computer screen. The man ducked and drew his gun, and Samantha fired again and again until she had emptied the magazine.

She tensed, holding her breath as the man gaped at her and then slowly crumpled to the ground. She stared at the spreading stain of blood on the center of his chest, and she swallowed back bile and dropped the empty gun from her shaking hands.

Dropping to her knees, she ran her hands over Rikist. She tested his pulse, found it to be weak, and then shook him.

"Rikist, come on, Rikist. Please wake up!" She sat up, wiping at her brow with the back of a hand. She thought back to Krissik's estimate of a twenty percent survival rate for an alien Rikist's age, and her stomach clenched. "Oh God, I hope I didn't kill him."

Samantha stood and stepped around the unnamed alien's body to the desk, looking for a phone. She grimaced as she saw that most of her shots had landed on or near the desk, destroying most of the electronic equipment and leaving almost nothing of value intact. She swallowed and rubbed at her face.

She glanced around the room. The only window had been boarded up, so that no air came in or out along the sealed seams. The door was across the room, and had also had flaps added to the edges, but did not look sealed shut.

"Probably to keep the light out," she muttered.

Samantha hesitated, and then crossed to the door and tested the handle. It turned. She undid the dead-bolt above with a slow click, and then slowly eased the door open. She peered outside, froze, and then pulled the door open completely to the vacant hallway. The hall was under construction, with plaster still visible on the walls and multi-colored carpet padding and nails lining the floor. Blue painters' tape edged the ceiling where the beginnings of yellow paint were visible.

"Oh my God," she whispered. "We're back at the hotel."

She glanced back at Rikist, and then stepped out and quietly shut the door. She headed down to her right, where she found the elevator and a directional map.

Second floor.

"So that's how they got in," she whispered. She hesitated outside the elevator doors, and then pushed the up arrow.

Nothing happened. She tried again, but the button did not even light up.

She frowned and pulled open the door to the stairs and headed up.

THE DOORS to most of the rooms on Samantha's floor were still open, making Samantha's heart race. The shadowed hall was quiet – not a soul in sight. The morning light from the open windows in the room cast elongated yellow boxes into the hall, and Samantha paused before stepping through each illuminated space. She peered into the rooms as she walked, surprised, and panicked that they had not been touched since the abduction.

She spotted her room and quickened her pace. She paused in the doorway and looked around.

The room was as they had left it: open bags at the foot of the beds, the dropped TV remote on the floor, and Carly's cell phone on the dresser. Samantha nearly dove for the phone, and then froze when she woke the lock screen and read the date.

"Monday?" Her heart dropped to her stomach. "I've... I've only been gone for three days?"

She looked around, wondering then where everyone was. If Krissik was right, and no one had been killed, then where was Carly?

Maybe everyone was taken to the hospital... That would make sense.

Samantha closed the door and slipped out of the dress. She pulled out a fresh change of clothes from her bag on the bed and slipped on jeans and a t-shirt over her underwear and a bra. She moaned happily at the support under her breasts, remembering how much she missed an underwire. Socks and tennis shoes followed, along with pulling her hair back in a low bun.

She dug out an envelope of cash she had stashed at the bottom of her bag and stuck it in her back pocket, grabbed her car keys off the nightstand between the beds, and hefted her duffle.

She knew she could leave the hotel; sneak downstairs past whatever security was in place and get to the parking lot where her car waited and get the hell out of Vegas. She could move on and pretend that the past week on another planet never happened and disappear in the hills of Colorado where no cat-like aliens could ever find her, and she would never leave her father's farm again.

She stepped out in the hall and hesitated.

She also knew that Rikist had risked everything in order to save her, and that he now lay unconscious and helpless in a room downstairs. If he were to wake up and leave, or be found by a wandering maid, or the police...

"Shit," she whispered. "They'd lock him up in some lab and he'd never get out."

She turned back into her room and opened the small refrigerator. Inside were several cans of soda and a few apples and muffins from breakfast the morning of check-in. She stuffed the food into her duffle and hurried back toward the stairs.

Footsteps down the hall sent chills up her spine, and she froze, listening. The footsteps were even and casual, followed by the squeaking of turning wheels. Samantha stepped back in a doorway and peeked around the corner as a male janitor pushing a laundry cart appeared and walked down the hall.

Samantha took a deep breath and stepped out as the man neared. The man cursed in Spanish and stepped back.

Samantha held out her hands. "Wait! I need your help!"

The man shook his head. "You not supposed to be here."

"I know, I know. My friend is hurt, can you help?"

He shook his head and turned to leave.

Samantha fished out the envelope of cash and pulled out a handful of bills, gaining an interested stare.

"I can pay you."

SAMANTHA FOUND Rikist just as she had left him, and she quietly knelt beside him. She set the duffle and keys down and checked his breathing and pulse. Nothing had changed. She frowned and turned to the man standing in the doorway, who had paled and looked ready to bolt.

Samantha fished out three twenty-dollar bills and handed them over. She showed him the full envelope. "You help me and it's yours."

The man hesitated, looking between Rikist's prone body and the envelope, and nodded.

IT TOOK A WHILE, but together, Samantha and the janitor got Rikist on the flat cart and down to the main level of the hotel. The janitor took her out of the back service entrance, away from the bustling lobby full of angry patrons and reporters asking questions about the gas leak that landed half of the hotel guests in the emergency room.

The wheels on the cart squeaked dangerously loud as they hurried through the parking structure to the fourth floor, Samantha sweating as they crested each level, knowing that they would surely get caught. Thankfully, the parking lot was quiet, with half of the structure empty.

Samantha nearly let out a sob as her gray SUV came into sight, and she quickened their pace to push them forward. She unlocked the car and reclined the back seat as far as it would go, and with the janitor's help, they managed to lift Rikist into the car to lie on the back seat and strap him in. Samantha straightened up, stretching her back, and wiped at the dew of sweat on her hairline.

The janitor's tan face was pale, and his eyes were wide. He muttered something about "el Diablo," and took off at a run, pushing the cart as soon as Samantha handed him the envelope.

Samantha took a shaky breath and tossed her duffle back into the passenger seat. She reached under the driver's seat and sighed in relief when she dug out her purse. She unzipped the top to spot her wallet and cell phone. She got inside the car, locked the doors, and turned the key in the ignition. The engine roared to life, and Samantha leaned her forehead against the steering wheel as the tears came in a sudden, relieving rush.

She wiped at her face and put the car in reverse, unwilling to get this far and have someone stop her in the parking structure. She peeled out, her tires screeching against the smooth concrete, and followed the arrows to the exit.

Samantha turned on the radio as the SUV pulled out onto the Vegas strip. The glowing lights of the tall casinos blurred together as she stared out her window, refusing to blink, and turned north onto Interstate 15 North. She glanced over her shoulder at the sleeping Rikist and forced a smile.

"I'm ready to go home."

IT WAS late afternoon when the tires of Samantha's SUV turned off the paved street on the outskirts of Grand Junction, Colorado onto a dirt road that led off the beaten path to her father's farm. Dust billowed out behind her car as she sped along the path, eager for the safety and security of home.

Samantha slowed as she reached the front gate, stopped, and got out long enough to manually open the chain-link drive gate, pull through, and lock it behind her. Her hands shook as she drove forward, her senses on high alert from an overdose of caffeine and her nerves shot from the reality of finally being free.

She pulled the car into the double garage and turned off the engine. She sat still for several minutes, listening to the end credits of a western audio book that she had snagged from her father's extensive collection, and then shut off the radio and sagged against the seat. She sniffed and wiped at her eyes. Then she pressed the remote clipped to her visor to shut the rolling garage door and got out and turned on the overhead lights on her way into the door to the house.

Inside, Samantha went through every room and closed all of the blinds and turned on all of the lights so that no corner of the spacious single-level ranch house was left in shadow. She flipped on the TV, turned on a national news station for background noise, and set her bag on the couch and looked around.

The house was simple, with a mixture of new and antique furniture that she had salvaged from her dad's use and the move from her city apartment. A TV sat in one corner with a collection of penguin figurines that her mother had collected, and no one had bothered to pack away.

She walked back to the garage and opened the car doors to let fresh air in. She knew there was no way she could move Rikist on her own, so she figured for now he could sleep where he was. She unbuckled him so that he was more comfortable and undid his laces and pulled his boots off. She propped open the door leading into the house so that she could listen for him, and then plopped down onto the couch in the living room.

She pulled out her cell phone and searched for Las Vegas-area hospitals as she watched the scrolling news stories at the bottom of the TV. Her first two phone calls to hospitals in the area were dead ends. She sighed and rubbed at her temples, pain building between her eyes, as she dialed the third hospital.

"Please be there," she whispered. "Please..."

"Sunrise Medical," the female operator answered.

Samantha sat up. "Hi, I'm trying to reach a patient there."

"Room number?"

"I... I'm not sure. They didn't tell me."

"What's the name?"

"Carly Michaels."

"We can't give out medical information over the phone..."

"Please don't hang up! It's my... sister. Step."

There was a pause. "I'm going to transfer you to the nurse's station. Please hold."

Samantha closed her eyes and pressed her lips together. This was further than she had gotten with the other two hospitals, so hopefully that was a positive thing.

"Nursing station, this is Adrianne, how can I help you?"

"Hi, I'm trying to reach Carly Michaels. She's a patient there."

"What room?"

"I don't know. We were separated at our hotel during the gas leak."

"What relationship do you have with the patient?"

Samantha's lips trembled. "Sister."

"Your name?"

"Samantha Tucker."

"Hold on a minute."

Samantha stood and paced around the living room as she waited for the nurse to come back on the line. Her pulse pounded in her ears as she prayed that this would not be another dead end. She froze mid-step as the line clicked and she heard shuffling on the other end.

"Hello? Samantha?"

Samantha's eyes widened. "Mrs. Michaels?"

"Oh, my God, Samantha, where are you? Carly woke up asking for you and she's been worried sick."

"I... I'm at home." Samantha's mind raced. "I was really sick and wasn't up to the trip, so I came home early. Carly stayed with Julie. Doesn't she remember?"

"No—she doesn't remember anything after getting to the hotel." Mrs. Michael's voice wavered. "The doctor said she has a mild case of amnesia from the shock. Oh, sweetheart, I'm just glad that you're OK."

"I'm fine. I'm sorry I didn't call earlier, I just turned on the news after I haven't been able to get ahold of Carly," she lied. "Can I talk to her?"

"She's sleeping. But I'll have her call you when she wakes up."

"Thanks, Mrs. Michaels."

"You take care, Samantha."

Samantha hung up and sunk back on the couch. She let the phone slip from her fingers and curled up on her side against the decorative pillows. She changed the news to some nonsensical reality show and stared at the screen without blinking until she slipped into a restless sleep.

SAMANTHA JOLTED awake in the midst of a dream filled with gunfire and yellow cat-eyes. She gasped and sat up, the TV still on and the yellow light thrown from the corner lamps illuminating the now-darkened room. She twisted and pushed aside the drapes away from the window behind the couch to see blackness.

"I've slept all evening..."

She closed her eyes and took a steadying breath, and then stood and walked into the kitchen. She pulled out the bag of dry cat food and filled a bowl for the duo of farm cats that roamed the grounds for mice and other vermin and set it on the back porch. She closed the door behind her and locked it, not waiting to see if the animals were there or not.

Then she searched through the cabinets for dinner and frowned at the lack of choice. The refrigerator was not much better; she purposely had not gone shopping the last week before leaving for Vegas, knowing she would not be home to eat whatever she bought. She hated seeing food spoil.

"So, we have apples, cheese, and..." She picked up a container of something she could not identify, grimaced, and put it back on the shelf. "I don't wanna know."

She shook her head and frowned, settling on a peanut butter and jelly sandwich and an apple. She carried her plate to the couch and flipped through the TV, settling on a documentary show on antique collecting, and nearly inhaled her food. She licked jelly off her fingers, debating a second sandwich, when she heard movement in the garage. She hit the mute button on the remote to listen.

Something crashed against the aluminum garage door, and Samantha jumped off the couch. She darted toward the door in the kitchen that led to the garage and stopped in the doorway. She looked around, trying to find the source of the noise.

There!

Rikist sagged against the far-right corner of the garage, hands splayed out against the row of storage cabinets and the rolling garage door for support. His legs shook, and he fought to keep his head up. His eyes were glazed and unfocused and did not seem to register Samantha as she cautiously stepped into the garage.

"Rikist?" she said slowly, keeping her movements to a minimum.

He jerked his head in her direction without really seeing her and growled.

Samantha paused, the hair standing on her arms and neck. She looked to her right near the car door, where he had knocked over a row of gardening tools. She hesitated, and then picked up a heavy metal rake and held it out in front of her like a spear.

"Rikist, it's me, Samantha." She stepped around the car. "It's OK, the fight's over. You're safe."

Rikist's low growl continued, and he hunched his shoulders and scooted down against the wall. He lost his balance and fell against the SUV. He caught himself on the cool metal, hissed, and lurched back as if he had been burned. He scooted backward across the concrete floor until his back hit the cabinets and then stood into a protective half-crouch.

Samantha stopped near the car, trying to gauge his awareness. His head kept drooping; his eyes were unfocused and rolling around as if he had suffered a concussion. She wondered if the thump she had heard had been him falling out of the car and wanted to check—but the constant animalistic rumble emanating from his throat made her pause. The last thing she wanted to do was surprise a wounded alien and have her innards torn out.

"Rikist? Can you hear me?"

Rikist's head turned toward her, his nostrils flaring. He blinked several times and shook his head as if to clear an unpleasant image. He slid down the wall to sit on the floor and let his head roll back to rest against the cabinets, his eyes closed.

"S-Sam-ntha?" came the slurred reply.

Samantha stepped warily around the SUV. Rikist looked up at her wearily from where he sat against the cabinets. His eyes were bloodshot, and his face pale.

"Are you OK?" she asked, lowering the rake.

"Where... where are we?"

She hesitated. "We're safe."

Rikist's eyes went in and out of focus. He rubbed at them with a clumsy hand. "I... I feel strange..."

Samantha propped the rake against the wall and then knelt by his side. She put her thumb under his chin and tilted his head, so she could see his face in the light. His eyes wandered, and his pupils dilated to different sizes. He coughed, and a line of blood dripped from one nostril.

Samantha blanched. "Oh, crap."

She ran her hands through his hair, feeling his skull. She frowned when she did not feel any bumps.

"If it's not from falling," she muttered. "Then it must be from the jump." She eyed him fearfully, hoping that the effects were not permanent. "Are you alright?"

Rikist's eyes slipped open lazily, his throat constricting as he swallowed. "I don... I not feel..."

"Do you feel sick?"

Rikist leaned toward her and emptied his stomach on the garage floor. Samantha jumped back, trying not to get hit by the spray as he vomited several times before shuddering and falling forward.

Samantha gasped and reached out to catch him before he hit the concrete. She grunted and shifted her grip to under his armpits, and managed to drag him away from the puddle, gently laying him on the ground beside the SUV. She shook his shoulder, trying to rouse him.

"Rikist. Rikist, wake up!"

His eyes fluttered open.

"Do you think you can walk?"

Rikist blinked, and then nodded sleepily.

Samantha frowned. "Oh, that's encouraging." She shook her head and grabbed under his arms. "Come on... up!"

SAMANTHA LOWERED Rikist's head to the pillow and pulled the blanket higher up around his neck. It had taken a while and a few near spills, but she had managed to guide him onto the living room couch where he could stretch out. She sat on the edge of the cushion and patted his feverish face and neck with a warm, wet cloth.

"Krissik said I was out for two days after my jump to your planet," she said softly. "Hopefully you'll be up and around soon."

She gazed down at his sleeping face with hope and fear, praying that he would suddenly open his eyes and shoot her one of his crooked and masculine-laced grins. She bit back an unexpected rush of tears and leaned down to kiss his brow.

"Don't die, Rikist," she whispered. "Not after crossing the universe with me."

She swallowed back the lump that had built in her throat and lay down beside him, burying her head in the crook of his arm. She rested her arm across his chest, measuring the rise and fall of his chest against her own breathing. She felt his heartbeat through his shirt against her wrist, and she ran her hand down the side of his cheek. She gave him a squeeze, then turned so that she could face the TV while pressing the back of her body against him and settled down for a long night of waiting.

FOURTEEN

The next morning Samantha started about her regular routine in an attempt to return to normalcy. Rikist slept through the night and did not even stir when she stood from the couch. She checked his pulse and breathing before getting dressed and heading outside. Her neighbor had agreed to take care of the animals while she was away, and she planned to call him later in the day to let him know he need not come by.

She left a voicemail for her neighbors to let them know she was home on her way to the barn and greeted the two buckskin mares and appaloosa stallion. She petted their noses and scratched under their chins, enjoying the feel of their stiff coat beneath her fingers. She gave them a quick rubdown each, trying to spread out the attention between the needy horses.

She set out a new bowl of food and water for the farm cats, surprised that there were now two tabbies and a calico waiting on the porch for her. She frowned at the size of the calico's stomach, realizing that she might need to put out a covered box to make a safe place for the inevitable litter of kittens she so did not need to deal with at the moment.

The long walk out through the three long rows of orange and lemon trees helped her clear her head, and by the time she had passed the grids of strawberries and squash she felt refreshed and elated to be back on the small farm. She looked forward to getting back to work.

While her education spent on her unfinished Masters in English and past work as a legal secretary was not much help when it came to planting and watering her crops, she actually enjoyed the small co-op farm her father had run for years, which provided enough crops to be self-sustaining for herself and to pay the rent, if not much else. It gave her time to focus on her own writing and get away from her past life plans that had fallen apart when, after continually suspecting that her ex was cheating on her due to multiple unexplained overnight trips to expensive hotels and suspicious credit card charges, she had left him. Before she had had to worry about work, school, her failed relationship, and unfinished wedding plans. Now, her simple goal was to increase production and sales enough that she could start putting money away and improve the house and land, instead of living month to month on the weekly local produce customers.

That, and figure out what to do with the resident alien sleeping on my couch.

She smiled at the four goats she had added to the back pen by the small chicken coop that had sat empty for years under her father's care. They looked up from chewing their grass, bleating in greeting, and then went back about their business. The chickens clucked noisily as she passed, stirring up feathers as she reached in for the six brown eggs. She checked the feed, saw that it was low, and made a note to take care of it in the evening.

She used her shirt as a basket, and pulled out a small white onion, carrots, and two zucchinis, and then picked a handful of vine-ripened strawberries and headed into the house with the eggs. She washed the produce and heated a skillet as she chopped up the veggies to sauté. She buttered the last piece of bread in the cupboard and added it to her plate, along with a small dish of sliced strawberries, and sat alone at the dining room table.

She glanced across the room at Rikist's sleeping form, a sense of dread building in the pit of her stomach. He had not moved since she had set him there the night before, and though she knew Krissik had said the jump was rough going to a new planet if unprepared, she also knew that neither brother had high expectations on Rikist ever surviving a jump again. The fact that he had woken in the garage gave her hope, but until he was up and moving around...

Please, just help him be OK.

Finished eating, Samantha went into the second spare bedroom where she had placed her father's things while she decided her next steps. She was not sure what she was going to do with Rikist if and when he woke up, but she sure was not going to have him grow moss lying still on her couch. She happened to enjoy writing reclined on that couch very much.

She looked around the space, eyeing the stacked cardboard boxes along the far wall and on the bare mattress in the center of the room. She sighed and started in on the first box, opening the top to peer inside.

SAMANTHA WAS ACTUALLY PLEASED with her progress by early afternoon. She had cleared out the bedroom and placed her father's things in the garage and dressed up the bed with clean sheets and blankets. She hung up the clothes in the emptied closet and opened up the window to let fresh air into the stuffy space. Her father, while not nearly as wide in the shoulders and chest as Rikist, had not been a small man, and she found several shirts and pants that would most likely fit him while she held off going into town for a much-needed shopping trip.

She found a frozen meal in the freezer behind the icemaker and nuked it for a quick lunch. She sat in her father's armchair—as the couch was taken—and put her feet up on the coffee table to watch a courtroom drama while she ate, sipping on an iced cola.

When she was finished, she wet a washcloth and dabbed at Rikist's face and neck, checking his breathing and pulse again. Though he still had not woken, at least it seemed his fever had gone down. She sighed, satisfied by at least a little progress, and then stood to grab her cell phone when he stirred.

Samantha knelt by the couch and put her hands on his chest. "Rikist?"

Rikist's eyes fluttered open, and he blinked against the sunlight. He closed his eyes and let out a soft whine as he shifted position on the cushions. He grimaced and tried to concentrate on his surroundings.

"R-raki si... sa tir..."

"Rikist? Can you hear me?"

His bloodshot eyes slid toward Samantha. He seemed to take a moment to focus, and then recognition brightened his face.

"Samantha," he said slowly, his words groggy.

Samantha tittered nervously and fought to keep her face neutral and her tears of relief at bay. "I'm so glad you're awake. I thought... I wasn't sure if you were going to be OK."

He licked his dry lips. "Where are we?"

"At home." She hesitated. "My home. On Earth."

Rikist's eyes shot open and his face paled further beyond its sweaty pallor. He turned his head to stare straight at her and gaped. He seemed lost for words, and then pushed himself up to a sitting position. Once upright, his eyes rolled back, and he caught himself against the back of the couch. Blood dripped from his nose and he wiped at it with a shaky hand. He glared at Samantha.

"I cannot be here! You should not... why did bring me here!"

Samantha's face reddened. "I saved your life!"

"You..." He took a deep breath and sunk back against the cushions, his eyes drooping, and strength spent after his outburst. "I... do not remember."

Samantha sat back and rubbed her face. "What's the last thing you remember?"

He thought about it. "We got to the base for the jump. I..." He searched, and then shrugged. "That is all."

Samantha frowned. "There was a fight. We were followed by soldiers and you were shot with one of those laser things." She pressed her lips together, deciding to hold back Krissik's arrival and involvement. "They were going to kill you, and I... pulled you onto the platform with me."

Rikist's stomach rumbled. He sniffed and wiped at his dripping nose again, a red trail visible on his upper lip.

Samantha lifted the wet washcloth to his face and wiped away the smear of blood. She pulled back quickly when she caught him staring down at her and stood.

"Are you hungry?"

He shook his head, his face blank, eyes unreadable.

Samantha quirked an eyebrow when his rumbling stomach betrayed him. "I don't have much here. I need to go to the store, but I can whip something up to last you while I'm gone."

"You want me stay here?"

"You're sure as hell not coming into town with me. Aside from the fact that you look like you're going to pass out at any minute, my nerves are not ready to have you free on the street yet."

If ever, she thought, glancing at his claws.

He looked concerned. "You are going alone?"

"Yeah. What's the big..." She paused when she met his eyes. "That's right. On your planet females don't... Here it's fine. I mean, this house is mine. I live here alone, and that's pretty normal here. Females don't require males to function or..." She trailed off, realizing she was losing him. "Didn't Lindsey explain how things work here?"

"A little." He shrugged, seeming a little shaken by the mention of her name. "She lived with her parents in a large family. She was never alone."

Samantha waited for him to continue, then after several moments of silence, twisted and snatched the remote off the coffee table and turned the TV on. "Here. This is to change the channel."

Rikist looked at the dated remote in her hand but made no move to take it.

Samantha grabbed his wrist and turned his palm up and dropped the remote into his hand. "The arrows on the left change the channel, the right is volume."

She spun on her heel and hurried into the kitchen to see what stock she had.

I forgot that this is probably as much of a culture shock for him as it was for me. Strange customs. Strange food.

Strange feelings...

There were several cans of veggies and beans, and she had a pack of hot dogs in the freezer she could defrost if she really wanted to...

"All they ate was fish," she mused. She opened another cabinet and pulled out two cans of tuna. "Bingo."

She was out of bread, but had soda crackers, and prepped the two cans of fish in a bowl with mayonnaise and pepper. She cut up the last of the strawberries and put them on a plate next to a stack of crackers and took the food back into the living room.

Rikist sat reclined against the couch, his eyes closed.

Samantha set the plate down on the coffee table. "You awake?" she asked.

"Hmm?" Rikist forced his eyes open. He stared at her, bleary eyed. "Surtis ka..."

"English, please. You'll probably feel better after you eat. I remember I was starving when I came to with Kris."

She sat on the couch next to Rikist and pulled the coffee table closer. She shook his shoulder when his eyes slid closed.

"Hey," she said. "Wake up."

She piled tuna on a cracker, and then held it up toward his mouth. She poked his side to get his attention, and then touched the cracker to his lips. Rikist flinched, and then looked down his nose at the cracker.

"What is this?" he said.

"Tuna," she responded. She pressed more firmly against his lips. "Open up."

He looked at her sideways, and then opened his mouth to allow Samantha to push the entire cracker inside. He chewed cautiously at first, and then picked up the pace as he finished.

"That..." he grinned. "Is very good."

Samantha smiled. "Much better than the plain food back home, eh?" She picked up a sliced strawberry and held it up. "Here, I grew these myself outside."

Rikist glanced at the strawberry in her fingers by his face, hesitated, and then stretched his neck forward the last few inches and took the strawberry from her hands with his mouth. His lips grazed her fingers as he sat back.

Samantha fought unsuccessfully against the blush that crept up her neck and cheeks. She lifted her eyes to Rikist's, only to find his gaze glued to the bowl of strawberries.

"What is this called?" he pointed, his nostrils flaring as he sniffed the air.

"Strawberries," Samantha sighed, realizing she was the only one affected by the brief but intimate contact. "You like them?"

"Yes. Actually..."

"I'll pick up a mix of things from the store." She stepped back and wiped her hand on her jeans, willing herself to forget the tingling sensation in her fingers. "Will you promise me you won't leave the house? I don't want to go if you're just waiting for me to leave so you can explore."

Rikist lifted the bowl of tuna closer to his mouth so that the loaded crackers did not have to travel far as he nearly shoveled them into his mouth. He glanced up and nodded. "I will stay. Until we learn how to get me home."

Samantha frowned, and then waved him away as she grabbed her keys and purse and headed out the door.

"Until then."

SAMANTHA ARRIVED home an hour and a half later with her arms laden with plastic grocery bags. She struggled to set her keys and purse on the counter as she waddled in through the garage door and set the bags down on the tile. She groaned at the state of her kitchen; several open cabinet doors revealed dry goods out of place, an empty cracker box lay on the counter, and several dented and clawed canned goods had been left near an empty pot after obviously outwitting the inquisitive alien.

She glanced over the tiled island countertop to the

living room and froze when she saw the couch was empty. Her heart flipped.

"Rikist?"

No answer.

"Oh, shit."

She stepped over the bags and ran into the living room, and then down the hall. She opened doors to the closets and hall bathroom as she passed, hoping to catch a glance of the absent alien. She poked her head into the guest bedroom, and then spun in the hall to push open the door to the master bedroom.

"Rikist, where—"

Rikist looked up from where he sat on her bed. He looked worn and sweat speckled his brow and temples. He had several of the photo books that she kept stacked on her dresser open on his lap. He smiled at her and held up a photo from when she was a child on a tricycle.

"This is you?" he asked, as he looked between the photo and the scowling Samantha to compare.

Samantha stormed up to him. She snatched the photo away and collected the albums. "Don't you understand the meaning of privacy? You can't just waltz into someone's house and go through their stuff—"

"I did not... *wallzs*, you brought me here," he said. "And the books were in the open."

"It doesn't matter..."

"This though," he shot her a mischievous grin and

pulled an open hat box from behind him and set it on his lap. "I found by the bed."

Samantha's jaw dropped, and she felt her knees go weak. She swallowed and closed her eyes. "That is, um... that's personal..."

His eyes glinted with humor, and his dimples dotted his cheeks as his smile spread. "I have not seen things like these before, but I can imagine their purpose."

Samantha cleared her throat and reached out to jerk the box away, though his hands held the box firmly against his lap. She glanced down at the assortment of flavored lubes and dildos as she shoved the lid back on, her face burning with embarrassment. She gritted her teeth and glared up at him.

"Let go."

"Who is the male beside the bed?"

Samantha glanced past Rikist to the framed photograph of her and John on the deck of a cruise ship. They had taken the picture the night he had proposed.

"No one..." She looked away. "My ex. He's a veterinarian in town. We were... supposed to get married. You know... be mates."

The color in Rikist's cheeks deepened. "Why did you not?"

"Because he was a jerk who didn't respect me or my personal space!"

Rikist released the box. Samantha cursed under her breath and shoved the box under the bed and crossed her arms. She tightened her jaw, unsure why she suddenly felt ashamed for still having John's picture. She glanced at Rikist, who sat glaring at the photo.

"Listen," she said. "You can't go through my things."

"Fine."

"Because it's not..." she paused. "Fine? Just like that?"

He nodded, looking toward the door. "I was bored. And hungry."

Samantha closed her eyes and counted to ten. "Well I just brought back enough food to feed an army, so that won't be a problem anymore."

Rikist pushed himself to his feet, wobbled, and then limped toward the door. Samantha caught his arm as he teetered and held him still. His eyes rolled, and he blinked to clear his vision.

Samantha tightened her grip. "Are you OK?"

"Room is spin..."

She veered him into the bedroom next to hers where she had prepped his bed.

"Here, you can stay here and rest. I cleared it out for you, and there are extra clothes you can try on to see if they fit. If not, I'll get you some new stuff in town."

Rikist nearly collapsed on the bed, his leg brace squeaking under the pressure. He grunted and turned onto his back, fumbling with the buckles. Samantha sat on the mattress and helped him.

"Are you sure you want this off?" she asked as she removed the side frames.

"Uncomfortable. I no need it right now."

"Don't."

"What?"

"You *don't* need it right now."

Rikist glared at her, and then rolled over onto his side away from her. "Give me a break."

"Sorry, habit." Samantha bit her lip. "Are you still hungry?"

He nodded against the pillow, though his breathing had already begun to deepen.

"I'll look out in the barn and see if I can find you some crutches." Samantha patted his back and left.

RIKIST FELL ASLEEP before Samantha had finished heating the canned soup on the stove, so she covered his bowl up for later and sat on the couch with her laptop.

She had always loved to read, and over the past few years had taken to writing after encouragement from one of her undergrad professors before she had dropped out of school to tend to her ailing father and take over the house. After her dad passed, she just could not bring herself to go back to school, but she had managed to snag a part-time online gig writing how-to articles. She did not make much, but it was enough to pay for clothes and other extras above the income from the farm.

And for saving passed out aliens...

Two hours into writing she sat back and stretched her arms over her head, bored. She glanced down the hall, listening to the silence.

"It's hard to find anything more interesting than an alien lion-god sleeping in my spare bedroom," she muttered.

A knock on the front door made her jump. Samantha set her laptop down on the table and walked cautiously to the door. She sucked in a breath and glanced through the peephole in the door. Her shoulders slumped, and she relaxed as she unlocked the deadbolt and opened the door.

A short Hispanic male in his late fifties wearing faded jeans and a cowboy hat greeted her. "Samantha. I saw your car out front and wanted to check. I wasn't expecting you 'til Monday."

"Hi Rodolfo." Samantha smiled, suddenly fighting back tears. "I came home early—been pretty sick. I left you a message—"

"You know I don't know how to use that damn phone." He shook his head. "That's too bad, though. You could have used the vacation."

Samantha frowned. "Why does everyone keep saying that?"

Rodolfo laughed, raspy and heartfelt. "You take on too much yourself, Samantha. You need to find a man to help you out around here."

She put a hand on her hip. "Rodolfo—"

"And I don't mean that asshole you had before."

"I can take care of things just fine." She rolled her eyes, though she knew Rodolfo's concern was genuine —even though her neighbor could be a tad blunt. "Thanks for taking care of the animals."

Rodolfo nodded and turned to go. "Let me know if you need anything. Maria's been asking when you're going to come over for dinner."

"Soon, I promise." She hesitated as he stepped off the porch. "Rodolfo?"

He turned, and his eyes widened in surprise as Samantha's arms flung around him in a tight embrace. He chuckled and pushed her back gently.

"Are you alright?"

Samantha guffawed and wiped at her face. She nodded. "Yeah. I'm just... It's just good to be home."

Rodolfo's brow creased, and he looked down at her with concern. "It's good to have you back. Are you sure you're alright?"

"Really, I'm fine. I'm just tired."

"Well... get some rest. If you need help with the animals for the next few days, you know where to find me."

Samantha waved as he climbed into his old Ford pickup and drove off. She rubbed at her face and sank down on the front step to stare at the orange glow beginning to burn at the tops of the trees in the distance as the sun slowly lowered toward the horizon.

"Who was that?"

Samantha jumped to see Rikist standing at the side of the doorframe, his body hidden from view. She stood and walked back into the house.

"My neighbor, Rodolfo," she said. "He was watching over the animals while I was gone."

"So, you do rely on him."

"Now and then. Rodolfo was my father's best friend for years, and he's always kept an eye out for me. Especially after Dad died…"

She trailed off, studying his face. If she was not mistaken, there seemed to be a hint of jealousy in Rikist's eyes and in the set of his masculine jaw. She smiled and wrapped her arms around his waist and pressed her face against his chest.

"You look a lot more alive than you did earlier." She stepped back. "I'm glad you're feeling better."

Rikist smiled back, and then cleared his throat and looked away. "I'm feeling hungry."

"I thought you hated my cooking?" Samantha chuckled.

He shrugged, grinning. "You didn't cook the staw-berys, you picked them."

Samantha laughed, and took his hand and pulled him toward the kitchen as he limped behind. She smiled when she felt his fingers tighten gently over hers.

FIFTEEN

Rikist had downed two family-size cans of tomato soup and sat at the table holding a small glass of wine as Samantha turned the light on in the oven to peek at her cookies. He swirled the inch of merlot around in his glass, sniffing the fumes.

He wrinkled his nose. "This smells."

Samantha straightened and picked up her own glass. She took a sip. "Tastes good though."

"Why did you give me so little?" He pointed to her glass. "You filled yours."

"Because I had your guys' version of alcohol." She smirked. "And this is much stronger. You need to ease into it since you're not—"

"I can handle whatever you can." He gave an arrogant lift of his chin, and then tipped his head back to down the wine at the bottom of his glass. He fought back a grimace. "See?"

"It takes a minute or two to kick in..." She looked

up at his raised glass and the set to his jaw. She shrugged. "Fine, you want to be a stubborn tough guy about it? Knock yourself out."

She grabbed the open bottle on the counter and filled his glass. She pressed in the blown glass stopper and leaned against the counter. She sipped on her wine, her eyes twinkling as she observed him. Though his English was a little rusty at times with a word here and there, she assumed he must have gotten pretty good at it with Lindsey for all those years.

"How many languages do you speak?" she asked.

"Four." Rikist took another drink, slower this time, and licked his lips. "What are you doing?"

Samantha furrowed her brow. "What?"

He pointed to the oven.

She looked to where he was pointing. "Ah. I'm making cookies."

"What is that?"

"They're dessert. I figured since you had a stash of chocolate at home you'd like these." Samantha winked at him, and then ran the sink and filled it with soapy water. "So, on your first jump here." She glanced over her shoulder as she dropped dishes in the sink. "When you... found Lindsey. Did you enjoy Vegas?"

"I didn't jump the same as Krissik," he said. He took another drink of wine.

"What do you mean?"

"Lindsey was from New... New Jor..."

"New Jersey?"

He shook his head, tapping one claw on the table as he thought. "York. New York."

Samantha started, and then scrubbed the dishes and mixing bowls with a vengeance. "You mean to tell me that you guys have multiple jump points set up here?"

"Four, I think, on your planet. Las Vegas, New York, Beg... Uh, Beg-ging... Is that correct?"

Samantha's eyes widened. "You mean Beijing?"

"Yes. Beijing. And one other major spot I do not remember."

"So... technically Krissik could come through another of those jumps if he wanted to?"

Rikist seemed to think about it. "Yes. But this is not near a jump site, at least not anymore with the hotel down. How will he find you? Easier just to find another female."

"But what if he tried to come through—"

"Then I will protect you."

"While you're here that is," she muttered. "Before you go home and leave me looking over my shoulder at every turn."

"Do you miss him?"

"Who, Krissik?"

"No. The one in the picture."

Samantha froze. She took her time putting the soup bowls in the dishwasher and hand drying her baking tools. Her heart raced.

"I... No. I don't miss him." She grabbed her wine

glass and took a big gulp. "Sometimes. But he wasn't any good for me. He was a jerk, and a cheater."

"What did he cheat at?"

She nearly choked on her wine. "Us. He... slept around."

Rikist did not seem to understand, and Samantha paled a shade. She closed her eyes.

"He kept going on secret business trips and had sex with other women."

There was a long pause. "I am sorry."

"It's not your fault. It's not anyone's but mine for trusting him."

She finished cleaning, and then patted her hands and eyes on a hanging towel, glancing over her shoulder at Rikist as she checked on her cookies.

"Another minute," she muttered. She closed the oven and walked toward Rikist.

Rikist's glass was half empty, and his eyes drooped. He sat more relaxed in his chair, and his face had a dreamy look to it. He caught Samantha staring, and sent her a wide, playful grin.

Samantha laughed, finding his lopsided smile both charming and boyish at the same time. It seemed to lift the raincloud that had been forming over her head. The wine had done its job, and his relaxed posture made her feel so much better after his anger for being brought to Earth.

"Are you OK?" she asked.

"Mm-hmm... I really feel very good right now."

Rikist nodded at her, glassy eyed. He took another sip of his wine. "Can I have more?"

She shook her head, smiling. "I think I'm going to cut you off at one. You're still coherent enough to watch a movie with me."

"On the couch?"

She smiled and opened her mouth to speak but stopped at the lost look on his face.

"Lindsey used to like movies," he said slowly, staring at his wine glass. "She... she made it a game hiding the disks and games in the apartment when Krissik came by."

Samantha frowned. "Krissik moved out?"

"He was at university." He held up two wobbly fingers. "Three years."

Samantha laughed, and he joined her. He sniffed and wiped at his glassy eyes.

"I miss movies on the couch," he said suddenly. He downed the rest of his wine with a grimace and glanced at Samantha standing beside him. His eyes slid down from her face to the middle of her chest, wavered, and then looked away.

Samantha swallowed down the butterflies in her stomach and turned to pull the pan of chocolate chip cookies out of the oven.

"How is your leg feeling?" she asked to change the subject.

Rikist grunted, and then sat up in his chair and sniffed the air. "Is that the cuck-ee?"

"Cookies." Samantha nodded. "You'll die for these."

Rikist gave her a look. "No one dies for food unless—"

Samantha shoved half of a hot cookie into his mouth. Rikist closed his eyes, moaning. He chuckled and nodded.

"You are right." He reached for the spatula as she placed the cookies onto cooling racks centered on the table. "Can I have more?"

She shook her head as she set the empty pan down and popped the other half of the cookie in her mouth. She hissed as the hot chocolate morsels burned her tongue, and she opened her mouth to let out the steam.

"Ha-ha-hot!"

"I will help."

Samantha looked up as Rikist quickly grabbed her shoulders, pulled her close, and pressed his mouth against hers. His lips locked around hers, opening her mouth wider as his tongue slipped around hers to lap up the cookie bits and run along the roof of her mouth. She closed her eyes and sucked in return, relishing in the mix of dark chocolate and wine over the taste that was all *him*.

She shuddered as Rikist pulled his head back and swallowed, his fangs grazing against her as he sucked off the last trace of chocolate off her bottom lip. She gazed wide-eyed and awestruck as he rolled his tongue over his sharp teeth to savor the sugary sweetness.

Rikist's heavy-lidded eyes were a darker amber

than Samantha had ever seen them, bordering on a deep, sunset orange. His lips twitched, and she felt his arm reach around her onto the counter toward the racks of cookies. She gasped as she felt warm chocolate smear against the side of her neck.

"Rikist, what—"

Rikist smiled at her roguishly and his breathing quickened. "You... have some right..."

He trailed off, and leaned forward to suck at her neck, his tongue rolling in hot, wet circles across her skin. He bit down gently, his fangs sending sharp pinpricks of pain that made Samantha hiss.

Samantha opened her eyes and looked down at her hand as Rikist lifted her two chocolate-smeared fingers toward his lips. She swallowed as he slid her fingers into his mouth and sucked; she had been so focused on his play bite that she had not even noticed him spreading more chocolate across her skin. She bit her lip as his tongue licked between her two fingers, working the webbing as if trying to burrow into a non-existent hole.

Rikist sucked her fingers clean, provocatively pulling them in and out of his mouth once slowly as he eyed her with a heavy gaze, and then let her hand drop.

"I..." he started, a dimple forming between his eyebrows as he frowned. "Sam-ntha, I am..." He motioned toward his empty wine glass on the table.

Samantha snaked her arm around his neck and leaned closer to press her lips against his, tilting her head to the side to get a better fit against his mouth.

Rikist moaned against her open mouth, and his hands lifted to grab the sides of her face. He kissed her back, tentatively at first and then with savage passion as his breathing quickened and his skin heated. He broke the kiss first, pulling back long enough to suck in a breath before trailing his kisses down Samantha's neck and across her collarbone. He pulled on her shirt to reach lower, and Samantha pushed him away long enough to struggle out of the top and toss it aside.

Rikist made a high-pitched primal whine in his throat as he stared down at her black bra and ran his hands over the rounded tops of her breasts, sliding his thumbs just inside the top lace to brush against her nipples. He scooted his chair further away from the table, giving them room to move.

Samantha reached up and unbuttoned the top of his shirt, working her way down. She was on the fourth button when Rikist grunted and grabbed the shirt with both hands and jerked it over his head. She yipped in surprise as he tugged her forward to straddle his legs. She grimaced at the awkward angle of the leg brace on his thigh and shifted her hips for a better seat over his raised crotch.

"I thought you said I was off limits?" she whispered, meeting his eyes.

He hesitated, and then kissed her again. He gave her a humorless grin. "I broke enough rules today. One more will not matter."

Rikist's hands slid from her shoulders to her back,

and he fumbled with the back of her bra with a look of annoyed concentration.

"Need help?" Samantha said after a moment, ginning.

Rikist grunted. "We do not have such... *things* at home."

He growled and grabbed the straps with both hands and yanked it apart, snapping the connectors. Samantha gasped in protest, but he covered her mouth with his and gently slid the straps off her arms and tossed the bra to the floor. He hissed through his teeth as he looked down at her front, his eyes round and his smile widening from ear to ear.

He grabbed Samantha around the waist and easily hoisted her onto the table, spreading her legs so that he sat between her knees. He put her hands on his shoulders and reclined back in the chair, forcing her to lean forward to keep her balance. He grinned, admiring the view of her arched torso and firm breasts near his face. He kissed each one in turn, his tongue flicking out to lap across her hardened nipples.

Rikist stood suddenly and pushed the cooling racks out of the way and laid Samantha flat on her back. Samantha looked up in question, and then her heart raced as his hands went to the button on her jeans. Rikist pulled the jeans down her hips and off her ankles in one smooth movement. The underwear came next, following the path of the discarded bra across the floor.

His eyes took her in, roaming from her flushed face

down her breasts and flat abdomen to the trimmed triangle of dark hair between her parted legs. His nostrils flared as he breathed in, his throat bouncing.

He reached down and cupped her, smiling at her warmth. His thumb gently circled against her clit as the hot skin of his knuckles caressed her soft folds. Samantha's breath left her at the savage look of lust he shot her, his eyes no longer alien but completely male.

"I can stop," he said in a low, husky voice. The look in his eyes clearly said he did not expect to.

Samantha swallowed and shook her head, her heart racing. "You better not."

Rikist sat in the chair and leaned forward, then pressed his nose close to Samantha's skin and breathed in. He made a small sound in his throat and kissed the crease where her thigh met groin, and his kisses worked their way closer in, deeper between her legs. He brushed his nose against the stubble on her bikini line and rolled his eyes up to gaze at her through the valley between her breasts.

Samantha gasped and grabbed his shoulder out of reflex as his exploring tongue slipped between her legs. His tongue was hot and wet, and lightly textured with what felt like millions of small, gentle bumps seemingly built with this single purpose in mind. Her heart leapt in her throat as his tongue rotated in slow, long circles.

"You taste 'mazing," he mumbled against her thigh.

He moaned, and his hands shot up to grab at her hips, forcing her legs further apart as his mouth worked her. His lips and tongue sucked and pulled at every fold until finally finding the small round nub near Samantha's front that made her squirm violently in his grasp.

He shoved his face deeper between her legs, sucking and licking her clit in a fevered pace that pushed every thought aside from him out of Samantha's mind. She cried out and dug her nails into his shoulder as he shoved his tongue deep inside. She grabbed a handful of his hair and ground her hips against his working mouth as his long, ribbed tongue worked faster, moving in and out in a rapid continuous motion, electricity shocking every nerve in her body and sending her floating on a wave of amber heat.

Samantha felt him smile against her as her legs trembled and she felt herself getting close. He shifted his attention back to her clit and massaged her opening with his chin. The double sensations of rolling and sucking heat nearly sent her over the edge, and she writhed on the table and raised her hips as she tilted her head back and moaned.

Rikist pulled back, his lips slick, breathing heavy with wild eyes. The cat-like pupils were dilated to the point they nearly overtook the glimmering irises that stared down at her as he wiped his mouth with the back of one hand. Rikist's nostrils flared as his hands went to the front of his pants and dropped them as far as the leg brace would allow.

Samantha lowered her eyes from his broad chest to his tapered waist above long, muscular thighs. The wound on his left thigh was healing, but the jagged line of stitches that was surely going to scar stood out starkly beneath the layer of mostly-absorbed protein bandage. She started to inquire about his leg when she gasped at the sight of his beginning erection and struggled to look away. She felt herself tighten again and quickly slid off the table to stand in front of him.

My God, that is one big cock.

She laughed at Rikist's shocked and disappointed expression. She touched his chest reassuringly. "I'll be right back."

She hurried into her bedroom, practically dove for the box under the bed, and grabbed a jar of warming lube. She thought about grabbing a condom, but considering the revelation of her recently discovered sterility, she did not bother. Besides, skin on skin felt much better anyway.

Rikist looked up as she entered and pushed away from where he leaned against the table, holding his pants up. He looked annoyed.

"If you do not want to," he said slowly. "You could have—"

Samantha popped the lid off the lube with her thumb and squeezed a quarter-sized amount into her palm.

"Relax, Romeo," she said.

She glanced between his legs again, and then poured out more.

She stepped closer and gently ran her fingers across his tip in a circular motion, and Rikist shuddered at her touch. She smiled, drinking in the pleased and slack expression on his beautiful face, as she slid her hand down the curved length of him, pressing against the matt of fur as she slicked him up. The thrill of having so much power over him heightened her excitement, and she fought to control the urge to just pounce on him. She pulled back slowly until her palm slid across the ridged head, smearing a drip of slick fluid that leaked out of his tip. Her skin tingled with heat as the warming agents in the lube kicked in, and she slid her hand back down toward his body.

Rikist closed his eyes and swallowed, his body trembling at her touch. "What... what is that?"

"Something to help things move easier."

Rikist licked his lips and opened his eyes to slits as Samantha's hand picked up speed, and he reached out to cup one of her firm breasts. His thumb ran back and forth across the round nipple, and he bent and licked a wet line up Samantha's neck to suck gently on the underside of her jaw.

Rikist's skin was hot within her hand, almost feverish, and she ached to squeeze that heat between her legs. Samantha's mouth went dry and her vision swam against the ache in her core, her body seeking a need that she had left unfulfilled for too long. Even the last few times with her ex had been brief and angry, and never so... thrilling and exciting. She longed to be able to be held in a man's arms again. To feel loved and wanted. To let go and feel that connection with someone again.

Rikist suddenly lifted Samantha and laid her onto the table so that her legs and ass hung off the edge. He scooted closer and then leaned over so that her breasts pressed up against his chest as he kissed her neck and collarbone. Samantha pressed on his chest.

"Is your leg OK for you to stand and—"

"It's fine."

"I'm just saying..."

"You talk too much!"

Samantha stilled as she felt Rikist's erection rub against her inner thigh as he gently lifted her legs to wrap around his waist. He used one hand to guide himself, and rubbed his slick tip against her folds, teasing. Samantha groaned and reached for him.

"God, Rikist—"

He slowly pressed his length into her, hissing with delight.

Samantha let out a moan as he pressed up against her cervix; his length sheathed and wide width stretching her beyond what she thought capable. She wiggled against the table, the sheer size of him enough to make her writhe and moan on the borderline between pleasure and pain as he filled her. She patted one of his shoulders when he simply stood there breathing.

"You can move now."

Rikist shook with effort as he slowly pulled out, every thick inch of him, until just the tip grazed the edges of her folds. He grinned and lifted her right leg to rest on his shoulder so that she spread wider to accommodate his size. He let out a loud, shaky breath, and entered her again, slower than before. His eyes watched her carefully with a ferocity that made Samantha's skin crawl with anticipation. Samantha writhed and wrapped her legs tightly around his waist and shoulder, her insides aching at the tight fit, yet screaming out for more.

After a few more slow rounds, she loosened up enough for Rikist to move more freely, and he gradually picked up speed. He wrapped one arm around her narrow waist and lifted her lower half higher off the table so that he could have more control over his thrusts, and eventually he picked up a rhythm that sent shockwaves through both bodies at each meeting of skin.

Samantha tilted her head to look down her front past her bouncing breasts, to his flat abs as the muscles tightened and bunched as he thrust into her, and she got the quickest of glimpses of his slick penis as he pulled out before ramming harder and faster into her. The sight thrilled her, and she felt herself rising once again on a cresting wave, ready to burst.

Rikist's left foot slipped on the tiled floor, and he gasped as he fought to keep his balance. He grimaced apologetically as he leaned his hands heavily onto the table, putting his weight on his right side as he caught his breath.

Samantha touched his face. "Is your knee hurting?"

He nodded, his cheeks red. "Sorry..."

She lifted her head and kissed him. "Pull out."

Rikist hesitated, his face ashamed, and then did as she said and stepped back. Samantha climbed off the table and guided him back to his chair.

"Sit," she said.

Rikist sat back, grimacing as he stretched out his left leg. "Samantha, I—"

"Oh, shut up already."

Samantha put her hands on his shoulders and hoisted herself up into his lap. She batted her eyelashes seductively as she lowered herself onto his still erect penis. Rikist closed his eyes and smiled as she slid down toward his base. He let out a strangled guffaw as she wriggled her hips, and his hands gripped her waist and rotated her in a figure eight across his lap.

Samantha cried out, the alternating pressure on her insides hitting spots she had never thought possible. Jolts of burning energy shot up her spine and made her legs quiver. She dug her nails into his skin as she gripped his neck and back and buried her face in his hair as she suddenly came with an intensity that she had never experienced before. She let go of her inhibitions and cried out, her mouth open and eyes squeezed shut as she pulsed against him.

For a few brief moments the only things that mattered to Samantha were Rikist and the thrusting cock between her legs. The walls around them could crumble, the house could catch fire, or the sun could smash against the moon. None of it mattered. Nothing except the rolling amber waves and bursts of sexual fireworks bouncing around inside her skull.

Rikist moaned, and he looked down as he felt her wetness drip down the center of his groin. He swallowed, and his eyes rolled back as his grip shifted to the back of her ass, cupping her cheeks, and ramming her up and down his throbbing length.

Drifting back to Earth, Samantha smiled and kissed Rikist's parted lips. She ran her tongue along his lips, tracing the outline of his fangs, and sucked on his tongue. She scratched her nails down his chest, making him cry out, and then pressed her elbows against his shoulders to give her leverage to control her movements as she rotated her hips in a small circle.

"Shri tsi ka..." Rikist cursed, his eyes closed. "Tra si..."

Rikist's shoulders and back worked as he voraciously thrust again and again against Samantha's rotating hips. Samantha grinned, wanting him to come as hard as she had, and tightened her inner muscles as she bore down on him. Rikist let out a moan, and his lips parted as his jaw went slack and his eyes closed. He buried his face in Samantha's neck as his body quivered for the last few strokes. Gold stars dotted Samantha's vision, and she dug her nails into his striped back as she felt him finish in a rushing gush of liquid heat that filled her and left her limp on his trembling lap.

Samantha's heartbeat slowed as she leaned against him, and a tear rolled down her cheek as she opened her eyes. Rikist's face came in and out of focus, and she blinked several times to clear her vision. His eyes were closed, and a bead of sweat dripped from his temple down his relaxed and very satisfied face. He took a deep breath, and his eyes fluttered open, the amber irises alive with more raw emotion than Samantha had ever seen: possession, happiness, and uncertainty.

He opened his mouth to speak, and then looked away, his jaw tight.

Samantha touched his cheek, turning him back to her. "What's wrong?"

"I... I never thought I would do this again." He kissed her and leaned his forehead against hers. "Just... been hard."

"We both have ghosts we're dealing with." She pressed her lips together and nodded against him. "Let's leave them in the closet for tonight."

She ran her hands up his arms, fingers tracing the defined patterns of muscle, and pushed gently on his shoulders.

"Help me off."

Rikist licked his lips, and then slowly pushed upward on her hips and helped her step to the side. Samantha stepped back and hissed, pressing her thighs together. Rikist's hand hovered in the air above her, as if wanting to touch her but afraid to make contact.

"Did I hurt you?"

Samantha smiled and then giggled uncontrollably as she wobbled to the nearest chair and sat. She shook her head and waved him away.

"No, no... that was freaking out of this world." She snorted as she fought to keep from laughing. "Literally.

I'm just not going to be able to walk right for the next week." He did not seem to understand, so she pointed to his crotch, "You are very large."

Rikist's mouth twisted in a proud, sideways grin. He shifted on the chair and smirked. "You seem to have enjoyed it very much."

Samantha blushed, and then stood. "I'm going to go shower. Do you want to watch a movie after?"

"Yes."

"What kind do you like?"

"No matter." Rikist shrugged. "Only one rule."

She lifted on eyebrow. "And that is?"

"I get to shower with you."

SIXTEEN

Rikist's leg still had not loosened up two days later, and Samantha began to worry that he had caused irreparable damage to his knee during their escape. He had blown her off, waving away her concern, though he did not complain when she suggested he take another day off to rest. So, they had spent the morning together at her stand and the afternoon canning strawberries. Samantha tried to teach Rikist how to bake—a treat considering wheat flour and sugar were not present on his home planet. He had been in seventh-heaven doing constant taste tests—to the point nearly half of the ingredients never made it into the oven.

An apple pie cooled on the window ledge as Samantha and Rikist reclined on the back-porch steps, sipping glasses of wine and watching the final rays of sunset. Samantha fought back a grin as she glanced down at the bubbles in Rikist's glass; he had snuck in some of the lemon-lime soda in the back of her fridge to take off the edge.

Rikist took a sip of his drink and idly ran the back of his hand against Samantha's calf, letting his left leg fully extend. In the dying light, his profile seemed exceptionally sharp and square, his shoulders solid rocks beneath the red sky and floating dandelion seeds. He leaned his head back to peer at her on the steps above him and smiled softly.

"You are very beautiful in this light, you know that?"

"Only in this light?" Samantha laughed. "You do realize it's pretty much dark."

"All the time then." His smile spread. "Especially when you blush."

"I'm not blushing."

He chuckled and looked out into the dark back-yard. "So, is this all you do?"

Samantha frowned. "What do you mean?"

"This. What we have been doing the last few days."

She glowered down at him. His English had finally smoothed out for the most part, so now anything he said could not be blamed on his poor translation.

"I don't just sit around on my ass all day, you know." She crossed her arms. "Just because I don't man some ship and command—"

"I did not say it was bad!" He laid a hand on her thigh and squeezed. "I think it's nice."

"Nice."

"The quiet and slow pace." His face went solemn. "A serenity I have never had before."

Samantha licked her lips. "Is that something that you could get used to?"

Rikist hesitated and took a long drink of his wine. Samantha frowned, knowing he was buying time. They had not fully discussed the option of Rikist living there permanently. Samantha secretly hoped that he would give up the idea of trying to get home he had hinted at while they had baked, though she was not about to put herself fully out there only to meet with disappointment. Rikist glanced at her from over his glass and winked as he finished draining it.

"Not sure," he drawled slowly, a mischievous glint in his eye. "I was hoping to get a little more tail in my idea of paradise."

Samantha tried to fight back against the sudden grin that threatened to take over her face, and she shook her head and socked him in the shoulder.

"And I was hoping to have a little more manpower around here for such a high payment."

"You told me to take the day off!"

"Because you're hopping around like Forrest Gump—"

His face scrunched up. "Who?"

"He's a—"

A sudden crash in the field beyond the light of the back porch brought their heads up.

"What was that?" Samantha whispered.

Rikist sat up. He peered into the growing darkness

where Samantha pointed. "I think it came from the stables." He set his glass down and heaved himself off the porch, brushing off his legs. "I will go check on the horses."

"Do want me to come, too?"

He shook his head and gave a roguish grin. Even in the darkness, Samantha could see the heat smoldering in his eyes. "No. You can go inside and get ready."

She swallowed down the butterflies fluttering up into her throat. "For what?"

"For what I am going to do to you when I come back," he said in a low, even tone.

"That shop is closed unless the patron becomes permanent."

He tilted his head to one side. "I guess that depends on how convincing the buyer is." He grinned. "And I can be very convincing."

Samantha bit her lip and grinned as he turned and disappeared into the darkness toward the stables. She sat back on the steps and closed her eyes, sipping her wine and listening to the crickets and bullfrog as she enjoyed the heat of the beautiful summer night.

Samantha felt something move in the darkness to her right, just outside the low back fence. Her eyes popped open and she sat up alertly as her breathing quickened. She set her glass down and slowly stood and walked backwards toward the house.

Maybe a coyote?

She hesitated as the shadows moved and converged into a tall, male figure, slowly approaching with a stealthy grace. Gold eyes appeared amidst the blackness, and Samantha's heart flipped as reddish hair and striped cheeks appeared in the dim illumination of the back-porch light.

Krissik!

She whirled and ran up the two steps and jerked the door open, then shut and locked it behind her. She sprinted through the kitchen toward her bedroom where she kept her father's shotgun high in the closet.

Samantha could not remember if it was even loaded.

She heard the front door shudder under a heavy weight, and then the front window crashed open. She screamed and pumped her legs faster down the hall as the heavy boots quickly gained. She veered off and dove into the bathroom at the last moment, shutting the door and locking it. She clamored up onto the tub's edge and slid open the small overhead window. She stood on tiptoes to get as close as she could and screamed.

"Rikist!"

The doorknob jiggled, and Krissik let out a guttural shriek when he realized it was locked. He slammed his fist against the door.

"Samantha! Riki stra it si!"

"Krissik!" Samantha turned wide-eyed to the shaking door. "Please, don't do this!"

"Ir riki stra it si!"

Samantha screamed as claws dug into the edge of the door panel and forced it open. Krissik's angry and distressed face glared down at her, as he ripped the door off its hinges and threw it against the wall behind him. He stormed into the bathroom and stopped, his chest heaving.

In the lighting from above the sink, Samantha could see that the last week—or month, as it could have been back on his planet's time—had not been kind to Krissik. His gaunt face appeared spotted and pale in the incandescent light, probably from lack of sleep and food, and dark circles bruised under his eyes. His gold eyes were faded, the spark of color snuffed out by the hurt and betrayal swirling in their depths.

"Kri sa ti, Samantha?" he asked, slower. His eyes widened when he seemed to realize she did not understand.

He knelt close and took her face in his hands, turning her head to the side. His fingers touched the small bruised dot behind her ear, where the hole from the missing transmitter had closed and nearly healed.

He turned her back to look at him, and he frowned at her. He opened his mouth, hesitated, and then shook his head.

"Isk?"

Samantha stared at his torn face, and without understanding his words, knew exactly what he was asking. She reached up and touched his cheek.

"Because I don't love you, Krissik." Her chin trembled, and she struggled to hold the tears in. "And I can't go back with you."

Krissik's face crumbled, and he clamped his jaw together and closed his eyes.

"I... ir takir sirik sti..."

He took a shaky breath and stared at her sadly, and then pressed his lips to hers.

Samantha pushed at his chest and turned her head to the side. "Kris... no."

He glared at her with wet eyelashes and tried to kiss her again.

Samantha slapped him across the face. "I said no, dammit!"

Krissik's eyes went wide with surprise, and his nostrils flared as he took in a deep breath. He leaned in closer, sniffing at Samantha's neck and hair. He growled and pushed her roughly onto the floor. He ignored her objections and pressed his face against her stomach and then between her legs.

He jerked backward, his eyes narrowed, and lips curled back to bare his fangs. His chest heaved as he growled low in his throat.

"Rikist?"

Samantha's stomach dropped as he stood, fury clouding his face. She scooted back and cowered against the toilet base, her hands up to shield her face.

"Kris, please—"

Krissik bent and grabbed her ankle and jerked her forward. Samantha slid across the cool floor tiles, her hands and free leg scrambling to gain traction. She got to her knees when Krissik's hand latched onto the back of her hair, and he pulled her to her feet and toward the bedroom. Samantha's eyes burned as she struggled to breathe against the awkward angle in which he held her neck, and she clawed at his arms, but to no avail.

He kicked the door open to her bedroom and forced her to the bed. Samantha screamed and kicked out, but he slapped her leg away and grabbed her wrists, holding them above her head. Samantha shook her head from side to side, tears streaking her face as she bucked and twisted on the mattress.

"Get off me!" she screamed. "Get off!"

Krissik leaned over her, his cheeks wet and eyes narrowed to slits. He kissed her neck and clamped something hard and metal across her wrists before pushing away and standing back.

Samantha looked up at him, surprised, and then tried to lift her hands. They felt weighted and immobile, and she tilted her head back to peer at the blinking light on the thick metal cuffs. She glared at Krissik.

"What are you doing?" she yelled. "Why—"

"Samantha?"

She stilled as Rikist's call came muffled from down the hall.

Krissik pulled his laser pistol from his belt and pressed a button, the lights on the side illuminating as it charged. He tightened his jaw and stared down at her, fire blazing in his eyes.

"Rak iris tri, Rikist."

Samantha's jaw dropped at the venom in Krissik's voice as he turned and walked out the door, shutting it behind him. She took a breath, dread pooling in her stomach, and screamed.

"Rikist!"

She thrashed against the restraints on her wrists, rolling her body across the mattress. She froze at the sound of glass breaking somewhere down the hall, and then screamed as she put all of her weight into the next turn and rolled off the bed. She landed with a hard thump on her side, and quickly rolled to her knees. She grunted and brought her feet under her and got into a deep squat. She groaned and forced herself to stand, her hands feeling like they were strapped to eighty-pound weights. She stumbled and fell against the dresser.

"Rikist!"

She closed her eyes and began to sway her arms back and forth, starting an inch at a time and eventually graduating to long, sweeping arcs. She gritted her teeth against the strain on her shoulders and forcibly slammed the device against the side of the heavy oak dresser. The impact jarred her shoulders, and she let out a whimper, before slamming her wrists again.

On the fourth impact, the mechanism on the restraints beeped, and the lock hissed and flipped open. Samantha gasped and leaned against the dresser, cradling her sore wrists, and then stumbled out the door. She hurried down the darkened hall, her hands brushing against the walls to steady her.

Samantha reached the entrance to the living room and froze as a beam of green light flashed across her vision. She yipped and stepped back to the sound of a series of growls, dropping to a crouch just inside the hallway.

"Samantha, get back!" Rikist yelled from her right. "Stay down!"

She looked up as Krissik leapt over the sofa, landed on all fours, and brought up his pistol, aiming it at Rikist.

"Rikist look out!" she shouted.

Rikist's eyes went wide before bringing up his own gun. He rolled to the right as Krissik's laser charged and fired. The light beam cut through the leather sofa and burned a hole the size of Samantha's fist into the wall.

Krissik crouched and darted around the corner into the kitchen, putting his back against the refrigerator and charging his weapon. He peeked around the corner but stopped as a beam from Rikist's gun cut through the edge of the drywall, singing his right ear.

"Rak iris tri ta!" Krissik yelled out with a snarl.

"Ka raki si tris!" Rikist growled back, standing from his position behind the overturned dining table. He held his weapon at the ready and advanced toward the kitchen. "Ri ta, Krissik!"

Krissik growled low in his throat and dropped to one knee, where the green glow of his weapon reflected his image in the black dishwasher. He took a deep breath, shifted his grip on the gun, and then spun around the corner, firing. Rikist roared and returned the fire, light beams ripping through the darkness, illuminating the toppled furniture and charred walls.

Rikist cried out as the laser sliced across his left arm, and he dropped to all fours as another nicked the brace and shattered one side of the supports. He lifted his gun with one arm and fired again but realized he did not need to; Krissik lay sideways across the back of the sofa, his eyes closed and blood seeping from his open mouth and a large hole in his side. His pistol lay in a puddle of blood on the floor.

Rikist stared. He grimaced and coughed, cradling his left arm. Blood seeped through his fingers and dripped down his elbow. He glanced between his fallen brother and Samantha, his face torn.

"Samantha? Are you alright?"

Samantha stood and nodded, her hands shaking. She walked to her left and turned on the lamp in the corner, the yellow glow allowing them to see the full damage to the house. She covered her mouth and peered over at Krissik's still form.

She was almost afraid to ask, "Did you kill him?"

Rikist licked his lips, his eyes wary. He looked too scared to move. He shook his head. "I... I don't know."

He took a breath, used one of the standing dining chairs to leverage himself to his feet, and limped toward Krissik.

The front door suddenly burst open, and Rodolfo stood in the doorway with a shotgun raised and trained on Rikist.

"Get back, hombre," Rodolfo said evenly, his finger tightening on the trigger. "Drop the gun."

Rikist lowered his pistol to the floor and kicked it away, and then raised his hands and hobbled backward.

Samantha rushed in between them and lifted her hands toward Rodolfo. "Rodolfo! It's OK, put the gun down!"

"I heard you screaming, and then some kind of gunfire." His finger moved from the trigger, but he did not lower the weapon. "I told you he was trouble."

"No, it wasn't him!" Samantha stepped closer to Rodolfo. "His brother—"

Rodolfo's eyes twitched, and then swung to his left to where Krissik lay. His brow lifted in surprise at the sight of Krissik's stripes and visible fangs. "Madre de Dios..."

Samantha pressed her hands on Rodolfo's shoulders, trying to lower his aim. "Look, Rodolfo, please put the gun down and I will explain everything. I promise."

The older man hesitated, and then slowly lowered his gun while shooting a distrustful glare in Rikist's direction. He tapped his boot on the floor.

"I'm waiting."

Samantha nodded, her shoulders relaxing. She looked back at Rikist, who motioned toward Krissik. "I will. But first, we need to take care of him."

RODOLFO FINISHED off his second beer and shook his head. He sighed, and then looked across the table at Rikist as the shirtless alien bandaged his arm, eyeing the line of fur and stripes along his sides and shoulders. Rikist glanced up as Samantha handed him a pair of painkillers, and then looked away, doing his best to ignore the old man.

Rodolfo snorted in Rikist's direction and stood. He straightened his shirt and placed his empty bottle on the counter.

"What are you planning on doing with the other one? You can't keep him tied up in the stables forever." Rodolfo glowered. "If you want him gone for good, then you need to just—"

"I will take care of him." Rikist glared. "Do not worry."

"Of course, I am going to worry." He spun on Rikist. "I have known this girl since she was a child, and hell if I will turn and just—"

"Thank you."

Rodolfo paused, eyeing Rikist. His brow knotted. "Por que?"

"For caring. For tonight. If my brother had beat me, then you would have been here to protect her."

Rodolfo stared straight-faced, and then nodded and turned to the door. "Maria will be expecting you over in the morning. She's probably still up waiting by the door."

Samantha walked him out. "I'll come by first thing. I promise."

She opened the door for Rodolfo, and then wrapped her arms around his thin chest, hugging him tight. "Thank you."

Rodolfo returned the hug and kissed the top of her head. They separated, and he nodded as he left. Samantha flipped the lock, and then leaned against the door. She frowned at Rikist.

"Are you really OK?"

He shrugged, looking down at the remains of his leg brace. "I do not know what to do."

Samantha walked closer and knelt beside his chair. She rested one hand on his good thigh. She wanted to speak words of comfort, but she had none to give. She wanted to feel safe again, where no other alien knew where she was. She wanted her quiet, contented existence on her small farm with Rikist and Rodolfo and Maria to keep her company, and to live out her simple life in peace. She wanted—no, *needed*—Krissik to go away.

But kill him? She just could not condone it. He had been nothing but kind to her on their planet and had just come back to take back the woman he loved. She had seen the hurt and betrayal in his eyes, and the sorrow etched across his face once he realized that Rikist had laid claim to her.

She looked up to Rikist's face, and saw his own inner battle raging inside. With his face drawn and eyes dark, his lips trembled against the hard set of his jaw. He looked away, his nostrils flaring.

"He almost—"

"Krissik was not going to hurt me, Rikist," Samantha cut him off. "He smelled you on me and flew off the handle. Could you blame him if you were in the same position?"

He glanced down at her, his bloodshot eyes glinting wetly. "I would have killed him."

"My point exactly." She laid her head in his lap and sighed when he ran his hand over her hair. "He's your little brother, Rikist."

The hand on her hair stilled. "What are you saying?"

"I don't want you to kill him."

Rikist gently pushed her head off his lap, and Samantha sat up to stare at him.

"Is that what you want to do?" she asked incredulously.

He shook his head, and then shrugged. "No. I... Of course not. But I know now that if he could find us, and if he sent word back home... I do not know what else to do to keep you safe."

"Stay, for one."

Rikist stared down at her, his face guarded.

Samantha squared her shoulders and stood. "You heard me. If you really care about me that much and want me to be safe, then you can't just walk away."

"It is not as simple as that..."

"Why can't it be? You said that you enjoy the simple peace that I have here. You can have that, too."

"The jumps need to be closed."

"How?"

He shook his head, defeated. "I do not know." He clicked his tongue. "And what about Krissik? You heard Rodolfo, we cannot keep him held forever."

Samantha inwardly beamed, happy he did not dispute her earlier statements. "I... Maybe you can try to talk sense into him."

Rikist hissed and bared his fangs. "You spent time with him. You know he is stubborn as a wall and will not give up on you."

"Just like his ass of a big brother."

"I am not stubborn, I am practical." He shook his head. "He cannot live in a cage like one of your animals."

"People change, Rikist. You have."

He shot her a sideways glance, and then pushed himself to his feet. He tested his weight on his left leg and grimaced as the brace creaked dangerously. He did not look happy as he leaned against the table.

"Can you help me?" he asked. "I need to lie down."

Samantha took his arm and let him lean on her shoulder. "In your room?"

He looked down at her, his face tired and sorrowful. "I was hoping I could lie next to you."

Samantha frowned. "Rikist, I'm really not in the mood after all of this—"

"No. I just... I just want to hold you for a while."

She swallowed. "A while?"

"Forever."

SEVENTEEN

Samantha woke before Rikist, yawned, and quickly shut off her phone before the shrill alarm rang through the air. She rolled onto her side and stared at his sleeping face and frowned. She tested his skin, cursing at the radiating heat, and knew what she had to do.

It's only because I love him...

She paused halfway off the bed, and grinned. "Yeah, I could at least admit it to myself."

She dressed quickly and as quietly as she could, not wanting to disturb him.

Rikist had tossed and turned most of the night, his delirious moans and whimpers keeping her up as well. Around dawn he had woken needing to use the bathroom and had been unable to move. He had cried at the throbbing pain in his immobile leg, and she had held him for nearly an hour until the double dose of pain meds kicked in and he fell asleep in her arms.

Samantha just hoped once she fixed him this time he would be able to keep off his leg and finally let it heal for good.

She grabbed her cell phone and shoes and tiptoed out the bedroom door, closing it behind her.

OUTSIDE, she dialed the number from memory and closed her eyes, balancing the plate of food in her other hand as she walked.

The phone rang four times before a groggy male voice came in on the other end. "H-hello?"

"John, it's Samantha."

Silence, then the ruffling of sheets. "What... Samantha, what the hell are you—"

"I need your help."

John guffawed. "I tried calling for months after you left without a peep from you, and now you're suddenly calling me asking for help. That's rich."

"Look, you—" Samantha paused mid-step and closed her eyes. *One, two, three, four...* "John, I know we left on bad terms. You were cheating on me and broke my heart; I keyed your truck and disappeared off the face of the Earth. Literally... I'm sorry you felt slighted when I didn't stick around after your secretive overnight 'business' trips—"

"Samantha, I've told you before, I never cheated on you..."

"Listen, I really need your help right now." She

fought to control the emotion in her wavering voice, and knew she failed by the sharp intake of his breath. "Please."

He sighed. "What is it?"

"Can you do an on-site surgery?"

"Jesus, Samantha, what happened?" Suddenly, John's voice slipped into his professional vet mode; the one thing Samantha could count on was his dedication to animals. "Did one of the horses get caught up in your fencing?"

"Something like that," she muttered. "He's um... torn up pretty bad. Lacerations up the thigh—uh, rear leg and side. I believe the joint is broken and the tendons are lacerated... it's pretty infected. Can you bring over antibiotics and sedatives?"

"I can see what I can do. If the damage is severe, then I'll have to bring the animal in. When did it happen?"

Samantha thought about it. *Earth time?* "Few days ago."

"Few—why did you take so long to call?"

"I was out of town."

"Where?"

She sighed. "In Vegas."

John sucked on his teeth. "Vegas, huh?" He snorted. "You know it would be a lot easier at my office with all my equipment..."

"Can you come over today?"

Hesitation. "When?"

"Now?"

"Sheesh, Samantha, I...what time is it?" He sighed. "I have an appointment at nine. I'll try to make it out there afterward."

"Thank you."

"You're going to owe me."

She did not like the sound of that, though she knew she did not have a lot of options. "Please hurry."

Samantha hung up before he could respond, and shoved the phone in her back pocket, hurrying to the barn. She hated the fact that she had had to ask John—the one person she *never* tried to initiate contact with outside of her animals—for help, but Rikist needed more than a few pills and ice packs. More if he ever wanted to walk normally again.

She slipped through the barn's large swinging door as quietly as she could. The scratchy smell of hay hung thick in the warm air, mixing with the musky scent of horses and oiled saddles. The morning sun shone in through the thin windows high up near the rafters, illuminating the dust particles floating through the air. Several sacks of barley sat stacked in the corners between racks of tack and garden tools. One of the mares snorted and stomped its foot, and she deftly reached out with her free hand to caress the velvet muzzle.

"Hush!" she whispered, willing the horse to quiet.

She strained her neck toward the stall to her right and peered over the gate.

Krissik lay curled up on his side on the blanket she had tossed across the hay pile bed, his arms tied tightly behind his back. Rodolfo had seen to his bindings: nylon and chain hobbles on his ankles, a length of rope connecting the hobbles to one of Rodolfo's dog's prong collars around his neck, and a pair of police-grade cuffs tight on his wrists, courtesy of Samantha's private toy box. Rodolfo had given Samantha a suspicious and somewhat horrified look when she procured them, but to her relief had said nothing.

Krissik shifted in his sleep, rubbing his chin against the blanket, and pulling his knees closer to his chest, and Samantha was reminded of how young he really was. A fine sheen of sweat covered his brow and upper lip, and blood speckled the bandages she had applied on his ear and side. Samantha unlatched the door as quietly as she could, but the click of the lock cut through the silence, and Krissik's eyes snapped open.

Surprise flooded his face when he saw Samantha, before his cheeks reddened and his eyes narrowed in anger. He swallowed and tried to twist into a sitting position, but the restraints and rope Rodolfo had used to keep his elbows tight against his sides made movement near impossible. He settled with growling and baring his fangs at her.

Samantha hesitated, and then knelt in the hay just out of reach. She lowered the plate of eggs, bacon, and toast so that he could see.

"I thought you might be hungry."

"Sri ak ta risti," he hissed, venom dripping from his words.

Samantha pressed her lips together and tried to keep her face neutral. "How are you feeling?"

She peered closer at his ear, and carefully pulled at the edge of the bandage on his side. She sighed, relieved. Now that she could see the wound in good lighting, it really was not that deep—a flesh wound—and Rikist had said the laser cuts were sterile, so as long as they kept the area clean, it should heal without any issues except minor scarring.

Krissik's skin jumped under her touch, and he struggled to wiggle out of reach. "Riki sra, Samn-tha!"

"I'm trying to help you," she said, her voice rising higher than she had planned. She gritted her teeth and held out a forkful of eggs. "Here, take a bite so you can keep your energy up to heal."

Krissik pressed his lips together and narrowed his eyes. "Sitka ri arsta ki—"

"I don't understand what you're saying, you know." Samantha's shoulders dropped. "Unless you brought another translator with you..." She paused at his nod. "You did? Where is it?"

Krissik motioned with his head toward the barn doors.

"Outside?"

He nodded.

"Where?"

He shrugged, his face smug, and then leaned toward her and wiggled his hands in the restraints.

Samantha guffawed and shook her head. "Nice try.

I'll go searching for it on my own when I'm through here."

She held up the fork again. Giving a defeated sigh, Krissik nodded. He leaned forward toward the fork, his eyes never leaving Samantha's, and then lurched forward.

Samantha yipped and jerked her hand back just as his jaws snapped in the air inches from the skin of her wrist. She glared down at him and stabbed his shoulder with the fork.

"Son of a bitch!"

Krissik let out a pained mewl and then glowered at her. Pain, anger, and weariness waged war on his face, and he concentrated visibly to keep his composure.

Samantha shook her head. "Kris, please listen to me. I know you're upset, and I know you came all the way here to get me back. But I was never yours to take back." She paused, watching the emotions play across his face. "You stole me, took me to your home without my permission. I... I don't love you, Krissik. I care for you, I do. I think you're a great kid and would make someone very happy. But I can never be your mate."

Krissik's eyes went wide and wet as he stared at her, unblinking. His breathing quickened.

Samantha took a deep breath and decided it would be less painful to drive in the last stake now then drag things on. "I love your brother."

Krissik swallowed forcibly and tried to turn his body away but ended up stuck on his stomach. He buried his face in the blanket and let out a defeated scream, and then let his shoulders sag. He mumbled something unintelligible against the blanket, and then twisted his head to look back at Samantha with one red eye.

"S-sor... Sree."

Samantha blinked. "What?"

"Aye Sor...ree."

The devastated look on Krissik's face was heart-breaking, and Samantha ignored the fact he had just tried to bite her, scooting closer so that she could turn him sideways to face her. She wiped at his cheeks with the backs of her hands, and smoothed hay particles out of his short hair.

"I'm sorry, too," she said. She leaned forward and kissed his brow, and then settled back to grab the plate and hefted the fork. "Do you want to try again?"

Krissik closed his eyes and managed a half-shrug. He opened his mouth obediently when the loaded fork touched his lips and chewed mechanically.

By the third bite, he was already anticipating the food, revealing his true hunger. The plate disappeared quickly, and Krissik settled back against his arms. He shifted uncomfortably and looked at Samantha pointedly.

She sighed and shook her head. "Until we're sure you're not going to try anything, you're stuck." She hesitated. "Though I can see what Rodolfo says about loosening some of them."

Krissik rolled his tongue in his cheek. "Ra stikra, Rikist?"

Samantha noted the concern in his eyes. "He's sleeping. He's in pretty bad shape, and his leg..." She shrugged, and suddenly everything that happened after the fight last night came out: the drugs, the fever, Rikist being unable to walk. "I don't know what's going to happen. I have someone coming over later to see what they can do, but I'm afraid he won't be able to fix Rikist's leg."

For the first time since the fight Samantha allowed herself a bout of tears. Everything had happened so suddenly, and she had had to be so strong—for both her and Rikist. The lack of sleep from the last night ate at her, and Rikist's vulnerable condition tore at her heart-strings.

She jumped when Krissik's cheek rubbed against her leg, realizing he had inched his way closer. She wiped the tears from her cheeks and forced a smile down at him.

"I have to go and check in on someone. I'll come back later and see how you're doing." She stood and looked down at Krissik's annoyed and hurt look. "I'm sorry. Like I said, you tried to kidnap me back and almost killed Rikist. You're staying put until I'm sure you're harmless."

"Samn-tha!" Krissik protested. "I sor-ree! Sirta ri ka, Samn-tha!"

She picked up the plate and fork, and then waved to him on her way out of the barn.

SAMANTHA NEARLY JUMPED out of her SUV before she had fully put it in park behind John's company van, her heart racing when she realized he was not in the driver's seat.

"Shit!" she ran to the house. "John!"

The quick visit to calm Maria's fears had turned into a longer ordeal than Samantha had planned, morphing from a simple check-in to a detailed explanation of her living conditions off-planet and current relationship issues. She had seen John's van roll up her driveway from across the field separating the two houses through Maria's window, and nearly had a heart attack. Jumping into her car, she had sped down the road to intercept him, with Rodolfo and Maria in their truck not far behind.

But John had not wasted any time going up to the house.

Samantha skidded across the porch and reached for the doorknob, whispering, "Please, please, please, please!"

"Samantha?"

Samantha spun around to see John appear around the corner of the house. She gulped in surprise.

It had been nearly a year since she had seen John in person, and as much as she hated him for the choices he had made, having him suddenly in front of her made her heart flip. He was tall with a pale complexion, genes from his mother's German side, and a wide, even smile. He had always been on the slim side, but now his arms and chest had filled out, expanding nicely against his polo shirt and khakis.

She blinked, recovering from her surprise. "I—you're here."

John frowned at her. "You asked me to come as soon as I could. So, I rescheduled my morning appointment."

Samantha let her face break into a wide smile and fought the nearly overwhelming urge to throw herself into his arms in thanks.

No, she thought. *Nothing to give him the wrong impression. I already have an alien in my barn I need to reform. I don't need an ex-cheater on the roster.*

"You didn't answer the door," John said, "so I was going to try the back." He pointed to the barn as Rodolfo pulled up. "Is the animal in there?"

Samantha waited for Rodolfo to get out of his truck and help Maria down from the passenger seat, and then shook her head. She unlocked the front door and jerked it open. "Inside."

John gave her an incredulous look. "Excuse me?"

"Look, just please trust me."

"Samantha..." He glanced back warily at Rodolfo and the shotgun in his hand, all too clear of the other man's feelings toward him. "Rodolfo. You two haven't planned some type of get back at the ex—"

"This is not about you," Samantha cut him short and frowned. "You need to promise me you won't say a word about this to anyone."

"Look, if you're doing something illegal or...

attempting some sort of chainsaw massacre reenactment—"

"Promise me. It's very important that no one knows about this."

John studied her face, his eyes hard, and then he glanced at Rodolfo before nodding. "I'll make you a deal. I'll help you, because I want you to be able to trust me again."

"So, what's the deal?"

"And in return, I get to take you to dinner so that I can explain things."

Samantha sighed in exasperation. "John—"

"No. If this is the only way I can get you to sit and listen to me, then so be it. Do you want my help, yes or no?"

She gritted her teeth. "Fine."

John stepped aside, motioning for Samantha to go first, his eyes still darting to Rodolfo's gun. Samantha forced a smile and led him inside.

John caught her arm as she passed and leaned closer as he shut the door behind them. "Now," he whispered harshly, "can you please tell me why the hell he's carrying a gun?"

"It's not for you." Samantha took his wrist and pulled him toward the bedroom. She shot him a sideways glance and let a devious smirk tug at her lips. "Unless you decide to open your fat mouth."

SAMANTHA LET John into the room first, so that she could try to slow him down should he decide to bolt. She steeled herself against the doorframe, readying herself for the sudden blow as he backpedaled in surprise and disbelief.

"You've got to be shitting me."

Samantha's eyes snapped open. It was not the response she had been expecting, and she stood taller to peer at John in confusion. "What?"

John dropped his bag by the door and stepped further into the room. He paused at the side of the bed and looked down at Rikist, whose feverish eyes glared upwards to meet the man's gaze. John rubbed at the back of his neck and shook his head at Samantha.

"How the hell did you get mixed up with him?" he asked.

Samantha shook herself awake and approached John. "You... you know him?"

"No," he said quickly. "Not him, per se, but... his species."

Samantha blinked. *I must not have heard that right.* "Come again?"

John placed one hand on Rikist's brow to test his skin.

Rikist awkwardly swiped at John's hand with his claws, barely missing. "Sam," his throat sounded raspy. "What is... who is this?"

"Rikist, don't," Samantha sat on the edge of the bed beside him and smoothed back hair from his face. She took a breath. "Rikist, this is John. He's here to help you."

"Rikist?" John's head snapped up. "Captain Rikist Sa Tskir?"

"How do you..." Rikist stared up at John in surprise, and then his eyes registered recognition and distaste and anger flooded his face. "From the picture."

John's eyes widened. He glanced at Samantha. "Obviously, you've been telling him less than positive stories about me."

"Nothing you didn't deserve," she snapped. "How do you know his name?"

"Because I'm not just a vet, Samantha." He closed his eyes and sighed. He turned to Rikist and held out his hand. "We've never actually met in person, Rikist. I'm Jonathan Merrick. I'm one of your medical contacts here on Earth."

"YOU REALLY KNOW how to pick 'em."

Samantha glowered over at John as she followed him out of the bedroom.

"And what mental list are you checking off?"

"Assholes and trouble." He laughed. "And yes, before you say anything, I already put myself at the top of that list."

Samantha grimaced and glanced over her shoulder at Rikist as he stirred restlessly in his morphine-induced sleep and bit her lip. She closed the door behind them and leaned against the wood.

"So, what do you think?"

"Do you want my honest opinion of your chosen love interest or do you want me to lie—"

"Focus, John. His leg."

John snapped the top of his bag shut and set it next to his mobile ultrasound machine and box of used rags. He shook his head.

"He really did a number on it. He's running a high fever from the unchecked infection, and I'm draining brown liquid out of his knee by the cup, which hints at the beginning of sepsis. The destroyed ligaments need replacement by reconstructive surgery. He has completely mutilated his patella and meniscus, and he is already showing signs of arthritis in the knee from his femur slipping down against his tibia."

Samantha licked her dry lips. "So, what do you suggest?"

"Obviously he needs surgery, and IVs and antibiotics to stop the spread of infection through his bloodstream. You'll have to bring him to my clinic, so I can have all my equipment. I can perform a graft from muscle in his biceps to pass through and around the joint and tibia to stabilize his knee, remove the loose shards of his kneecap, and place sutures around the fabella to help facilitate the growth of scar tissue."

"How do you know how to do all of this?"

He shrugged. "It's really not that different than

operating on animals. Besides, aren't humans just another type of mammal?"

"Impressive." Samantha fought a smile. "Will that fix him?"

John hesitated. "Mostly. There's enough damage that I can't positively say it will be one hundred percent. It really depends on how bad it is once I actually start cutting him open. Lasting effects could range from a minor limp to chronic pain and arthritis. Or he could mend completely." He shrugged apologetically. "They heal better than we do, and faster, so I'm hopeful. I just don't want to make any promises."

Samantha's heart dropped to her knees. She slid down the door and sat on the floor and covered her eyes with the palms.

"This is all because of me."

"Unless you blew up his ship in the first place, I highly doubt that. From working for him, I know he's a stubborn ass, and I don't see him as one to follow doctor's orders easily." John knelt beside her, paused, and then gingerly brushed his fingers against her cheek. "So, I guess this means dinner's off."

She frowned up at him. "I promised I would."

"Yeah, but after seeing you with him, it's obvious there's no point anymore."

Samantha peered at him, and then let out a breath. "You wanted to try to fix things between us."

"I wanted to explain. You never gave me a chance."

She set her lips in a tight line and studied John's

face. "How did you get mixed up with Rikist in the first place?"

"It was about six or seven years ago. When I was going to school in New York."

"New York..." her eyes widened. "You were there when the first wave came through?"

John nodded. "I was meeting a classmate at the hotel. We were having dinner up on the rooftop garden when I saw the force shield appear around the building, and the lights went out." John pressed his lips together in a tight line and stood. "Long story short, they appeared out of nowhere in uniform and started snatching girls... but it became clear immediately that this was their first time, and several of the aliens got sick—I'm assuming from our atmosphere.

"Any who, I'm not really sure how I ended up treating them, but somehow I found myself working beside an EMT tech trying to resuscitate two of the aliens before getting knocked on the back of my head and waking up in the ER with a concussion. Three months later, I received an email from someone within the resistance acknowledging the risk I'd taken and was offered a handsome amount of compensation to provide medical support to on-planet staff and send medications through their jump sites."

"And you agreed?"

He grinned. "It was a... *very* handsome amount. How do you think I was able to take us to Paris for three weeks after graduation? And Hawaii?"

Samantha blushed. Paris had been an out-of-body

experience between the two of them, with lavish hotels, room service, and endless sightseeing. And Hawaii... those were probably the best two weeks of her life.

Before the secrets started taking over.

"And Rikist?" she prodded.

"Rikist took over as my main point of contact about two years ago. We've never actually met before today. Only communicated through emails and text messaging." He took one of her hands between his and gave it a gentle squeeze. "The last-minute trips between Las Vegas and New York were to treat the occasional incoming resistance soldiers and deliver antibiotics." His eyes saddened. "Not the secretive affair you assumed."

"Why didn't you tell me the truth?"

"I couldn't. For one, I didn't want you to get involved. Though that seems like a moot point now. And two..." He grimaced. "Your boyfriend threatened to jump over here and disembowel me if I decided to run off and spill secrets. Once in, always in kind of thing..."

Samantha wiped at her eyes. *Yeah, that sounded like Rikist.*

"I'm sorry for not telling you," John said slowly. "For not being honest about everything. I really screwed things up, didn't I?"

The apology loosened the tight knot in her stomach, and Samantha smiled. "Well I did get a refund of the five thousand you put down for the reception and your mother sent me the two tickets to Seattle she had bought for us. So, it wasn't a total waste."

John smiled, though his eyes wavered. "You love him, don't you?"

She thought about it, and then nodded. "Yeah."

"I guess I deserve that." He frowned, looked away, and then nodded and forced a smile. "I'm happy for you. Really. But am I wrong in being a little concerned the guy isn't human?"

"John..."

"You bet." He stood. "But considering he's both your boyfriend and my employer, we should probably get him over to the clinic before he keels over, and I lose my greatest source of income. I've gotten used to my quarterly, all-inclusive paid vacations."

AFTER HALF AN HOUR OF ARGUING, Rodolfo finally left with John to take Rikist to the vet clinic for surgery, while Samantha stayed behind with Maria and Krissik. Rodolfo had not wanted to leave the two women alone with Krissik, but Samantha and John convinced him that John could not move Rikist on his own. Rikist had been nervous as hell, stopping just short of begging Samantha to come along. John and Rodolfo finally managed to wrestle Rikist into the van, and John slipped him some Versed and after ten minutes the alien had mellowed out and fought hard to stay awake.

"I promise I'll get there before you wake up," Samantha told him with a kiss.

John just rolled his eyes and started the van, and Rodolfo slid the side door shut as they pulled out of the drive.

Maria helped Samantha clean up the living room and kitchen; making checklists in between sweeping and mopping of miscellaneous items that needed replacing. Samantha growled in frustration as the list grew to include her dishwasher and two dining room chairs.

"Those two sure had a bone to pick," Maria muttered as she finished wiping down the counters. She opened the refrigerator and began pulling out the bags of groceries she had brought over that morning. "Are they at least on talking terms yet?"

Samantha stood and stretched her sore back. She tossed a singed pillow onto the couch and shook her head. "I honestly hope they do soon though. I don't think I could take another fight in my living room..."

"I'm sure everything will work out. I'm going to make us something for lunch, and then get something going for dinner." Maria hummed as she moved about; nothing seemed to phase her for long. "Do carnitas sound OK?"

Samantha smiled at Maria's infectious, positive mood. "That sounds great. Thank you."

"Do you want to take something out to the younger one? What is his name?"

"Kris."

"Ah, Kris. Do you think he's hungry?"

Samantha nodded and headed toward her room. "I'm going to go change, and then I'll take him his food."

"SO, you really don't have a translator with you?"

Krissik looked away from where Samantha sat and shook his head. He shifted against the handcuffs and rested his cheek on the blanket.

Samantha tapped her nails against her knee, clicking her tongue against her cheek. She was surprisingly disappointed; she had hoped Krissik had been truthful in bringing the equipment along so that she could communicate with him. Granted, he understood everything she said, but that made for a pretty one-way conversation.

"How hard is it to get one?"

Krissik frowned at her. "Isk?"

"Why?" She had been around the brothers long enough to recognize a few words. "So that we can talk —and so I can understand what you're saying. Especially if..." She hesitated, motioning with her hands as she reached for the proper words. "If you would like to stay."

Krissik's eyes went round, and his pupils dilated in surprise, enough that Samantha nearly laughed aloud. She grinned and held out her hands toward his face.

"Don't move."

Krissik tensed as her hands went to his neck, and his entire body stilled as she gently loosened the pronged chain around his neck and carefully lifted it over and off his head. Krissik swallowed and rolled his neck, testing the newfound freedom. He glanced curiously at Samantha, who shrugged.

"Look, I know you came here to take me back to your planet," she started. "But I'm not going anywhere, and you know Rikist would never let you leave with me. So, you have two options."

She paused, as if considering, and then began loosening the knots on Krissik's torso and legs. She left the hobbles and handcuffs on, and then helped him into a sitting position against the stall wall. Krissik hissed in discomfort as he stretched his legs out, and he shifted against the warm wood. He licked his lips and looked at Samantha expectantly.

Samantha squared her shoulders. "One, you stay here until Rikist is back, and then you can say goodbye and you go home and never bother us again. Because I'm pretty sure if you try to come back under the same circumstance Rikist won't stop until you're dead. And I'd really hate to see that happen." She softened at the shocked and touched look in his eyes. "Or two, I let you go now so you can go take a shower and get some true rest in a real bed, and you can get acquainted with your new room."

Krissik started. "Ri tas sirta rat, isk?"

Samantha shrugged. "You're Rikist's brother. And

that makes you part of my family. You, me, Rikist, Rodolfo, Maria..."

Krissik lowered his gaze and seemed to lose himself to his thoughts. Samantha knelt beside him and laid a hand on his shoulder.

"I know it would mean a lot to Rikist if you would stay," she whispered. "So, he has his brother beside him. But I understand if you would rather be with your own kind."

Krissik's eyes met hers, and he nodded.

"S-ste... stay."

EIGHTEEN

The bell jingled as Rodolfo unlocked and opened the front door to the clinic when Samantha and Krissik arrived. His eyes widened at the sight of Krissik, and his hands went for the shotgun resting by the wall to his right.

"It's fine, Rodolfo!" Samantha assured. She took Krissik's elbow and pulled him into the clinic. "Don't worry, we worked things out."

"I'm getting too old for this crap," Rodolfo muttered as he relocked the door and took a seat in the small waiting room, fanning his face with his hat.

"Samantha?" John called from around the corner. "Back here."

Samantha led Krissik to one of the back rooms, where Rikist slept on his back on a hospital bed surrounded by beeping monitors. Several IVs stuck out of his left arm, and a long, clear tube snaked into his mouth and down his throat. A thick, white bandage wrapped around his right bicep, where Samantha knew John had taken a muscle graft to use in Rikist's leg. The leg in question had been set in a plaster cast from below the knee down to the foot to splint the fractured bone, and an industrial-style knee brace had one end drilled into the top of the cast and the other fitted snugly against his cleaned and bandaged thigh.

John turned from the sink, and he started at the sight of Krissik. "Ah, what the hell—"

"Don't worry." Samantha held a hand up. "It's fine, they're brothers. What's that in his mouth?"

John shook himself as if ruffling his feathers, and then looked where she was pointing as he dried off his hands. "Endotracheal tube. It delivers oxygen, sevoflurorane and nitrous oxide directly to his lungs so he doesn't aspirate—"

"Nitrous oxide?"

"Laughing gas. Along with the Versed and Propofol, he went down quick. He's a big guy, so I'm just glad I factored the dosages correctly." He reached for the tape holding the tube in place and gently peeled it off. "I already cut the gas off about ten minutes ago, and he's breathing on his own, so I can take the oxygen out."

Samantha looked away as John began slowly pulling the tube from out of Rikist's throat. She glanced at Krissik, who looked about ready to pounce on John and tear him to shreds.

John caught the look as well and froze. His eyes darted to Samantha. "Can you please explain to him that I'm not hurting his brother before he tries to eat me?"

"He's just trying to help." Samantha grabbed Krissik's arm and pulled him about. "*Help*, Krissik."

Krissik nodded curtly, letting her know he was aware; the low growl from deep in his throat made it clear he did not like it.

She rubbed Krissik's arm and chest, trying her best to calm him. "How did the surgery go?"

"Uh, pretty good actually." John set the tube down on a tray and turned the dials on the IV drips, testing them. "I was able to clean up the tissue damage around his knee and removed a hell of a lot of infection. The graft went well, and with some consistent therapy he should be able to regain most, if not all motion in his leg. There's a risk of some stability issues, but we won't know that for a while as he heals. A brace will help with that, though."

John pulled out a bottle of clear fluid and a needle and began filling the syringe.

"What's that for?" Samantha asked.

"He should be stirring any time." He set the bottle on the counter and tapped the bubbles out of the syringe. "This is morphine, and it's in case he wakes up in combat mode and starts swinging. Happens sometimes, usually with cops, soldiers, or athletes. And a right hook from this son of a bitch could land me in the hospital."

Krissik pulled away from Samantha and slipped to

the other side of the bed. He shook Rikist's arm. "Ra irit sa, Rikist?"

"Let him wake on his own!" John cursed and stumbled around to the other side of the bed, reaching for Krissik. "His awareness isn't in place, you're just going to confuse him—"

Rikist screamed. He thrashed against the bed, swiping his claws as if to push something away as he howled. He kicked his foot out, knocking over the nearest metal table and scattering trays of surgical equipment across the floor. Krissik hissed and clambered on the bed to hold Rikist down from struggling off the bed. The heart rate monitor beeped at a rapid pace, and an alarm clicked on another machine as an IV chord ripped free.

"Shit!" John cursed and fought to keep Rikist's arm still. "Hold him!"

Krissik pressed all of his weight on Rikist's upper body, and John jammed the needle into Rikist's exposed shoulder. Rodolfo appeared in the hall behind Samantha, shucking the shotgun barrel. Samantha gasped and flung her arms around Rodolfo, blocking any chance for him to use the weapon. Rodolfo growled and moved his hand away from the trigger.

"Dammit, Samantha—"

"Don't even think about it!" she cut him off.

The men continued to struggle for another minute, and then Rikist slowly settled back onto the bed, breathing heavily.

John wiped a shaky hand across his brow and

stepped back as Krissik eased off the bed. Samantha blinked, realizing she had a death grip on Rodolfo's arms, and forced her hands to her sides. She glared at Rodolfo until he set the gun to the side with a sigh.

John stepped closer to the table and stuck a hand out to check Rikist's pulse against the quieting machines. "Jesus, that was close."

"S-sirt... ka sita rits..." Rikist mumbled. He lifted his head groggily, and then let it fall back on the pillow. He began to shiver violently, so hard that his teeth chattered. "Rak ir... isik tsi..."

Krissik snapped his gaze to John, concern plastered across his face.

John bent and opened a cabinet and produced several folded blankets. "Don't worry, feeling cold is a pretty common side effect of the anesthesia. Here, wrap these around him."

Krissik took the blankets. He spread them out over Rikist's legs and tucked them in around his brother's neck. His hand wavered, and then gently brushed the underside of his wrist against Rikist's jaw in greeting.

"Stri kis, Rikist?"

Rikist's head lolled to the side, and he did several long, drawn-out blinks. "Sti iris..." His voice rasped between shivers. His gaze wandered, disoriented, as he slurred, "W-where am... Ir tsra, Samn-tha?"

"I'm right here." Samantha pushed past Krissik and rubbed Rikist's shoulder through the blanket. "You're at John's clinic."

He lifted his head and frowned at the cast. "What happened to my leg?"

"You had surgery, remember? And you did good—"

"Why?"

Samantha eyed John. "Is he OK?"

"He's fine." John fixed the IVs in Rikist's arm. "The Versed causes temporary amnesia, so that his body doesn't remember the surgery itself. It'll probably wear off in an hour or so."

Rikist's hand swayed in the air as he tried to touch Samantha's face, his fingers brushing air a foot to her right. "H-hi... Hiya." Rikist's punch-drunk smile reached from ear to ear, and he tried to lift his head to sit up. "W-what happened to my leg?"

John smirked. "Shark bit it off."

Rikist's eyes went wide. "What?"

"Stop, it, John." Samantha laughed, and pushed Rikist down against the bed. "Just lay your head back, Rikist."

Rikist suddenly broke into a bout of giggling, which just as suddenly melted into annoyance as he shivered. "Why's so... fuckin' cold in here?"

"Moody bastard, isn't he?" John smirked and reached out and turned Rikist's head to face him. "Rikist, look at me. I want you to try to follow my finger with just your eyes."

John held up one finger and slowly moved his hand back and forth. Rikist blinked and tried to lift his own finger to touch John's. John chuckled and pushed Rikist's hand away.

"Alright, E.T., keep your hand down. Just follow with your eyes."

"You got handsome fingers..." Rikist muttered.

Krissik guffawed beside Samantha, who had covered her mouth with one hand. The younger alien closed his eyes and shook his head, laughing. "Ta irtis, Rikist!"

John grinned and put a blood pressure cuff on Rikist's arm. "So, I've been told." He winked at Samantha.

"What..." Rikist tried to pull his arm away from John's grip, his eyes locked on John's fingers. "What are you doing?"

"Checking your blood pressure."

Rikist's sloppy grin widened. "Are you gonna take advantage of me?"

Rodolfo leaned against the doorjamb, amused. Krissik nearly crumpled on the foot of the bed, his face red as he guffawed hysterically.

John dropped his stethoscope and tried to keep a straight face as he undid the cuff as quickly as possible and stepped back. "I think your blood pressure's fine—"

"My throat hurts." Suddenly, Rikist's chin trembled, and his face crumpled as he sucked in a shaky breath.

Rodolfo's leathery face flashed a grin. "Is he crying?"

"It's the meds talking," John said, his composure back. "Some people are more susceptible to emotional outbursts after waking. It's just the body's way of reacting to trauma." He paused, a roguish grin on his lips, and then leaned close to the bed. "Hey Rikist, what happened to your leg?"

Rikist tried to weakly lift his sluggish limbs to wipe at his face as started to sob. The other men doubled over in laughter. Especially Krissik, who seemed to be thoroughly enjoying himself.

Samantha stifled a laugh. "John, you're an asshole!"

Annoyed as she was that they were laughing at Rikist's expense, she had to admit that it *was* pretty damn funny.

And all I want to do is lick those tears right off his cheeks and lips.

"You're alright, Rikist," Samantha cooed, struggling to keep the smirk off her straight face. A snort of laughter escaped, and she buried her face in the pillow to regain her self-control as she stroked his face and arm. "It's gonna be OK."

John cleared his throat, though the humor did not leave his eyes. He slipped several bottles of pills into a plastic bag and held it up to Samantha.

"Right now, he's on Dialaudid to keep him down for the next twenty-four hours. After that, he'll be on Vicodin for the pain, and Xanax to minimize anxiety and keep him down so that his leg can heal. The two meds together will increase drowsiness and most likely dizziness and difficulty concentrating, so he'll probably be knocked flat for the first few days." He handed her the bag. "Then of course there's antibiotics, and you can give him Ibuprofen if he needs it. I wrote every-thing down for you, so you know when and how much to give."

"Thanks, John."

"You know can call me anytime if you need anything."

"What did you do my leg?" Rikist moaned behind them.

Samantha rolled her eyes at Krissik's hyena-like laugh and allowed herself to break into a wide grin. "Alright, Kris. Let's get him home."

NINETEEN

John had not been kidding about the potency of the medication he had prescribed. The drugs had kept Rikist in pretty much a sedated state for the first three days, not waking for much more beyond taking his pills with food and enjoying an ear rub from Samantha before slipping back out. Though it was probably for the best; the antibiotics and pain meds made him nauseated beyond help, and sleep seemed to be the only reprieve available.

Krissik decided to stay and had been extremely helpful around the house. His natural talent in architecture came to light when he redesigned an impressive irrigation system for Samantha's gardens and orchards that would cut down on her watering bill, and made plans for improvements to the barn and a standalone guesthouse for himself that would be built once Rikist was up to helping... If he was *ever* up to helping.

Rikist made it a clear point to avoid his brother at

all costs, even stubbornly refusing Krissik's help moving around the house, which effectively grounded him to the living room couch most of the time. Samantha was able to help Rikist with the daily physical therapy John had prescribed, and to and from the bathroom, but nothing beyond that. Krissik had offered to accompany Rikist on the short walks around the house John had recommended, but of course, the bullheaded alien had refused and even suffered a nasty fall that backslid his recovery by several days.

Two weeks later, Rikist's health had improved greatly, and for the most part, he was back to being his old self, though by the end of the first week the restrictive bed rest had made Rikist agitated as hell, and Samantha was silently glad for the pills that still knocked him on his ass twice a day.

It allowed her to catch up on work and spend some quality time with Krissik.

SAMANTHA QUIETLY TURNED off the television in the living room and covered Rikist's sleeping form with a blanket. Satisfied he was out, she tiptoed her way from the couch into Krissik's room, where he lay on his stomach in the middle of the bed, waiting. He pointed at the clock on the wall, showing the time as half-past nine. Samantha smiled at him and crawled onto the bed beside him and rubbed behind his ear, gaining a purr.

"Sorry, he took a while to go out tonight." She mirrored his pose and stretched her legs out behind her, propping her upper body up on a pillow so that their shoulders touched. "So, you ready to get started?"

Krissik smiled and nodded, and then reached beside the bed and pulled up a notepad and short stack of children's books. He flipped through the books and handed one to Samantha.

Samantha frowned. "We've already read this one. Six times."

Krissik shrugged. "Ike it."

"Like," Samantha said. She pressed her tongue to the bottom of her front teeth and exaggerated the movement, "La-la... *like*."

Krissik scrunched his brow as he worked to conquer his uncooperative mouth. "El...la-ike. Like"

"Good." Samantha opened the book to the first page and pointed to the first line.

In return for Krissik's hard work with his brother and helping out around the house, Samantha had been giving him speech and reading tutoring sessions. Since he was going to stay, the first thing he needed to do was to learn the language. Rikist had not been exaggerating when he had called his little brother a genius; in two weeks, Krissik had picked up a basic understanding and substantial vocabulary of English. He still needed a lot of practice—especially with 'l,' 'v,' and 'f,' as their native language did not have any equivalent sounds—but his dedication was admirable, and Samantha had no doubt that given another month, he would be able to hold a conversation with the average Joe.

Krissik studied the page and slowly sounded out the letters, his voice thick with accent. "The cat ran fa...fat...fs—"

"Fast."

"—Ran fast..." He glanced up at Samantha's lips just inches away trying to illustrate the correct sound. He stared and swallowed, licked his lips.

Samantha caught his look and frowned. "Kris?"

Krissik blinked back to reality, and then groaned and let his face fall on the book. He mumbled against the pages, before managing, "Saw-ree."

Samantha sighed and rubbed his back affectionately. "I know it's been hard." She smiled when he purred and rubbed his cheek against her arm, and then ruffled the soft fur on his head. "Just keep it in check, OK?"

Krissik rolled sideways, so that Samantha's hands could reach a preferred spot under his chin. "I jus' miss... uh..."

"You're homesick, huh?"

His gold eyes looked incredibly sad, and he made no effort to hide it. "L-own."

"Huh?"

Krissik sat up, the wheels obviously turning in his head as he searched for the right words. "Lone. Ah-lone."

Samantha's eyes softened. She sat up and touched

his cheek so that he faced her. "You're not alone, Krissik. You've got me and Rikist—"

Krissik shot her an annoyed but tired look and shook his head. "You and Rikist. Me?" He sighed again. "None."

Samantha opened her mouth to respond when her cell phone rang from down the hall. She gave Krissik an apologetic smile and planted a firm kiss on his forehead. "I'll be right back."

Krissik forced a smile, and looked down at the pages, his finger moving across the words as he went back to studying.

Samantha sprinted through the living room and into the kitchen, even though she knew the shrill ringing would not bother Rikist; the pills would probably allow him to sleep through an earthquake. She glanced over at his sleeping form on the couch as she picked up the phone and swiped her finger across the front without looking.

"Hello?"

"Sam?"

Samantha's heart did a little flip. "Carly? Oh... oh my God I've been trying to reach you forever!"

"I know, I got your voicemails. Sorry, I... I've just been busy the last few weeks recovering from the hotel and... then the therapy afterward..."

"Therapy?"

"Yeah." Carly sighed, and her voice became lost for a moment behind the blaring of a radio. The music died, and Carly grunted. "Well, my mother felt it necessary. My version of events didn't seem to match most everyone else's."

What... what version does she remember? "Carly, I'm... Look, I'm sorry I left early. I wasn't feeling well, and I—"

"Yeah, well if you're that sorry then you can make it up to me."

Samantha's palms began to sweat. "What did you have in mind?"

"Well I figured if I ever wanted to visit you sometime then I could crash with you and you could show me around."

Samantha closed her eyes and smiled. That was not a favor; that was Carly's way of justifying another vacation on her parent's wallet.

"Deal. When were you thinking about coming out?"

Carly laughed, her throat rich and mischievous.

"I'll be there in half an hour."

RIKIST STRUGGLED to open his eyes at the insistent shake on his bare shoulder. He grimaced and lifted his head.

"What... Samantha, what's wrong?"

"Sorry, I know you're tired," Samantha said hurriedly. "But I need you to get up and go into the bedroom."

Rikist sucked in a breath and pushed himself to a

reclined position after two attempts. He forced his eyes open and groggily looked around the room. "What?"

Samantha frowned. Rikist always slept soundly for several hours almost immediately after taking his meds, and she checked her phone to see the time.

Forty-five minutes ago... Damn! You've got the worst timing ever, Carly.

She rubbed his shoulder and helped him sit up. "Carly is almost here."

"Who?"

"My friend from the hotel."

Rikist's chin snapped up, and he cleared his throat as he tried to wipe the sleep from his eyes. "I... The one you thought Krissik shot?"

"Not Krissik, but he was right there when it happened." She shook her head. "Anyway, yes, that Carly."

It seemed to take several moments for her words to register. He swallowed. "Does she remember?"

"I don't know."

Samantha grabbed Rikist's discarded shirt from the back of the couch and tossed it to him. He looked down, bewildered, as the shirt bounced off his chest and fell in a pile on his lap. Samantha groaned, and then shook the shirt out and shoved it over his head.

"Come on, you need to move."

She helped Rikist into the shirt, fixing the right side when it caught the bandages on his arm. She pulled the blanket back and slid her hands under his cast and knee brace and helped him swing his legs off the side of the couch and sit up. Rikist's eyes rolled back and he swayed, and Samantha caught his shoulders and helped him lean against her for support.

"Sorry, too fast?" she whispered.

He mumbled in reply.

Samantha ran her fingers through his mane to pat down the mussed bangs from his short nap and then slowed, her hands at the back of his neck as she gazed down at his face while he tried to gather his bearings. Rikist looked up at her, dreamy eyes expectant and struggling to focus on her face. When he realized she was staring, he smiled.

"Hey."

He wrapped his arms behind her waist and pulled her closer. He rubbed his cheek and chin affectionately against the front of her breasts, a motion Samantha had come to realize was the equivalent of a cat scent marking. Though the way he moaned as he slid the stubble on his chin against her skin felt much more titillating than something as simple as animal instincts.

Samantha caressed the side of his face and leaned down for a gentle kiss. "I love you, too."

Rikist smiled against Samantha's lips, slow and lazy, and spread his legs. His hands slipped further down her hips to slide under the hem of her jogging shorts and gripped the crease between her butt and thighs. He squeezed and pulled her against his body, so that the front of her legs rubbed against his crotch, letting her feel the beginnings of his erection.

Heat rushed up Samantha's neck and cheeks, and

she suddenly felt light headed. The regimen of drugs and Rikist's slow healing had kept the physical aspect of their relationship on the back burner. Until that moment, it seemed Rikist's libido had been completely shot from either the Vicodin or annoyance at Samantha's close contact during Krissik's tutoring—something he had jealously commented on several times. The hard knot pressing against the front of his sweats let her know whatever had been keeping her lion down was not strong enough to tame him any longer.

The intimacy of his nearness stole her breath away, and she felt heat pool in her belly and moisture gather in her silk underwear. Heat radiated off his skin in waves, and she felt his otherworldly golden sunshine bathe her skin in tingling warmth. For a moment, she let herself bask in his glow. She unconsciously ran one hand down his tight abs and into the waistband of his pants. She smirked and felt him up through the cotton underwear, fondling his heavy sack and thick base. She rubbed her thumb across his wide tip and felt a slick wetness dampening the material.

"Happy to see me?" she whispered.

He chuckled low in his throat, his nostrils flaring. He leaned forward and pressed his nose against the warmth of her neck, breathing in deeply. His tongue shot out and licked a long, wet line on her collarbone, followed by a quick nip of his fangs. His hands shook on her thighs, and his claws twitched dangerously against her bare skin.

"I've really missed you." A low rumble rolled from

his gut and danced across Samantha's skin. "Tsi raki... I want you so bad right now."

Samantha swallowed the lump in her throat and pulled her hand free of his sweats, cupping his face in her hands. She kissed his pouting lips, and then gently bit the scar on his jaw.

"Take it easy, tiger," she spoke in his ear. "I'll put you back to bed nicely tonight."

Rikist smirked, his eyes heated as he pulled back to gaze at her. "Nice is not the word I was thinking when imagining you above me."

Samantha crooked an eyebrow, fighting a smile. "Me on top, again? Man, you're getting lazy."

His grin widened, revealing his dimples amidst the week's worth of beard growth. "That laziness only extends to my leg. My mouth, on the other hand, is salivating for some hot, wet—"

A frantic knock on the wall made them jerk, and an annoyed growl escaped Rikist's tight lips.

"Samantha?" Krissik's voice came from behind them. "I...T-there some... something that side..."

Samantha turned to peer over her shoulder, noting the way Krissik kept his eyes on his brother. He almost looked pleased he had interrupted. She frowned and stepped away from Rikist.

"He is improving," Rikist muttered as he glared at his brother, obviously upset by his presence. "What are you planning on telling her?"

"I don't know." Samantha shook her head. "I guess

I want to see what she remembers first. Krissik, can you help him?"

Krissik nodded and strode across the room, his long legs eating the distance in only a few steps. He bent to rest his brother's left arm over his shoulders, when Rikist's hand shot out and clamped down on Krissik's throat. Rikist bared his fangs and let out a low, bestial growl, as his claws bit into the soft skin of Krissik's throat. The younger alien yelped, and his body rolled into a curled, submissive position as he held his clawed hands out in front of his belly.

"Si trak ri siti," Rikist's gravelly voice rumbled. "Tsrik ti risa."

"Rikist!" Samantha yelled. She leapt forward and grappled at his shoulder. "Let him go!"

Two weeks of tension crackled through the darkened room like firecrackers on a hot, summer night. Some part of Samantha knew this moment would come eventually, but now really was not the right time. The brothers needed to confront the elephant in the room standing between them, and address their issues in a civil, heart-felt discussion, a conversation that did not involve fangs and claws and blood on her freshly-mopped wood floors with her best friend standing outside.

Samantha jumped as the dark, amber eyes slid toward her, and her skin crawled at the savage fire burning in their depths. She balled her hands into fists.

"Let him go. Now!"

Rikist narrowed his eyes, and then grunted and

pushed his brother away. Krissik collapsed to the floor, gasping, and cradled his bruised neck. Fear seeped out of his pores, and his eyes appeared unnaturally wide in his pale face. Samantha knelt beside Krissik to push his hand away from his neck and was relieved when she saw Rikist had not broken skin. She glared at Rikist.

"What the hell is wrong with you?"

"Stay out of this, Samantha."

"No, this is my house! You've already trashed the place with your first sibling quarrel, and I'm not going to sit by while you two continually try to kill each other."

"He doesn't know his place."

She glared at him. "Are you referring to me?"

"Have you seen the way he still looks at you?" Rikist growled, his face distorting in distress. "I don't trust him."

Samantha moved to stand when Krissik grabbed her wrist and pulled her back down. He coughed and shook his head, his breathing settling.

"No... Rikist is ro...rotect his. You..." He let out a frustrated sigh at her confused look, and touched the spot over Samantha's heart, his eyes resigned. "Dis not mine."

He glanced at Rikist and then stood, rubbing his wounded neck, and cowered as he shuffled toward his brother, upturned wrist out. Rikist watched him approach without blinking, his nostrils still flared in anger. Krissik hesitated, and slowly leaned forward, head down, and extended his shaking wrist to Rikist's chin.

"Ta rik stri istik, Samantha," he whispered. He swallowed and passively tilted his head just enough to peer up with one eye. "I saw-ree, Rikist."

Rikist's frown deepened, the muscle in his jaw bouncing. After a moment, he closed his eyes and breathed out deeply through his nose and leaned forward to rub his chin against Krissik's wrist.

The anger in Rikist's face snuffed out like an expired candlewick at their touch, and he grabbed Krissik's extended arm and pulled him closer. He rubbed his cheek against Krissik's, his puffing coughs rolling through Krissik's swallowed whimpers. He closed his eyes tightly, the corners creasing in concentration, and then wrapped his arms around Krissik's narrower shoulders, pulling him into a firm embrace.

"Sirtki si raki, Krissik." His arms tightened as he rubbed the underside of his chin against the side of Krissik's neck possessively. "I'm sorry, too."

"And I'm sorry I took so long!"

All heads turned toward the new voice, and Samantha nearly collapsed as Carly dropped her bag just inside the front door, her wide eyes all for the two men embracing on the couch. Her shocked face turned to Samantha.

"Holy shit, you've got two of them."

TWENTY

"What I would have paid to see John's expression when he saw Rikist."

Carly pouted her lips as she mulled Samantha's story over in her head, and then took another sip of her coffee. One manicured finger tapped the edge of the mug as her mascara-lined eyes roamed the faces at the kitchen table. Samantha wiped at her eyes with a napkin, upset at having to relay a summary of her adventures over the last few weeks to the friend she had left behind in a hallway full of aliens. Krissik sat sideways in his seat, his elbow hooked over the back of the nearest chair and eyes carefully watching the blonde's every move, as if Carly were a coiled viper. Rikist looked tired and apathetic, cradling his head in his hands with his elbows on the table.

"Is he drunk?" Carly asked, giving Samantha a look.

Samantha snorted. "No. I told you, it's the meds."

She rubbed Rikist's back. He sat up straighter and tried to look interested. She smiled at him. "You should go back to bed."

Rikist cast a wary look toward Carly, who sneered gleefully.

"Do I make the big, bad alien uncomfortable?" she teased.

"You're... taking this really well," Samantha cut in. She shook her head. "I was a mess at first."

"Sweetie, you're a mess when it comes to men in general." She waved Samantha away. "Thing is, I am actually a little relieved to see them. See, when I was at the hospital I kept waking up to nightmares of giant cats trying to paw at me and rip my clothes off. I'd wake up screaming and yelling things about green lights and such... they tried giving me meds, but once I got home I refused to take them."

She glanced at Krissik. "I remember you." She grinned at his surprised expression. "I didn't at first, but then as more time went by, the dreams became clearer."

"You are not supposed to remember..." Rikist muttered, his brow drawn.

Carly nodded. "I figured that. And in all reality, I thought I was going crazy. But then Samantha just calls me out of the blue and starts leaving me worried voice-mails..." She shrugged and smiled at Samantha. "And here we are."

Samantha smiled, relieved beyond belief that she had someone else to share this secret with. She patted Rikist's arm, and he forced a worried smile back.

Rikist yawned, and then reached for his crutch and lurched to his feet. "Krissik, take the couch."

Krissik furrowed his brow. "Why?"

"Because Carly needs a place to sleep."

Carly took a slow sip from her mug, a wolfish grin on her lips. Her eyes had not left Krissik for more than a few seconds after the initial shock of the men's presence had worn off. The piercing blue gaze seemed to try hard to peel away every thread of clothing.

Krissik had noticed the hunger in her eyes, and the young alien had surprisingly backed away; most likely because the look on her face said she wanted to eat him alive and lick the spoon. He had made it a point to keep Samantha or Rikist between him and the curly-haired predator.

Samantha, on the other hand, thought that a run-in with her... *energetic* best friend would probably work wonders on the angst-ridden alien. She smirked as she watched Krissik squirm in his seat under Carly's heated gaze.

"Go to bed, I'll be there in a few." She gently kissed Rikist's lips, and then patted his back as he passed.

Rikist glanced back at Carly, and then his brother, and Samantha could see the concern in his eyes. She winked at him.

"Don't worry. She doesn't bite."

Carly leaned across the table, her breasts pressing against her folded arms and nearly popping out of her satin bra. She smiled wide when Krissik licked his lips and his breathing quickened, obviously thinking she was winning him over.

Samantha knew Krissik well enough to know that Carly was scaring the shit out of him.

She walked behind Carly's chair and pressed her lips against her friend's ear. "Take it easy, you're scaring him."

"I want to do more than scare him," Carly whispered back. "Did you see what those men were capable —oh, screw seeing. You've done it!"

Samantha clamped a hand over Carly's mouth. She smiled sweetly at Krissik. "Kris, can you please turn down the bed in your room?"

Krissik nodded, a little too quickly, and disappeared from the kitchen in a blink.

Carly shook Samantha off and glared at her. "What is your problem? Can't you share?"

"I... Damn, Carly, get a hold of yourself!" Samantha lowered her voice. "You need to slow down. He's never..." She trailed off, not really sure how she should explain.

Carly's eyes doubled in size. "He's a virgin?"

"Yes."

"Well, that's a very significant detail you left out."

Samantha rolled her eyes. "I didn't think it was necessary."

"Samantha?" Rikist called from the bedroom.

Samantha sped past Carly before she could be stopped and slipped through the bedroom door. The lamp on the bedside table cast Rikist's broad shadow across the dim room as he dug through the drawer from his sideways position on the bed, his left leg propped on a pile of pillows. She padded closer to him.

"What are you doing?"

He grimaced and rolled to his back, pressing on his thigh. "Damn, that hurts." He motioned for her to come closer. "Here, give this to Krissik."

Samantha held her hand out, and gasped when he dropped a little glass vial in her palm. She sloshed the tiny bit of liquid around, the scent of mint wafting up from the cork. She stared down at Rikist.

"Where did you get this?"

"Had it in my pocket when you brought me here. I'd swiped it from him back at the apartment." He smirked. "I think he could use the confidence boost."

She opened her mouth the respond, but he held up one hand.

"Just... hurry up and take it to him. He looks ready to explode."

Samantha laughed, and held the vial up to the light. "With this, they're both going to."

Her gaze slipped from the vial to the dark, amber eyes reflecting the yellow light of the lamp like miniature suns, the glow drawing her in like a delicate moth.

"You know I need to leave."

Samantha's head jerked up. Her skin cooled, and her stomach seemed filled with lead. "What... what are you—"

"I need to close the jump sites." He sighed and

shook his head, his jaw tight. "With Carly remembering, and Krissik coming through..."

"Rikist, I..."

"I will not let anyone take you away from me."

Samantha fought back sudden tears, unsure where the conversation was going.

"So, you're leaving."

Rikist looked up at the tone in her voice and reached out and wrapped his arm around her waist to pull her close. He kissed her stomach through her shirt and peered up at her face.

"Samantha, I will come back. I promise. But I cannot sit here, terrified that one day someone else will come through that jump site and find us. Find you."

Rikist's eyes creased at their corners and he leaned his head back, staring up at her from over his straight nose.

"I love you, Samantha. And if you're willing to put up with a crippled, bad-humored asshole—"

"You're not—"

"I take that back." He grinned. "Not the asshole part, but the willing part. Because I am here to stay whether you like it or not."

Samantha sighed, a weight rolling off her shoulders, and she felt dizzy with the release of tension she had been fighting off all week. She leaned toward the bed and kissed his brow.

Rikist's hand twitched on her side as he gently pushed her away and waved her out of the room.

"Hurry up. It's getting late."

Samantha smiled. "I'll be right back."

Outside the bedroom, Krissik paced the kitchen as he put away mugs and wiped up coffee rings on the table. He glanced up as Samantha appeared, and his hands shook as he pulled her behind the counter.

"Samn-tha," he stuttered, his practiced vocabulary slipping along with his nerves. "I... I not know what..."

"Just breathe."

Samantha took his face in both hands and kissed between his eyes, holding the kiss until he slowed and took a deep breath. She pulled back and smiled at him, letting her thumbs caress his cheeks.

"What happened to the conqueror who yanked me through a third-story Las Vegas hotel window?"

He shook in her hands. "Sh-she berry strong."

"*Very*, not berry," Samantha laughed. "You're so adorable sometimes, you know that? Listen, don't worry, she's not going to eat you." She hesitated, and then pointedly glanced down at his crotch. "Unless you ask her to."

Krissik's eyes registered panic, and Samantha let go long enough to hold up the vial in front of his face. The gold eyes widened.

"How?"

"Rikist."

Krissik blinked, and then a sheepish grin pulled at his lips. He glanced at his closed bedroom door and set his shoulders a little straighter. He took the vial, tested the contents, and then popped the cork and let half of the contents slip between his lips. He swished the contents around in his mouth before swallowing.

Krissik smiled at Samantha and leaned in just enough for her to smell the familiar minty aura laced with sunbeams. "Thank... you."

"No, thank you." Samantha wrapped her arms around his neck. "You brought me to Rikist."

Krissik hugged her back, sighing as he rubbed his cheek against hers, purring. He kissed the side of her neck before stepping back. He winked as he walked backwards toward his door, an eager grin plastered across his face.

"Sis."

THE LIGHTS WERE off when Samantha quietly stepped into her bedroom. Rikist's slow, even breathing filled the dark silence, and Samantha sighed in disappointment as she undressed for bed, trying to ignore the muffled giggling through the walls.

I should have known he'd be sleeping. Serves me right for thinking that after all this mess tonight he'd be up to anything.

She slipped a silk gown over her head and smoothed the edges out just above her knees. She let her hair fall down around her shoulders, scratching at the spot the rubber band had held her bun, and then slipped between the sheets. She scooted closer to Rikist, staying just out of reach so as not to wake him, and let his radiant body heat comfort her as she acclimated to her chilled side of the bed.

A hot hand slid up her knee and thigh toward her groin, and she gasped as Rikist pressed his nose to the crook of her neck, his warm breath rolling across her bare skin.

"Sorry, did I wake you?"

"No."

She hesitated. "When are you leaving?"

He shrugged against her back. "Probably a week. Maybe two. I need to let my leg heal enough to travel."

Samantha tried to sit up, but his hand moved from her thigh to her breasts, trapping her against the pillow. Her heartbeat hitched as a single claw delicately traced patterns around her nipples through the silk, and his body shifted to close the inch gap between them.

"Oh," Samantha gasped. Her cheeks flushed as his wide, erect penis slid wetly against her leg.

He's naked.

And very lubed up.

Samantha felt him smile against her neck, and he twitched against her leg in anticipation. She bit her lip and grinned, knowing very well his feline eyes could see her clearly in the dark.

"Shouldn't you be sleeping?" she whispered, wiling her heart to slow before it burst.

He let out a deep throated puffing sound; the two-hundred-and-fifty-pound beast's equivalent to purring. "Shouldn't you be screwing me already?"

Samantha gasped in surprise as the fresh scent of

mint and cinnamon enveloped her, and amber fireflies swirled around in the black hole that threatened to caress her into oblivion. She closed her eyes and struggled to focus against the instant ache in her core and the dampness gathering between her legs.

He couldn't resist a quick taste...

She threw her head back and guffawed, her entire body filling with waves of rolling honey and her toes curling in expectancy. She could not fight the stupid grin that took her lips hostage, so she did not try.

"You son of a bitch," she laughed.

Rikist chuckled and lifted on one elbow to kiss her as he used one hand to shove her panties to the side and rub his palm against her groin.

"I couldn't let Krissik have all the fun."

He pressed his mouth against hers, parting her lips and letting his tongue explore. Liquid fire spilled into her mouth and seared her throat and set her blood boiling, bringing her to the edge before her next breath.

Samantha groaned against his mouth and arched her back, her hands curling in his hair and pulling him down on top of her. She broke the kiss, panting, and her reason managed to struggle to the surface long enough to stare at his face. She used one foot to carefully tap at his cast.

"You think you can handle this?"

Rikist's lips pulled back in a predatory snarl as he forced his eyes away from his hand in her groin to meet her eyes. His feral expression melted any future words on her mouth as he pushed himself into a pushup position above her, letting his erection slide thick and heavy against her belly. He balanced on one hand and his good leg, the round muscles in his arms and shoulders bunching as he reached down to rip her underwear off, followed quickly by the silk gown.

"I think I can manage."

The amber eyes glowed in the dark as he took her completely in, his breathing slow and even. His lips spread into a wide smile, and he adjusted his hips so that his slick head rubbed against her clit. His fangs bit into his lower lip as he watched her tremble beneath him. He kissed her gently on the lips.

"I was teasing you in the kitchen," he breathed against her skin. "Tonight, I'm going to fuck you out of this world like you've never imagined."

"Arrogant, aren't we?" She grinned. "I don't know, I've read some pretty kinky stuff throughout my years."

His hot tongue lapped across her neck and chin before slipping between her teeth. He groaned and pulled back, letting her see the promises in his eyes. He reached between his legs and guided himself in, easing into Samantha slowly and relishing the ecstasy on her face as he filled her inch by inch. He bared his fangs and let his eyes flash in the dim moonlight reflecting in from the window, reaffirming his otherworldly origins.

"Sweetheart, I promise your books just won't be the same after me." He smirked as Samantha let her lips part in a blissful, open-mouthed smile when he rotated his hips, pushing her along the tide of honey waves lapping at the inside of her skull. "And this story doesn't end after tonight."

Samantha dug her nails into his lower back and squeezed, gaining an encouraging grunt from the man inside her.

"You talk too much," she whispered. "Just shut up and show me how much you love me."

Rikist's eyes creased at the corners as he smiled and moved to oblige her.

THANK YOU FOR READING!

Thank you for supporting independent authors with your purchase!

If you enjoyed the book, please take a moment to review it online. Reviews are golden to authors and help show your support!

HERE'S A SNEAK PEEK OF THE KEEPING: BOOK TWO OF THE SA TSKIR BROTHERS CHRONICLES

THE KEEPING:
BOOK TWO

Dinner at Samantha's house tended to fall into two camps: Rikist and Samantha ate at the kitchen table while Carly and Krissik retreated to the den. The room held an upgraded flat-screen television—courtesy of Rikist's connections—and a jumble of mismatched furniture and decorations from Samantha's father. Carly knew better than to call it a storage room, but that was effectively what it had become.

Once Krissik figured out how to work the television, he had claimed the place as his own, taking it over every evening to practice his English.

Krissik made sure Carly was comfortable beside him, and then switched on BBC America.

"Time for *The Chemists*," he said, not bothering to restrain his glee.

Carly shook her head, not entirely understanding his obsession with the show. As far as she could see, *The Chemists* was about a bunch of British pharmacists who could not seem to keep their heads or their pants on. It was the sort of salacious, slightly deranged television she would have loved in college—and probably would have loved now, if life had not gotten quite so serious lately. But Krissik had discovered reruns of the show a week or so prior, and now he watched it religiously.

When the episode ended, Krissik turned to her with a smile. "That's ace!"

Carly held back an eye roll and reached out to ruffle his soft, red hair. Krissik leaned into her embrace, a slow, rumbling purr rising out of his chest. Carly shifted her attention to scratch at the underside of his jaw, and Krissik rumbled on contentedly, twisting his head to get her to hit the right spots. Carly grinned. The sound coming out of the gratified alien seemed like something she should have heard from a giant cat, a tiger perhaps, and it never ceased to please her.

"You probably shouldn't use a British show to learn your colloquialisms," Carly said. "Americans don't say *ace*."

"Maybe should."

The show ran its end credits, a montage of Big Ben, London Bridge, and some additional scattered scenery of Great Britain.

"You know, not all of these places are even in the show," Carly said. "They're just slamming them all in there to appeal to the average American."

Krissik sat up and looked thoughtful. "Are *you* average American?"

She thought about it. "No. I've been to London and the rest of Great Britain. Several times as a child, actually. I *know* all those places aren't in the same area. And you, well..."

"I am a purist," he said with a grin. "Learning about your world."

Carly smirked. "You mean a tourist?"

She ruffled his hair again, then began rubbing just behind his left ear when he laid his head in her lap. The purring started again, and Carly's smile widened.

A European newscaster came on, reporting on the business going on across the pond: something important in Rome, followed by the obligatory imagery of the Coliseum and the Vatican.

Krissik sat up very straight and leaned forward, his attention at once captured by the images floating across the screen. Excitement rippled off him in almost visible waves.

Carly almost laughed. *God, he's such a nerd!*

But such a cute nerd...

"Are these same places you show me in your pictures?" he asked, without taking his eyes off the Vatican. "The ancient holy places?"

"That one is."

Krissik had been a student of architecture in his world. He often spoke of his work there and had shown Carly some recreated sketches of projects he had been working on before coming to Earth. It had all looked very impressive to Carly, though her only experience with building anything had involved trying to create a pillow fort with her nanny back in grade school. Samantha had described Krissik as tremendously gifted—nearly a genius. Carly supposed it was not entirely out of the question for him to be interested in the architecture of Earth, which, he had told her, was far more graceful and attractive than the buildings in his homeworld.

We build for strength and function, he had said, *to withstand battles...your buildings, they such beautiful, as like dreamers designed them.*

The people of Earth fascinated Krissik; that much was clear. That a species could *dream* and create beautiful things was of tremendous excitement to him. Whatever concept he had previously formed of Earthlings before his stay had clearly been abstract.

"What did you think of the hotel you found us in?" she asked.

Krissik glanced at her in surprise. She had not brought up Vegas to him outside of their nightly rendezvous; the nightmares were quite enough. But while awake, Carly could block the images of the hotel hallways and the military invaders—and hoped that by finally addressing things in daylight, she might eventually heal. Besides, she was looking for Krissik's professional opinion about the structures, not his recollection of the transpired events.

Krissik thought about her question. "I did not see much. The place was dark, and, you know." He paused. "The bedrooms I saw—"

"Hotel rooms. Not bedrooms."

"The rooms I saw," he winked at her, "were nice. Very soft. Whole building is made for comfort. No weapons, no shields, no big walls to stand against blasts. Pictures and hanging cloths everywhere, water fountains... Very different from home." He watched the broadcast for another moment, his claws briefly stretching out before retracting, in what Carly had come to recognize as a sort of stimming mechanism. "People go to hotels to relax. My world had such places once. I studied them."

"How far back are we talking?"

Krissik shrugged. "Too far. I only see pictures. But I always want to build something like that...something more than just—just getting along?" He frowned, mouthing the words he had just said. "No, that is not what I mean. I want to do more. Our buildings were made to survive. Not to create beautiful things."

"I understand," Carly said. "At least, I think I do. You wanted more than the life you had?"

"No, I wanted more than the work I had. I did not think about life... until now."

Carly bit back a sigh. At least Krissik was not looking at her now, so he could not see her struggling to not close off from him entirely. She knew Krissik wanted more than she gave of herself emotionally. But the catastrophe with her ex, Andrew—even now, five years later, she cringed to think of his name—had taught her to build walls so high that even Krissik might not be able to scale them.

And even if I wanted to let someone entirely in, I don't know if I honestly could.

The Rome segment ended, and a Russian reporter in front of St. Petersburg continued the news coverage. Some sort of banking scandal, maybe. Carly was only half paying attention, running her fingers through the soft fur on Krissik's ears, and tracing the tiger stripes along his neck.

"I want to see these places," Krissik said suddenly.

Carly kept stroking his hair, considering his appearance. Rikist had ventured off the farm a handful of times since Carly had arrived, usually to meet one of the human handlers for intel, but always near sundown and behind sunglasses and collared jackets. Krissik could probably do the same with his golden cat eyes—contacts, maybe—but there was no saying his eyes could handle contacts at all. Krissik's fur-like hair could be gelled back into a more maintainable style...

But the stripes. The dark tiger stripes covering Krissik's skin from nearly head to toe would prove difficult.

Krissik sat up and twisted around to look at her. "Why you always so quiet when I talk about seeing your world?"

Uh-oh. He was onto her.

"We could travel together," he said. "It'd be a cracking good time."

Another *Chemists* reference. If Krissik was looking to television to improve his dialect, Carly figured he might have done better going after something more mainstream American...or maybe not. She was not sure she would live with herself if Krissik started talking like something out a reality dating TV show.

"Carly," Krissik said, a little more annoyed now.

Carly started, realizing she had spaced out for a moment. "Sorry. I was just thinking."

"What about?"

Was honesty the best policy here? She used another precious second to gather her thoughts. "Kris, we still haven't figured out all the specifics about...well, about what you're going to do here."

Krissik's mouth flattened into a firm line.

Carly continued. "You have to understand how difficult it is—I mean, your appearance—we can talk about things, sure, but..."

She was floundering now; she had never been much good at disappointing people. It had been easier to cut and run rather than stick around and watch those she cared about to realize she would just let them down.

"Can we talk about this later?" she asked.

Krissik sighed, nodded, and patted her hand. Then he rose and took himself out of the den without another word.

"Sorry," Carly murmured.

She heard the bedroom door close.

Carly picked up the remains of dinner and brought the plates into the kitchen. Rikist stood alone at the sink, washing the dishes. Even standing there barefoot, in jeans and a T-shirt, he was a formidable presence that seemed to fill the small space.

Carly hesitated in the doorway. For the most part, Carly made it a point to never be alone with the massive predator, which Krissik seemed to appreciate.

Probably still stinging from Rikist stealing Samantha away. He's probably still on edge.

In that regard, she knew Krissik had nothing to worry about. While she had to admit Rikist was drop-dead sexy, and the idea of being dominated by such an exotic beast twisted Carly's stomach into a frantic whirlwind of butterflies, the sheer intensity of Rikist's amber stare scared the living shit out of her.

Rikist's head jerked toward the sound of Carly's soft steps, though his hands never faltered. He offered her a faint nod.

"Hello," he said, his polite voice tinged with reservation. "Do you want me to wash those?"

Carly handed him the dishes. "Thanks. Sam putting you to work?"

"She's not feeling well." Rikist shrugged. "Said her stomach is upset."

Rikist scrubbed the dishes in silence for a moment. Carly considered following after Krissik but also felt some compulsion to talk to Rikist. It did not seem fair to just ditch him while he was trying to clean up after everyone. Besides, he *was* her best friend's boyfriend, and she *was* living in their spare bedroom. She ought to put in some effort to make nice.

"So," she said. "How's your leg doing?"

"Fine, for the most part."

"Does it still hurt?"

Rikist shrugged. "Now and then. Usually just when I overdo it."

Rikist had been seriously wounded during a battle on his home planet and exaggerated the injury during his and Samantha's escape to Earth. Samantha's ex—John, a veterinarian and an ally to the alien resistance—had patched up Rikist wounds and helped ease the pain. Over the past two weeks, Rikist had been finally able to get around without the help of crutches and had downgraded to a simple sports' knee brace. Carly had to admit that Rikist looked much better, and the freedom to move around had brought a shine into his piercing eyes.

Carly smiled. "How do you like living on Earth so far?"

Rikist scrubbed at an incredibly tough spot on a pan with the sponge, then gave up and used one sharp claw to scratch at the offending stain.

"Nice. I actually find farm life peaceful and very... not regimented." He made a face. "That is not even a word, is it?"

Carly shrugged. "I think that's probably true of non-military life in general, right?"

"No. Not where I come from."

The edge to his voice at once warned her away and lured her in. Samantha had recounted stories of the brothers' home while she was on their planet; many of the residences were shelled beyond habitation, nearly no vegetation surviving, and a strictly enforced curfew. Carly was quite curious to know more about the brothers' backgrounds, but Krissik seemed to dislike her asking too much, and so Carly had laid that topic to rest.

Though if Krissik would not talk, maybe Rikist would?

"So..." Carly leaned against the wall. "Your planet is in a civil war?"

"You could call it that." Rikist did not look her way. "It happens every fifty years or so, though this one is considerably larger... No one is happy with the factions in power, and with the disease and scarcity of females..." Rikist's scratching at the plate quickened, the thick tendons in his forearms flexing. "The leaders have become petty, ravenous bastards. Each attack against the citizens is just a flexing of power."

Carly stared. She knew Rikist's English skills were well above Krissik's, having been mated to a human before Samantha, but the outburst surprised her. In fact, she tried to recall another instance where he had said nearly as much in one sitting.

Rikist looked up as if catching himself. He chuckled, flashing fangs. "I didn't mean to explode like that. I guess I've been saving it for a while. There is no use in talking to Samantha. She thinks we are alone and safe. But I wish she would listen when I tell her I am worried."

"About them coming after you? Her?"

"Both. Or punishing Earth as a whole for my treason." He turned off the sink and grabbed a daisy-printed hand towel from the counter. "I did not leave on good terms."

Carly watched Rikist as he dried the plates and proceeded to put them into the cupboards in a casual and very domesticated manner. In Carly's opinion, it was an odd sight, considering the man's size and permanently extended claws.

Will Krissik's claws eventually be unable to retract?

She knew Rikist was almost ten years older than Krissik, and that physical changes—like the fading stripes and inability to purr—came with full maturity. She glanced again at Rikist's sharp fingertips and shuddered.

God, I hope Krissik's stays a little softer around the edges when he hits thirty.

Rikist finished drying his hands and leaned back against the counter. He slipped a cookie from the nearby rooster tin and winked at Carly, putting a finger to his lips.

Carly smirked. She had overheard enough of Samantha's comments about Rikist's obsession with her baking to know she had tried hiding the treats throughout the house. Though with the aliens' sharp noses, Samantha's attempts had been futile. Samantha had finally given up trying to be tactful and had begun nagging her mate about his sugar intake. Krissik took her words into full consideration. Rikist did not seem to give a damn.

Rikist sniffed the cookie before breaking it in half.

"So," he said. "What does my brother have up his ass this time?"

Carly stared at him. *How did he know we were fighting?*

"I don't—" she began.

"My brother is completely inept at hiding his feelings." Rikist tossed half of the cookie into the air and snapped at it with his teeth. "I am just assuming it has something to do with you."

"It's nothing," Carly sighed. "He's just... he's feeling cooped up here at the ranch."

Rikist studied for a moment, making Carly almost cringe under the intensity of his stare. The muscles in his jaw worked as he chewed. Then he frowned and shoved the second half of the cookie in his mouth and brushed his hands off on his jeans.

"Krissik cannot leave the farm. So, do not even entertain that notion of his."

"You leave," Carly noted.

Rikist's amber eyes narrowed, and a low growl emitted from between his snarling lips. "Krissik is not like me. Do not ever make the mistake of believing otherwise."

Carly's heart skipped a beat, and she took a step back. Rikist blinked, and he forced his face to go neutral.

"I am sorry. I am just a little on edge right now, and that was not fair." He dipped his head toward Carly and started toward the hall. "Good night, Carly."

Carly sputtered an affirmative and watched him go.

That guy is fucking crazy.

She stood in the kitchen for a moment, twiddling her fingers in thought. Deciding movement was better than standing alone, she retreated into the living room. She made sure the couch and coffee table were tidy and turned off the lights. Afterward, she headed down the hall to the two guest bedrooms. Rikist had given up his room to Carly and moved into the master with Samantha. Krissik had the third room—though he rarely slept in his room at all.

Carly's room was large, spacious, and pleasant, with several feminine touches, and right now, Krissik seemed to take up half of it. He lay on her bed, arms tucked behind his head, staring up at the ceiling. Carly closed her eyes.

Great. I've gone from talking to one brother about fears of military action to actually facing a war with the other. A battle we are both very ill-equipped to fight.

Rikist, she knew, understood how to fight on human terms, and did not seem to get bent out of shape when someone got emotional. As much as Krissik tried to act human around Carly, he had not yet figured out how females ticked, and their spats usually ended with him puzzling over Carly's behavior. He was far too used to everything being calculated and orderly, and any deviation on Carly's part seemed to confuse and frighten the hell out of him.

It's like I'm dating a striped Spock, Carly thought.

She closed the door behind her and leaned against the warm wood. "Kris," she said. "Can we not fight?"

"You are one who makes a fight," he said.

"Only because you don't understand."

"What is to understand?"

Carly groaned.

Oh, here we go again. Fine, if he wants a battle, well...I'll give him one.

"Krissik," she said. "You know you don't look human."

"I can wear some-gasses," he said. "Like Rikist."

"Sunglasses," Carly corrected.

This argument almost bubbled up a few days before, but Samantha ran into the room, needing help with one of the goats. Since then, it simmered; with Krissik obviously not forgetting.

Krissik frowned. "Why you not want us to go these places? Do you not want to show your world?"

"It's not that," Carly said. "I did show you some of them."

"Pictures," he said dismissively. "They just pictures, Carly. I want to *see* these places. View their arch-tech. Learn how they is made."

"And how do you expect to pay for all of this globe-trotting without a job?"

Krissik hesitated, pressing his lips together as he met Carly's eyes.

Carly crossed her arms and glared at him. "Of course—your sugar momma."

"Is not...I just want us to do these things together."

Us, us, us.

Krissik kept repeating that mantra as if it might stick—as if Carly felt the same. Carly could not entirely say she *did not* feel something for Krissik. Still, it had been so long between boyfriends that she could not quite tell whether she felt love, or just the addictive rush that came with excellent sex—and with Krissik, sex was *always* outstanding. But what about beyond that? The reality was that he was an alien; without a home, without a job, and seemingly without a daily purpose beyond dreaming of traveling the world and bedding Carly.

Is that what I want for myself long-term? A boy-toy who I have to keep hidden from the world and support for the rest of my life? I can barely manage myself, let alone another person.

"Because we just can't," Carly said flatly, with more force than she had intended.

Krissik sat up. "Why not?"

"Look in the mirror, Krissik!" She held out her hands, exasperated. "You have goddamn stripes and fangs, and golden eyes—"

"Rikist does it."

"You are not Rikist!"

The four words struck Krissik as if Carly had slapped him. His eyes widened, and his face blanched before he steeled his shoulders and shut his expression down.

Carly's stomach flipped, realizing her error.

Krissik sighed as if reading her thoughts. "Is all right. I no want to argue tonight."

"I'm sorry," Carly said, and meant it. "It's not that I don't think you're a great guy. But—this is hard for me. I don't know what they do on your planet, but here—"

"Yes, here you sit and think and try to make choice to be with this man or that man, or if what you feel is real feeling, or what is it word—passion?" He cocked his head to the side, stumbling slightly over the word. "That's ace, Carly, that's just ace."

Carly closed her eyes. "I don't think that's meant to be used sarcastically..."

Krissik choked down a howl and swatted angrily at a pillow on the bed, sending it flying into the corner. Krissik leaned over his knees and clutched at the top of his head.

"*Isk ti raka,*" he muttered. "No luck at all..."

Maybe he was not over Samantha.

The thought gave Carly a start. Krissik had sworn again and again he was done with Samantha, but every now and then he pulled something in front of Rikist— from slipping an arm around Carly, to making sure to place a hand on her leg while they were eating, to the obvious kiss good morning in the kitchen. Maybe it was just about proving something to his brother.

But what if it was still about Samantha?

Why do I even care? Carly wondered. *We're not married or anything...even if he did care about Samantha more than me...*

Irrational anger temporarily flooded through her,

and she quickly shut it down. Samantha had nothing to do with this. Her friend had not asked to be abducted by Krissik in the first place and had made her feelings known upfront that she loved *Rikist*.

But Carly knew, from what Samantha had said, that Krissik had fallen for her quite hard. Samantha's later infatuation with Rikist had broken his heart and driven a wedge between him and his brother. Carly had known that much from the beginning and had not expected much of anything from Krissik, for that very reason. He needed a rebound, and it had been a while since Carly had let herself have a good time with a man.

So why does it bother me now?

Krissik kept his back to Carly. His entire body trembled with minute, almost invisible tremors. Carly hesitated as she watched him shake his head as if trying to clear away an unwanted image, and her shoulders sank.

He's already been hurt badly enough. He doesn't deserve me jerking his chain, too.

"Kris, I'm sorry," she said. "I'm...I'm all mixed up right now. Have been for a long time."

"Complicated," Krissik mumbled. "You females are *complicated*."

Carly nodded. "I think that's been a common complaint of men across the centuries—and probably all the galaxies."

Krissik snorted.

With a sigh, she placed her hands on his muscled

back. She felt the tension beneath her fingers shift. "Kris, don't do this," she said. "Don't get angry. You knew from the start we weren't... you know. A thing."

Krissik's shoulders heaved, and he swung around, his golden eyes blazing. The feral look took Carly's breath away, and then he brought his head down to hers, capturing her mouth in a hard, almost painful kiss so that his fangs nearly bruised her lower lip. He pushed her back down onto the bed, kneeling between her legs. Carly heard the distinct snapping of her jeans button, followed by the zipper as he pulled them to her ankles.

"I want to taste you," he said in a low growl.

Carly knew he was trying to end the fight, in the same manner that most of their arguments ended; by him winning her over with sex.

As if I'm that one-dimensional, Carly thought, frowning.

She let Krissik yank off her shoes, jeans, and underwear.

At least...I hope I'm not.

They practiced this position only once before. Krissik showed good instincts but dove in headfirst and full throttle—the concept of teasing seemingly quite beyond him. He messily dug in like a starving man at a buffet table, leading Carly to eventually prop herself up on her elbows to gawk at him, not entirely sure if he even knew what he was trying to do anymore.

"I'm ready this time," Krissik informed her. "I was reading some of Samantha's books."

Carly blinked. "Samantha has books about this?" She pictured a battered copy of *The Joy of Sex* hidden away under a floorboard somewhere.

Krissik's golden eyes twinkled, and his tongue darted out to touch his lips. "The books with the many strong men on the pictures."

Carly managed to choke back her laughter. She knew Samantha enjoyed reading the occasional romance novel on her tablet, but the image of Krissik curled up in the corner with an erotica novel made Carly want to break into giggles—probably not the sexiest thing she could do right now.

"They are *very* learning," Krissik went on, his face earnest.

"Oh, I bet they are," Carly said, trying not to laugh at his serious expression. "What are you going to do?"

He wiggled his eyebrows at her. "You see. And now, I shall explore you... honey pot."

Carly's sidesplitting laughter slowed as Krissik lowered his head between her legs. Carly tapped his hair, then paused when she felt his breath against her most sensitive spots.

"Gently," she said. "*Gently*, Krissik. Don't just try to touch everything at once."

He pushed her legs further apart, looking at her for directions.

"*Gently*," she said. "Just don't...bite this time."

Krissik's eager expression dimmed slightly. "I am sorry about that."

"I know." Carly smiled and ran her fingers along his forearms "I trust you. Go to town."

Krissik's tongue felt hot and strong, gently ribbed like his feline equivalents, and he traced her first along the edges of her outer thighs, leaving a warm, wet line that cooled in the window's breeze. He slipped in closer, his tongue flicking against her opening, and Carly nearly jumped off the bed at the sudden rush of heat.

He has been reading!

"Oh—that's good. That's *good*—"

Krissik's tongue slipped inside her, at once insistent and gentle.

"Just taste," Carly panted. "Just...taste..."

Krissik encircled her, flicking the tiny nub that made her jump. Carly squeaked, shoving a fist up to her mouth to keep from making too much noise. Who knew how thick the walls in this house were, with Rikist and Samantha in the room next door?

Krissik crawled onto the bed, kissing his way along Carly's body and to bury his face under her shirt. Carly propped herself up to yank her shirt and bra away, then settled back against the pillows. Krissik's hot mouth sealed shut around her left nipple, his fangs gently scraping against her feverish skin, and he gave a long, strong pull. Carly moaned softly as her nipple stretched until she felt it would tear away. Krissik did the same with the other side, pulling and stretching until Carly cried out. He squeezed both breasts together, forming an ample mound in the center of her pale chest, and let his hot tongue snake down her cleavage as his thumbs circled her reddened nipples.

Carly fumbled with Krissik's jeans as he reached into his pocket and took out a small glass vial, barely filled with a clear, sloshing liquid. Krissik uncorked the top, put the bottle to the tip of his tongue, and tipped his head back. Satisfied, he corked the bottled and set it on the bedside table. Carly closed her eyes as the scent of mint and kittens trickled down across her neck and face, and she breathed in the welcome aroma with a broad smile in preparation for the liquid's effects.

It took them a moment to get him to lose his clothing, and then Krissik's naked body pressed down against hers, the soft, white patch of fur in the center of his chest tickling her breasts. The scent of kitten and mint enveloped her senses. Krissik reared back to lick his way down her body, allowing her the opportunity to study him, to take in his frame.

Krissik's powerful shoulders and chest seemed to have grown in the past two weeks of working on the farm. Carly marveled at his form. The dark stripes that curved around his face and arms continued down his back and sides, accentuating the curve of muscles. Forget about a six-pack—she could have bounced quarters off his friggin' eight-pack.

Carly ran her hands down Krissik's slender waist, and her gaze alighted on the patch of fur circling the base of his cock. He was huge—bigger than any other man she had been with. Sam had murmured about Rikist's size during a late-night giggle session, and Carly could only surmise that the entire species was physically gifted.

Carly ran her fingers along Krissik's tip, a mischievous smile on her face as she slid her fingers further down to the soft fur on his heavy sack. God, what a remarkable specimen he was. Carly wanted to lick him, suck on him, make love to him until her body gave way, and they melded together into one boneless, copulating mess.

Krissik made a different sound as she stroked his velvety skin—not quite a purr, but not a growl, either. Some strange, alien sound that was entirely masculine —and it brought a surge of wetness between Carly's legs. She bucked slightly, longing for his hands on her.

"Kris..."

Krissik pulled Carly into his arms, embracing her, his weight pressing her hard against the springy mattress. Carly slipped her arms around his neck, kissing him, tasting her own essence on his lips.

Carly's vision exploded in a burst of golden stars and honey waves. Minty fire spilled between her lips as Krissik transferred the intoxicating liquid from his tongue to hers. Heat rose from Carly's groin, stroking between her legs and radiating up to her stomach and chest in a rush of wildfire that nearly left her senseless. She sucked in air, the fragrances of mint and kitten fur barraging her senses, and she felt herself running her fingers up and down his back in an almost frenzied rush.

"Inside," she hissed. She would not be able to hold on much longer.

Krissik reached between her legs, testing her readiness with his knuckles. He nudged Carly's legs apart a little more and began easing into her, inch by inch, letting her adjust to his size.

Krissik placed one hand on either side of her head and pushed fully into her. Carly gasped, lifting her legs up to wrap them around his firm backside. He slid in and out, and then lowered his face to her neck, puffing against her throat. She felt his hips pumping into her, his length sliding in and out, and she began to move with him, matching his thrusts, using her heels against his ass to push him deeper inside.

Krissik reached one hand down to grasp Carly's hip, squeezing almost painfully. Carly knew his claws were digging into her skin, bruising her, and she loved it, relished the sensation of *feeling* so much. Krissik drew back and pounded into her, stretching her open, flooding her with his very being. Fiery stars whirled around her head as honey waves rolled across her skin like ripples from Krissik's every thrust. Carly could not see, could not breathe, could only sense the heat from between her legs moving up through her body in powerful, never-ending shockwaves.

Krissik brought Carly to hurried, frenzied orgasm almost immediately. The first climax had just started to fade when she felt the second wave of golden honey begin, and Krissik drove faster in response to her strangled cries.

They came together, and he slid in and out of her a few more times, his face replaced by dazzling stars.

After a moment, Krissik withdrew and pressed his head against Carly's breasts.

Carly stroked his hair, running her fingers through the thick fur as the gold stardust slowly faded. Here, in the darkness, he could be any man—a perfect, human man—and no one would ever know the difference.

"Good job," Krissik said drowsily.

Carly blinked. "Did you just tell *me* good job?"

"Four out of five, I say."

"You're grading our sex?"

Carly felt Krissik smile against her breasts.

"You turkey," she said, because there was really nothing else left for her to say.

Krissik's tongue flicked out again, catching one nipple. "You like."

He was right, of course. She did.

She liked it too much. Every time he shared the minty, alien substance, Carly's brain simply stopped functioning, turning her into a wild, lust-crazed sex fiend, and every finale was more mind-blowing than the last.

"If you could bottle that stuff, you'd make a fortune," she murmured.

Krissik slid off, wrapped his arms around her

middle, and draped one leg across hers, effectively locking her against him.

"Good night," he murmured into her hair.

"Good night," she mumbled, already halfway into a dream.

The fight, for now, appeared to be over.

ALSO BY DANIELLE KAHEAKU

The Sa Tskir Brothers Chronicles

The Scouting

The Abduction

The Keeping

The Remaining

The Recruit (2026)

The Daemon Progeny Trilogy

Artificial Selection

Cells of Time (2026)

The Dark Clone (2027)

Standalone Novels

He Rode a Dark Horse

Anthologies

In Love with an Alien

Alien Embrace

California Screamin'

Abaculus

Abaculus II

Abaculus III

The Axels and Allies Trilogy As Dani Kane

Wormholes: Book One